Walter Henry Howe

Scotch Wit and Humor

Classified under appropriate subject headings

Walter Henry Howe

Scotch Wit and Humor
Classified under appropriate subject headings

ISBN/EAN: 9783337411473

Printed in Europe, USA, Canada, Australia, Japan

Cover: Foto ©Andreas Hilbeck / pixelio.de

More available books at **www.hansebooks.com**

Scotch
Wit and Humor

CLASSIFIED UNDER APPROPRIATE SUBJECT
HEADINGS, WITH, IN MANY CASES, A
REFERENCE TO A TABLE OF AUTHORS

PHILADELPHIA
GEORGE W. JACOBS & CO.
103-105 S. Fifteenth Street

Preface

Scotch Wit and Humor is a fairly representative collection of the type of wit and humor which is at home north of the Tweed—and almost everywhere else—for are not Scotchmen to be found everywhere? To say that wit and humor is not a native of Scotch human nature is to share the responsibility for an inaccuracy the author of which must have been as unobservant as those who repeat it. It is quite true that the humor is not always or generally on the surface—what treasure is?—and it may be true, too, that the thrifty habits of our northern friends, combined with the earnestness produced by their religious history, have brought to the surface the seriousness—amounting sometimes almost to heaviness—which is their most apparent characteristic. But under the surface will be found a rich vein of generosity, and a fund of humor, which soon cure a stranger—if he has eyes to see and is capable of appreciation—of the common error of supposing that Scotchmen are either stingy or stupid.

True, there may be the absence of the brilliancy which characterizes much of the English wit and humor, and of the inexpressible quality which is contained in Hibernian fun; but for point of neatness one may look far before discovering anything to surpass the shrewdness and playfulness to be found in the Scotch race. In fact, if Scotland had no wit and humor she would have been incapable of furnishing a man who employed such methods in construction as were introduced by the engineer of the Forth Bridge.

W. H. HOWE.

Contents

Contents

Contents

Contents

10 Contents

Contents

LIST OF KNOWN WORKS AND
AUTHORITIES QUOTED

(Indicated in the Text by a Corresponding Number)

1 *Life and Labor* . . . . (SMILES)
2 . . . . . (ROBERT BURNS)
3 . . . . (PALL MALL GAZETTE)
4 . . . . (DR. CHAS. STEWART)
5 . . . . . (NORMAN MACLEOD)
6 . . . . (DR. BEGG)
7 . . . . . . (DEAN RAMSAY)
8 *National Fun* . . . (MAURICE DAVIES)
9 *Anecdotes of the Clergy* . (JACOB LARWOOD)
10 . . . . (WILLIAM ARNOTT)
11 . . . (MONCURE D. CONWAY)
12 *Rab and His Friends* . (REV. JOHN BROWN)
13 *Memoir of R. Chambers* . (WILLIAM CHAMBERS)
14 *Memorials* . . . (LORD COCKBURN)
15 . . . . . (DR. GUTHRIE)
16 . . . . . . (ANONYMOUS)
17 . . . . . . (DAILY NEWS)
18 *Turkey in Europe* . . (COLONEL J. BAKER)
19 *All the Year Round* . (CHARLES DICKENS)
20 *Red Gauntlet* . . . (SIR WALTER SCOTT)
21 . . . . . (CHAMBERS' JOURNAL)
22 . . . . . . (DR. HANNA)
23 . . . . . . (SIR W. SCOTT)
24 . . . . . . (JAMES HOGG)
25 . . . . . . (REV. D. HOGG)
26 . . . . . . (J. SMITH)

12

Scotch Wit and Humor

Scoring a Point

A young Englishman was at a party mostly composed of Scotchmen, and though he made several attempts to crack a joke, he failed to evoke a single smile from the countenances of his companions. He became angry, and exclaimed petulantly: "Why, it would take a gimlet to put a joke into the heads of you Scotchmen."

"Ay," replied one of them; "but the gimlet wud need tae be mair pointed than thae jokes."

A Cross-Examiner Answered

Mr. A. Scott writes from Paris: More than twenty years ago the Rev. Dr. Arnott, of Glasgow, delivered a lecture to the Young Men's Christian Association, Exeter Hall, upon "The earth framed and fitted as a habitation for man." When he came to the subject of "water" he told the audience that to give himself a rest he would tell them an anecdote. Briefly, it was this: John Clerk (afterwards Lord Eldon) was being examined before a Committee of the House of Lords. In using the word water, he pronounced it in his native Doric as "watter." The noble lord, the chairman, had the rudeness to interpose with the remark, "In England, Mr. Clerk, we spell water with one "t." Mr. Clerk was for a moment taken aback, but his native wit reasserted itself and he rejoined, "There may na be twa 't's' in watter, my lord, but there are twa 'n's' in manners." The droll way in which the doctor told the story put the audience into fits of laughter, renewed over and over again, so that the genial old lecturer obtained the rest he desired. [3]

13

One "Always Right;" the Other "Never Wrong"

A worthy old Ayrshire farmer had the portraits of himself and his wife painted. When that of her husband, in an elegant frame, was hung over the fireplace, the gudewife remarked in a sly manner: "I think, gudeman, noo that ye've gotten your picture hung up there, we should just put in below't, for a motto, like, 'Aye richt!'"

"Deed may ye, my woman," replied her husband in an equally pawkie tone; "and when ye got yours hung up ower the sofa there, we'll just put up anither motto on't, and say, 'Never wrang!'"

"A Nest Egg Noo!"

An old maid, who kept house in a thriving weaving village, was much pestered by the young knights of the shuttle constantly entrapping her serving-women into the willing noose of matrimony. This, for various reasons, was not to be tolerated. She accordingly hired a woman sufficiently ripe in years, and of a complexion that the weather would not spoil. On going with her, the first day after the term, to "make her markets," they were met by a group of strapping young weavers, who were anxious to get a peep at the "leddy's new lass."

One of them, looking more eagerly into the face of the favored handmaid than the rest, and then at her mistress, could not help involuntarily exclaiming, "Hech, mistress, ye've gotten a nest egg noo!"

Light Through a Crack

Some years ago the celebrated Edward Irving had been lecturing at Dumfries, and a man who passed as a wag in that locality had been to hear him.

He met Watty Dunlop the following day, who said, "Weel, Willie, man, an' what do ye think of Mr. Irving?"

"Oh," said Willie, contemptuously, "the man's crack't."

Dunlop patted him on the shoulder, with a quiet remark, "Willie, ye'll aften see a light peeping through a crack!" [7]

A Lesson to the Marquis of Lorne

The youthful Maccallum More, who is now allied to the Royal Family of Great Britain, was some years ago driving four-in-hand in a rather narrow pass on his father's estate. He was accompanied by one or two friends—jolly young sprigs of nobility — who appeared, under the influence of a very warm day and in the prospect of a good dinner, to be wonderfully hilarious.

In this mood the party came upon a cart laden with turnips, alongside which the farmer, or his man, trudged with the most perfect self-complacency, and who, despite frequent calls, would not make the slightest effort to enable the approaching equipage to pass, which it could not possibly do until the cart had been drawn close up to the near side of the road. With a pardonable assumption of authority, the marquis interrogated the carter : " Do you know who I am, sir ? " The man readily admitted his ignorance.

" Well," replied the young patrician, preparing himself for an effective *denouément*, " I'm the Duke of Argyll's eldest son ! "

" Deed," quoth the imperturbable man of turnips, " an' I dinna care gin ye were the deevil's son ; keep ye're ain side o' the road, an' I'll keep mine."

It is creditable to the good sense of the marquis, so far from seeking to resist this impertinent rejoinder, he turned to one of his friends, and remarked that the carter was evidently " a very clever fellow."

Lessons in Theology

The answer of an old woman under examination by the minister, to the question from the Shorter Catechism, " What are the *decrees* of God ? " could not have been surpassed by the General Assembly of the Kirk, or even the Synod of Dart, " Indeed, sir, He kens that best Himsell."

———

An answer analogous to the above, though not so pungent, was given by a catechumen of the late Dr. Johnston of Leith. She answered his own question.

patting him on the shoulder: "Deed, just tell it yersell, bonny doctor (he was a very handsome man); naebody can tell it better."

A contributor (A. Halliday) to *All the Year Round*, in 1865, writes as follows:

When I go north of Aberdeen, I prefer to travel by third class. Your first-class Scotchman is a very solemn person, very reserved, very much occupied in maintaining his dignity, and while saying little, appearing to claim to think the more. The people whom you meet in the third-class carriages, on the other hand, are extremely free. There is no reserve about them whatever; they begin to talk the moment they enter the carriage, about the crops, the latest news, anything that may occur to them. And they are full of humor and jocularity.

My fellow-passengers on one journey were small farmers, artisans, clerks, and fishermen. They discussed everything, politics, literature, religion, agriculture, and even scientific matters in a light and airy spirit of banter and fun. An old fellow, whose hands claimed long acquaintance with the plow, gave a whimsical description of the parting of the Atlantic telegraph cable, which set the whole carriage in a roar.

"Have you ony shares in it, Sandy?" said one.

"Na, na," said Sandy. "I've left off speculation since my wife took to wearing crinolines; I canna afford it noo."

"Fat d'ye think of the rinderpest, Sandy?"

"Weel, I'm thinking that if my coo tak's it, Tibbie an' me winna ha'muckle milk to our tay."

The knotty question of predestination came up and could not be settled. When the train stopped at the next station, Sandy said: "Bide a wee, there's a doctor o' deveenity in one o' the first-class carriages. I'll gang and ask him fat he thinks aboot it." And out Sandy got to consult the doctor. We could hear him parleying with the eminent divine over the carriage door, and presently he came running back, just as the train was starting, and was bundled in, neck and crop, by the guard.

"Weel, Sandy," said his oppugner on the predestination question, "did the doctor o' deveenity gie you his opinion?"

"Ay, did he."

"An' fat did he say aboot it?"

"Weel, he just said he dinna ken an' he dinna care."

The notion of a D. D. neither kenning nor caring about the highly important doctrine of predestination, so tickled the fancy of the company that they went into fits of laughter.   [38]

Double Meanings

A well-known idiot, named Jamie Frazer, belonging to the parish of Lunan, in Forfarshire, quite surprised people sometimes by his replies. The congregation of his parish had for some time distressed the minister by their habit of sleeping in church. He had often endeavored to impress them with a sense of the impropriety of such conduct, and one day when Jamie was sitting in the front gallery wide awake, when many were slumbering round him, the clergyman endeavored to awaken the attention of his hearers by stating the fact, saying: "You see even Jamie Frazer, the idiot, does not fall asleep as so many of you are doing." Jamie not liking, perhaps, to be designated, coolly replied, "An' I hadna been an idiot I wad ha' been sleepin', too."   [7]

Another imbecile of Peebles had been sitting in church for some time listening to a vigorous declamation from the pulpit against deceit and falsehood. He was observed to turn red and grow uneasy, until at last, as if wincing under the supposed attack upon himself personally, he roared out: "Indeed, meenister, there's mair lears in Peebles than me."   [7]

A minister, who had been all day visiting, called on an old dame, well known for her kindness of heart

and hospitality, and begged the favor of a cup of tea.
This was heartily accorded, and the old woman
bustled about, getting out the best china and whatever rural delicacies were at hand to honor her unexpected guest.   As the minister sat watching these
preparations, his eye fell on four or five cats devour-
ing cold porridge under the table.

" Dear me ! what a number of cats," he observed.
" Do they all belong to you, Mrs. Black ? "

" No, sir," replied his hostess innocently ; " but as
I often say, a' the hungry brutes i' the country side
come to me seekin' a meal o' meat."

The minister was rather at a loss for a reply.

Scotch " Fashion "

The following story, told in the " Scotch Remin-
iscenses " of Dean Ramsay, is not without its point
at the present day : " On a certain occasion a new
pair of inexpressibles had been made for the laird ;
they were so tight that, after waxing hot and red in
the attempt to try them on, he *let out* rather savagely
at the tailor, who calmly assured him, ' It's the
fashion—it's the fashion.'

" ' Eh, ye haveril, is it the fashion for them *no' to
go on ?* ' "   [7]

Wattie Dunlop's Sympathy for Orphans

Many anecdotes of pithy and facetious replies are
recorded of a minister of the South, usually distinguished as " Our Wattie Dunlop."   On one occasion
two irreverent young fellows determined, as they said,
to " taigle " (confound) the minister.   Coming up to
him in the High Street of Dumfries, they accosted
him with much solemnity : " Maister Dunlop, hae ye
heard the news ? "   " What news ? "   " Oh, the deil's
dead."   " Is he ? " said Mr. Dunlop, " then I maun
pray for twa faitherless bairns."   [7]

Highland Happiness

Sir Walter Scott, in one of his novels, gives expression to the height of a Highlander's happiness :
Twenty-four bagpipes assembled together in a small
room, all playing at the same time different tunes. [23]

Plain Scotch

Mr. John Clerk (afterwards Lord Eldon), in pleading before the House of Lords one day, happened to say in his broadest Scotch accent: "In plain English, ma lords."

Upon which a noble lord jocosely remarked: "In plain Scotch, you mean, Mr. Clerk."

The prompt advocate instantly rejoined: "Nae matter! in plain common sense, ma lords, and that's the same in a' languages, ye'll ken."

Caring for Their Minister

A minister was called in to see a man who was very ill. After finishing his visit, as he was leaving the house, he said to the man's wife: "My good woman, do you not go to any church at all?"

"Oh yes, sir; we gang to the Barony Kirk."

"Then why in the world did you send for me? Why didn't you send for Dr. Macleod?"

"Na, na, sir, 'deed no; we wadna risk him. Do ye no ken it's a dangerous case of typhus?"

Three Sisters All One Age

A Highland census taker contributed the following story to *Chambers'*: I had a bad job with the Miss M'Farlanes. They are three maiden ladies—sisters. It seems the one would not trust the other to see the census paper filled up; so they agreed to bring it to me to fill in.

"Would you kindly fill in this census paper for us?" said Miss M'Farlane. "My sisters will look over and give you their particulars by and by."

Now, Miss M'Farlane is a very nice lady; though Mrs. Cameron tells me she has been calling very often at the manse since the minister lost his wife. Be that as it may, I said to her that I would be happy to fill up the paper; and asked her in the meantime to give me her own particulars. When it came to the age column, she played with her boot on the carpet, and drew the black ribbons of her silk bag through her fingers, and whispered: "You can say four-and-thirty, Mr. M'Lauchlin." "All right, ma'am," says I; for I knew she was four-and-thirty at any rate. Then Miss Susan came over—that's the second sister—really a handsome young creature, with fine ringlets and curls, though she is a little tender-eyed, and wears spectacles.

Well, when we came to the age column, Miss Susan played with one of her ringlets, and looked in my face sweetly, and said : "Mr. M'Lauchlin, what did Miss M'Farlane say ? My sister, you know, is considerably older than I am — there was a brother between us."

"Quite so, my dear Miss Susan," said I ; "but you see the bargain was that each was to state her own age."

"Well," said Miss Susan, still playing with her ringlets, "you can say—age, thirty-four years, Mr. M'Lauchlin."

In a little while the youngest sister came in.

"Miss M'Farlane," said she, "sent me over for the census paper."

"O, no, my dear," says I ; "I cannot part with the paper."

"Well, then," said she, "just enter my name, too, Mr. M'Lauchlin."

"Quite so. But tell me, Miss Robina, why did Miss M'Farlane not fill up the paper herself ?"—for Miss Robina and I were always on very confidential terms.

"Oh," she replied, "there was a dispute over *particulars ;* and Miss M'Farlane would not let my other sister see how old she had said she was ; and Miss Susan refused to state her age to Miss M'Farlane ; and so, to end the quarrel, we agreed to ask you to be so kind as to fill in the paper."

"Yes, yes, Miss Robina," said I ; "that's quite satisfactory ; and so, I'll fill in your name now, if you please."

"Yes," she uttered, with a sigh. When we came to the age column—"Is it absolutely necessary," said she, "to fill in the age ? Don't you think it is a most impertinent question to ask, Mr. M'Lauchlin ?"

"Tuts, it may be so to some folk ; but to a sweet young creature like you, it cannot matter a button."

"Well," said Miss Robina — "but now, Mr. M'Lauchlin, I'm to tell you a great secret"; and she blushed as she slowly continued: "The minister comes sometimes to see us."

"I *have* noticed him rather more attentive in his visitations in your quarter of late, than usual, Miss Robina."

"Very well, Mr. M'Lauchlin; but you must not tease me just now. You know Miss M'Farlane is of opinion that he is in love with her; while Miss Susan thinks her taste for literature and her knowledge of geology, especially her pamphlet on the Old Red Sandstone and its fossils as confirming the old Mosaic record, are all matters of great interest to Mr. Frazer, and she fancies that he comes so frequently for the privilege of conversing with her. But," exclaimed Miss Robina, with a look of triumph, "look at that!" and she held in her hand a beautiful gold ring. "I have got that from the minister this very day!"

I congratulated her. She had been a favorite pupil of mine, and I was rather pleased with what happened. "But what," I asked her, "has all this to do with the census?"

"Oh, just this," continued Miss Robina. "I had no reason to conceal my age, as Mr. Frazer knows it exactly, since he baptized me. He was a young creature then, only three-and-twenty; so that's just the difference between us."

"Nothing at all, Miss Robina," said I; "nothing at all; not worth mentioning."

"In this changeful and passing world," said Miss Robina, "three-and-twenty years are not much after all, Mr. M'Lauchlin!"

"Much!" said I. "Tuts, my dear, it's nothing— just, indeed, what should be."

"I was just thirty-four last birthday, Mr. M'Lauchlin," said Miss Robina; "and the minister said the last time he called that no young lady should take the cares and responsibilities of a household upon herself till she was — well, eight-and-twenty; and he added that thirty-four was late enough."

"The minister, my dear, is a man of sense."

So thus were the Miss M'Farlanes' census schedules filled up; and if ever some one in search of the curiosities of the census should come across it, he may think it strange enough, for he will find that the three sisters M'Farlane are all ae year's bairns!

Distributing His Praises with Discernment

Will Stout was a bachelor and parish beadle, residing with his old mother who lived to the age of nearly a hundred years. In mature life he was urged by some friends to take a wife. He was very cautious, however, in regard to matrimony, and declined the advice, excusing himself on the ground "that there are many things you can say to your mither you couldna say to a fremit (strange) woman."

While beadle, he had seen four or five different ministers in the parish, and had buried two or three of them. And although his feelings became somewhat blunted regarding the sacredness of graves in general, yet he took a somewhat tender care of the spot where the ministers lay. After his extended experience, he was asked to give his deliberate judgment as to which of them he had liked best. His answer was guarded; he said he did not know, as they were all good men. But being further pressed and asked if he had no preference, after a little thought he again admitted that they were all "guid men, guid men; but Mr. Mathieson's claes fitted me best."

One of the new incumbents, knowing Will's interest in the clothes, thought that at an early stage he would gain his favor by presenting him with a coat. To make him conscious of the kindly service he was doing, the minister informed him that it was almost new. Will took the garment, examined it with a critical eye, and having thoroughly satisfied himself, pronounced it "a guid coat," but pawkily added: "When Mr. Watt, the old minister, gied me a coat, he gied me breeks as weel."

The new minister, who was fortunately gifted with a sense of humor, could not do less than complete Will's rig-out from top to toe, and so established himself as a permanent favorite with the beadle.

Mallet, Plane and Sermon—All Wooden

In olden times, the serviceable beadle was armed with a small wooden "nob" or mallet, with which he was quietly commissioned to "tap" gently but firmly the heads of careless sleepers in church during the sermon. An instance to hand is very amusing.

In the old town of Kilbarchan, which is celebrated in Scottish poetry as the birthplace of Habbie Simpson, the piper and verse maker of the clachan, once lived and preached a reverend original, whose pulpit ministrations were of the old-fashioned, hodden-gray type, being humdrum and innocent of all spirit-rousing eloquence and force. Like many of his clerical brethren, he was greatly annoyed every Sunday at the sight of several of his parishioners sleeping throughout the sermon. He was especially angry with Johnny Plane, the village joiner, who dropped off to sleep every Sunday afternoon simultaneously with the formal delivery of the text. Johnny had been "touched" by the old beadle's mallet on several occasions, but only in a gentle though persuasive manner. At last, one day the minister, provoked beyond endurance at the sight of the joiner soundly sleeping, lost his temper.

"Johnny Plane!" cried the reverend gentleman, stopping his discourse and eyeing the culprit severely, "are ye really sleeping already, and me no' half through the first head?"

The joiner, easy man, was quite oblivious to things celestial and mundane, and noticed not the rebuke.

"Andra," resumed the minister, addressing the beadle, and relapsing into informal Doric, "gang round to the wast loft (west gallery) and rap up Johnny Plane. Gie the lazy loon a guid stiff rap on the heid—he deserves 't."

Round and up to the "wast loft" the old-fashioned beadle goes, and reaching the somnolent parishioner, he rather smartly "raps" him on his bald head. Instantly, there was on the part of Johnny a sudden start-up, and between him and the worthy beadle a hot, underbreath bandying of words.

Silence restored, the reverend gentleman proceeded

with his sermon as if nothing unusual had occurred.
After sermon, Andra met the minister in the vestry,
who at once made inquiry as to the " words " he had
had with Johnny in the gallery. But the beadle was
reticent and uncommunicative on the matter, and
would not be questioned at the reception the joiner
had given his salutary summons.

"Well, Andra," at length said the reverend gentleman, " I'll tell ye what, we must not be beaten in this
matter ; if the loon sleeps next Sunday during sermon,
just you gang up and rap him back to reason. It's a
knock wi' some *force* in't the chiel wants, mind that,
and spare not."

"Deed no, sir" was the beadle's canny reply.
"I'll no' disturb him, sleepin' or waukin', for some
time to come. He threatens to knock pew-Bibles and
hymn-books oot o me, if I again daur to 'rap' him
atween this and Martinmas. If Johnny's to be kept
frae sleepin', minister, ye maun *just pit the force into
yer sermon.*"

Using Their Senses

The following story is told by one of the officers
engaged in taking a census : One afternoon, I called
up at Whinny Knowes, to get their schedule ; and
Mrs. Cameron invited me to stay to tea, telling me
what a day they had had at " Whins " with the census
paper.

"'First of all,' said she, 'the master there '—
pointing to her husband—'said seriously that every
one must tell their ages, whether they were married
or not, and whether they intended to be married, and
the age and occupation of their sweethearts—in fact,
that every particular was to be mentioned. Now,
Mr. M'Lauchlin, our two servant lasses are real nice
girls ; but save me ! what a fluster this census paper
has put them in. Janet has been ten years with us,
and is a most superior woman, with good sense ; but
at this time she is the most distressed of the two.
After family worship last night, she said she would
like a word o' the master himsel'.'

"'All right,' says John, with a slight twinkle in his
eye.

"'When they were by themselves, Janet stood with her Bible in her hand, and her eyes fixed on the point of her shoe. 'Sir,' said she, 'I was three-an'-thirty last birthday, though my neighbor Mary thinks I'm only eight-an'-twenty. And as for Alexander '— this was the miller, Janet's reputed sweetheart—'he's never asked my age exactly; and so, if it's all the same, I would like you just to keep your thumb upon 'that. And then, as to whether he's to marry me or not, that depends on whether the factor gives him another lease of the mill. He says he'll take me at Martinmas coming if he gets the lease; but at the farthest, next Martinmas, whether or no.'

"'Janet,' said my husband, 'you have stated the matter fairly; there is nothing more required.'

"And John, there," continued Mrs. Cameron, "has made good use of Janet's census return. This very forenoon Lady Menzies called to see us, as she often does. Said John to her ladyship, says he: 'He's a very good fellow, Alexander Christie, the miller—a superior man. I'm sorry we are like to lose him for a neighbor.'

"'I never heard of that,' said her ladyship. 'He is a steady, honest man, and a good miller, I believe. I should be sorry to lose him on the estate. What is the cause of this?'

"'Oh,' replied my husband, 'it seems the factor is not very willing to have a new lease of the mill without one being built. Your ladyship,' added John, 'can see what Alexander is after.'

"'Oh, yes, I understand,' said she, laughing. 'I will try and keep the miller'; and off she set without another word. Down the burnside she goes, and meets Alexander, with a bag of corn on his back, at the mill-door. When he had set it down, and was wiping the perspiration off his brow with the back of his hand, Lady Menzies said: 'You are busy to-day, miller.'

"'Yes, my lady,' said he; 'this is a busy time.'

"'I wonder,' said her ladyship, coming to the point at once, 'that a fine young fellow like you does not settle down now and take a wife, and let me have the pleasure of seeing you as a tenant always with us.'

" ' You wouldn't, my lady,' said the miller, ' have me bring a bird before I had a cage to put it in. The factor grudges to build me a house; therefore, I fear I must remove.'

" ' Well, Christie,' said her ladyship with great glee, ' you'll look out for the bird, and leave it to me to find the cage.'

" ' It's a bargain, my lady,' said Alexander. ' My father and my grandfather were millers here for many a long year before me; and to tell the truth, I was reluctant to leave the old place.'

" In the course of the forenoon, the miller made an errand up the burn to the ' Whins,' for some empty bags; and as we had already got an inkling of what had passed between him and Lady Menzies, I sent Janet to the barn to help him look them out. When Janet returned, I saw she was a little flurried, and looked as if there was something she wished to say. In a little while — ' Ma'am,' says she to me, ' I'm no' to stop after Martinmas.'

" ' No, Janet ?' says I. ' I'm sorry to hear that. I'm sure I've no fault to find with you, and you have been a long time with us.'

" ' I'm not going far away,' said Janet, with some pride; ' the bairns will aye get a handful of groats when they come to see us !'

" So you see, Mr. M'Lauchlin, what a change this census paper of yours has brought about."

" Ay, ay, good wife," said Whinny Knowes, laughing; " Although you have lost a good servant, you must admit that I've managed to keep the miller."

Qualifications for a Chief

When Glengarry claimed the chieftainship of the Macdonald clan, the generally acknowledged chief wrote to him as follows: "My DEAR GLENGARRY: As soon as you can prove yourself my chief I shall be ready to acknowledge you. In the meantime, I am, *Yours*, MACDONALD."

A Beadle Magnifying His Office

The story of Watty Tinlin, the half-crazy beadle of

Hawick parish, illustrates the license which was, on certain occasions, supposed to be due to his office. One day Wat got so tired of listening to the long sermon of a strange minister, that he went outside the church, and wandering in the direction of the river Teviot, saw the worshipers from the adjoining parish of Wilton crossing the bridge on their way home.

Returning to the church and finding the preacher still thundering away, he shouted out, to the astonishment and relief of the exhausted congregation: "Say, amen, sir; say amen! Wulton's kirk's comin ower Teviot Brig!"

No Wonder!

The Lord Provost of a certain well-known city in the north had a daughter married to a gentleman of the name of Baird; and speaking of names of several friends, he happened to remark: "My grandmother was a Huisband, and my mother a Man," these having been the maiden names of the ladies.

"Why, in that case," said the celebrated Dr. Gregory, who happened to be present, "we may the less wonder at your daughter having got a Baird."

Virtuous Necessity

Robbie Fairgrieve was sexton as well as kirk-beadle in a Roxburghshire parish, and despite the solemn duties attaching to his vocation, was on the whole a genial man, about equally fond of a joke and a good dram. In fact, Robbie was affected with a chronic "spark in his throat" which was ill to quench, and was, indeed, never fairly extinguished during the fifty years he officiated as kirk-beadle and sexton. One day, the minister of the parish met Robbie coming home from a visit to Jedburgh fair much sooner than was expected, he (Robbie) having found the fair painfully *dry*, in the sense of an unprecedented absence of friendly drams. Curious to know the cause of the beadle's quick return, the minister inquired as to the reason of such correct conduct, since most of his fellow-parishioners would likely stay out the fair.

"Oh, sir," said Robbie, "huz yins (us ones) wha

are 'sponsible kirk-officers " (alluding to the minister
and himself), "should aye strive to be guid ensamples
to the riff-raff o' the flock."

Strangers—"Unawares "—Not always Angels

Dr. Ferguson's first residence in Peebleshire was at
Neidpath Castle, which was then just about to fall into
its present half-ruinous state. On settling there, he
told his family that it was his desire that any respectable people in the neighborhood who called should be
received with the utmost civility, so that they might
remain on pleasant terms with all around. Ere many
days had elapsed, a neatly-dressed, gentleman-like
little man was shown into Dr. Ferguson's own room,
and entered easily into miscellaneous conversation.
The bell for their early family-dinner ringing at the
time, the courteous professor invited his visitor to join
the family in the dining-room, which he readily consented to do. The family, remembering their father's
injunction, of course received the unknown with all
possible distinction, and a very lively conversation
ensued. Dr. Ferguson, however, expressed his con-
cern to see that his guest was eating very little—
indeed, only making an appearance of eating—and he
confessed his regret that he had so little variety of
fare to offer him.

"Oh, doctor," said the stranger, "never mind me:
the fact is, on *killing days* I scarcely ever have any
appetite."

Not small was the surprise, but much greater the
amusement of the family, on discovering that he of the
stingy appetite was Robert Smith, the Peebles butcher,
and that the object of his visit was merely to bespeak
Dr. Ferguson's custom!

"Reflections "

A young preacher was holding forth to a country
congregation, with rather more show than substance ;
after discussing certain heads in his way, he informed
his audience that he would conclude with a few reflections.

An old man, who seemed not greatly gratified, gave

a significant shrug of his shoulders, and said in a low tone of voice, "Ye needna fash. There'll be plenty o' reflections I'se warn ye, though ye dinna mak' ony yersel'."

An Observant Husband

Willie Turnbull and his wife used to sup their evening meal of brose out of one " cog," but the gudewife generally took care to place the lump of butter at one side of the dish, which she carefully turned to her own side of the table. One night, however, Mrs. Turnbull inadvertently turned the " fat side " from her, and did not discover her error till she was about to dip in her spoon. She could not, without exposing her selfishness, actually turn the bowl round before her husband, but the butter she must have, and in order to obtain it she resorted to artifice.

"Willie," said she, as if seized with a sudden inspiration, " isn't this a queer world ? I'm tell't that it just turns round and round about, as I micht take this bowl and turn it round this way," and she prepared to suit the action to the word.

Willie, however, saw this at a glance, and promptly stopped the practical illustration, saying, " Ay, ay, Maggie, the world's queer enough, but you just let it stand still e'enow, and the brose bowl, too ! "

"Bulls " in Scotland

Two operatives in one of the Border towns were heard disputing about a new cemetery, beside the elegant railing of which they were standing. One of them, evidently disliking the continental fashion in which it was being laid out, said in disgust, " I'd rather dee than be buried in sic a place ! "

" Weel, it's the verra reverse wi' me," said the other, " for I'll be buried naewhere else if I'm spared."

"Brothers " in Law

A countryman, going into the Court of Session, took notice of two advocates at the bar, who, being engaged on opposite sides of the case in hand, wrangled with and contradicted each other severely, each frequently, however, styling his opponent "brother." The countryman observed to a bystander that there did not seem to be much brotherly love between them.

"Oh," said he, "they're only brothers *in law*."

"I suppose they'll be married on twa sisters, then," replied he; "and I think it's just the auld story ower again—freen's 'gree best separate."

A Family Likeness

Some soldiers, quartered in a country village, when they met at the roll-call were asking one another what kind of quarters they had got; one of them said he had very good quarters, but the strangest landlady ever he saw—she always took him off. A comrade said he would go along with him and would take her off. He went and offered to shake hands with her, saying, "How are you, Elspa?"

"Indeed, sir," said she, "ye hae the better o' me; I dinna ken ye."

"Dear me, Elspa," replied the soldier, "d'ye no ken me? I'm the devil's sister's son."

"Dear, save us!" quoth the old wife, looking him broadly in the face; "'od man, but ye're like your uncle!"

"Unco' Modest"

A Scottish witness in the House of Lords once gave in a rather dictatorial style his notions as to the failings in the character of Irishmen and Englishmen.

He was allowed to say his say, and when out of breath Lord Lucan asked him to oblige the committee with his ideas relative to Scotch character.

"Aweel, my laird, they're just on the contrary, unco' modest and "—the rest of the sentence was drowned in uproarious merriment.

Objecting to "Regeneration"

"What is the meaning of 'regeneration,' Tommy?" asked a teacher in the north, of one of the most promising pupils.

"It means 'to be born again,' sir," was the answer.

"Quite right, quite right, my man. Would you like to be born again, Tommy?" said the examiner.

"No, sir, I wadna," replied the heretical youth, boldly.

"Indeed, laddie, and wha for no'?" inquired the astounded preceptor.

"Because, sir," answered Tommy, "I'm fear'd I might be born a lassie."

Reasons For and Against Organs in Kirk

At a certain gathering of Presbyterian clergymen one of them urged that organs should be introduced in order to draw more young people to the church; upon which an old minister remarked that this was acting on the principle of "O whistle, an' I'll come to ye, my lad!"

Too Much Light and Too Little

A parish minister in Stirlingshire, noted for his parsimonious habits, had his glebe land wholly cropped with corn upon one occasion. After the ingatherings of harvest, news reached him that a considerable fall in prices was expected, and he ordered his serviceable "man," John, to get the corn threshed and taken to market with all possible speed. Now the beadle, having a well-founded hatred for his master's greed, set about his work in his ordinary style—a slow, if sure, process. John's style, however, did not on this occasion please the minister, who ordered him to get through with the task, even though he should get it done by candle-light.

"Weel, weel," said the beadle; "say nae mair aboot it; it'll be done, sir, e'en as ye desire."

Next day the minister, hearing the sound of the flail, entered the barn to see what progress was being made with the work, when, to his astonishment and anger, he found his beadle "flailing" away with might and main, and a candle burning brightly on each side of the threshing-floor.

"What's this I see? What's the meaning of this?" demanded his master. "Candles burning in broad daylight!"

"Oh, contain yersel', sir—contain yersel'," replied John with provoking coolness. "I'm daein' nae mair

than ye bade me, for I'm daein' the job baith by day-
licht and by can'le-licht.''

The beadle, after being severely lectured on his
extravagant conduct, was ordered to take the candles
to the kitchen, and henceforth and at all times he was
to be deprived of their use.

One night shortly after, a message came to the minister that one of his parishioners, who lived at a distance, was supposed to be dying, and was anxious to
see him. John was dispatched to saddle the horse;
and his master set about equipping himself for the
journey. He then stepped across to where John was
waiting with the animal, and seizing the reins, was
about to mount, when suddenly, seeing a pair of horns
on the crest of the steed, he shouted : '' What in all
the earth is this you have done, John ? ''

The beadle, comically peering in the darkness at
the creature, exclaimed : '' I declare, sir, if I hav'na
saddled the coo instead o' the horse, for the want o'
can'le-licht ! ''

A Reproof Cleverly Diverted

The punctuality which reigned over the domestic
regulations of Dr. Chalmers was sometimes not a little
inconvenient to his guests.

His aunt, while living in the house, appearing one
morning too late for breakfast, and well knowing what
awaited her if she did not '' take the first word o'
flyting,'' thus diverted the expected storm.

'' Oh ! Mr. Chalmers,'' she exclaimed, as she entered
the room, '' I had such a strange dream last night ; I
dreamt that you were dead. And I dreamt,'' she
continued, '' that the funeral cards were written ; and
the day came, and the folk came, and the hour came ;
but what do you think happened? Why, the clock
had scarce done chapping twelve, which was the hour
named in the cards, when a loud knocking was heard
in the coffin, and a voice, gey peremptory and ill-
pleased like, came out of it, saying, ' Twelve's chap-
pit, and ye're no liftin' ! ' ''

The doctor was too fond of a joke not to relish this
one ; and, in the hearty laugh which followed, the
ingenious culprit escaped. [22]

A Scotch "Squire"

"What name, sir?" said a booking clerk at a coach office in Paisley, to a person who was applying for a seat in the Glasgow coach.

"What hae ye to dae wi' my name, gin I gie ye the siller?" replied the applicant.

"I require it for the way-bill; and unless you give it, you can't have a place in the coach," said the clerk.

"Oh! gin that be the case, I suppose ye maun hae't. Weel, then, my name's John Tamson o' Butter Braes, an' ye may put 'Esquire' till't, gin ye like; at least, I live on my ain farm."

Peter Peebles' Prejudice

"Ow, he is just a weed harum-scarum creature, that wad never take his studies; daft, sir, clean daft."

"Deft!" said the justice; "what d'ye mean by deft—eh?"

"Just Fifish," replied Peter; "wowf—a wee bit by the East—Nook, or sae; it's common case—the ae half of the warld thinks the tither daft. I have met folk in my day that thought I was daft mysell; and, for my part, I think our Court of Session clean daft, that have had the great cause of Peebles against Plainstanes before them for this score of years, and have never been able to ding the bottom of it yet." [20]

English versus Scotch Sheep's Heads

A Scottish family, having removed to London, wished to have a sheep's head prepared as they had been accustomed to have it at home, and sent the servant to procure one.

"My gude man," said the girl, "I want a sheep's head."

"There's plenty of them," replied the knight of the knife, "choose one for yourself."

"Na, na," said she, "I want ane that will sing (singe)."

"Go, you stupid girl," said he, "whoever heard of a sheep's head that could sing?"

"Why," said the girl in wrath, "it's ye that's stupid; for a' the sheep's heads in Scotland can sing;

but I jalouse your English sheep are just as grit fuies as their owners, and can do naething as they ocht."

Seeking, not Help, but Information, and Getting It

The landlord of the hotel at the foot of Ben Nevis tells a story of an Englishman stumbling into a bog between the mountain and the inn, and sinking up to his armpits. In danger of his life he called out to a tall Highlander who was passing by, "How can I get out of this?" to which the Scotchman replied, "I dinna think ye can," and coolly walked on.

Compulsory Education and a Father's Remedy

One of the members of a Scottish School Board was recently discussing the question of compulsory education with a worthy elector, who addressed him as follows: "An' that's gospel, is't, that ye're gaun to eddicatt my bairns whuther I will or no?"

The member proceeded to explain.

"Weel, I'll just tell ye. Ye say they're to be eddicatt; I say they're no' an' they sanna. I'll droon them first!"

"No Lord's Day!"

In a certain district in the Highlands, the bell-man one day made the following proclamation: "O yes, O yes, and O yes; and that's three times! You'll all pe tak' notice, that there will pe no Lord's day here next Sabbath, pecause the laird's wife wants the kirk to dry her clothes in!"

Dead Shot

An ironmonger who kept a shop in the High Street of Edinburgh, and sold gunpowder and shot, when asked by any ignorant person in what respect "patent" shot—a new article at that time—surpassed the old kind, "Oh, sir," he would answer, "it shoots deader."

Quid Pro Quo

An old Scottish beggar, with bonnet in hand, appealed to a clergyman for "a bit of charity." The minister put a piece of silver into his hand.

"Thank ye, sir; oh, thank ye! I'll gie ye an afternoon's hearing for this ane o' these days."

The Scottish Credit System

An intimation hung in a warehouse in Glasgow was to this effect: " No credit given here, except to those who pay money down."

Scotch "Paddy"

" Noo, my gude bairns," said a schoolmaster to his class " there's just another instance o' the uncertainty o' human life ; ane o' your ane schulemates—a fine wee bit lassie—went to her bed hale and weel at night and rose a corpse in the morning."

. The Importance of Quantity in Scholarship

Charles Erskine was, at the age of twenty, a teacher of Latin in Edinburgh University. On one occasion, after his elevation to the bench, a young lawyer in arguing a case before him used a false Latin quantity, whereupon his lordship said, with a good-natured smile, " Are you sure, sir, you are correct in your *quantity* there?"

The young counsel nettled at the query, retorted petulantly, " My lord, I never was a schoolmaster."

" No," answered the judge, " nor, I think, a scholar either."

Capital Punishment

Andrew Leslie, an old Scotchman, always rode a donkey to his work and tethered him, while he labored, on the road, or wherever else he might be. It was suggested to him by a neighboring gentleman that he was suspected of putting him in to feed in the fields at other people's expense.

" Eh, laird, I could never be tempted to do that, for my cuddy winna eat anything but nettles and thistles."

One day, however, the same gentleman was riding along the road when he saw Andrew Leslie at work, and his donkey up to his knees in one of his own clover fields feeding luxuriously.

" Hollo! Andrew," said he, " I thought you told me your cuddy would eat nothing but nettles and thistles."

" Ay," was the reply, "but he misbehaved the day ;
he nearly kicked me ower his head, sae I put him in
there just to punish him ! "

" Plucked ! "

Scotch parish schoolmasters are, on their appointment, examined as to their literary qualifications. One
of the fraternity being called by his examiner to translate Horace's ode beginning, " Exegi monumentum
ære perennius," commenced as follows : " Exegi
monumentum—I have eaten a mountain."

" Ah," said one of the examiners, " ye needna proceed any further ; for after eatin' sic a dinner, this
parish wad be a puir mouthfu' t' ye. Ye maun try
some wider sphere."

An Instance of Scott's Pleasantry

Sir Walter Scott was never wanting in something
pleasant to say, even on the most trivial occasions.
Calling one day at Huntly Burn, soon after the settle-
ment of his friend in that house, and observing a fine
honeysuckle in full blossom over the door, he congratulated Miss Ferguson on its appearance. She
remarked that it was the kind called trumpet honeysuckle, from the form of the flower. " Weel," said
Scott, " ye'll never come out o' your ain door without
a flourish o' trumpets."

Turning His Father's Weakness to Account

Many good stories are told of old Dr. Lawson, a
Presbyterian minister in Scotland, who was so absent-
minded that he sometimes was quite insensible of the
world around him. One of his sons, who afterwards
became a highly esteemed Christian minister, was a
very tricky boy, perhaps mischievous in his tricks.

Near the manse lived an old woman, of crabbed
temper, and rather ungodly in her mode of living.
She and the boy had quarreled, and the result was
that he took a quiet opportunity to kill one of her
hens. She went immediately to Dr. Lawson and
charged his son with the deed. She was believed ;
and, as it was not denied, punishment was inflicted.

He was ordered to abide in the house; and to make the sentence more severe his father took him into the *study*, and commanded him to sit there with him.

The son was restless, and frequently eyed the door. At last he saw his father drowned in thought, and quietly slipped out. He went directly to the old woman's and killed another hen, returning immediately and taking his place in the library, his father having never missed him.

The old woman speedily made her appearance, and charged the slaughter again upon him.

Dr. Lawson, however, waxed angry—declared her to be a false accuser, as the boy had been closeted with him all the time—adding: " Besides, this convinces me that you had just as little ground for your last accusation; I therefore acquit him of both, and he may go out now."

The woman went off in high dudgeon, and the prisoner in high glee.

Curious Idea for the Evidence for Truth

Jean M'Gown had been telling a story to some friends who seemed inclined to doubt the truth thereof, when Jean, turning round quite indignantly, said, " It mon be true, for father read it out o' a *bound book!* "

Dry Weather, and Its Effects on the Ocean

The family of Mr. Torrance were about leaving the town of Strathaven, for America. Tibby Torrance, an old maiden sister of Mr. Torrance's was to accompany them.

Before they left, some of the neighbors were talking to Tibby of the dangers of the " great deep," when she suddenly exclaimed, " Aweel, aweel, it's been a gay dry summer, and I think the sea'll no' be very deep! "

Laughing in the Pulpit—With Explanation

A Scotch Presbyterian minister stopped one morning, in the middle of his discourse, laughing out loud and long. After a while he composed his face, and finished the service without any explanation of his extraordinary conduct.

The elders, who had often been annoyed with his peculiarities, thought this a fit occasion to remonstrate with him. They did so during the noon intermission, and insisted upon the propriety of his making an explanation in the afternoon. To this he readily assented; and after the people were again assembled, and while he was standing, book in hand, ready to begin the service, he said:

"Brethren, I laughed in midst of the service this mornin', and the gude eldership came and talked wi' me aboot it, and I towld them I would make an apology to you at once, and that I am now aboot to do. As I was preaching to you this mornin', I saw the deil come in that door wi' a long parchment in his hand, as long as my arm; and as he came up that side he tuk down the names of all that were asleep, an' then he went down the ither side, and got only twa seats down, and by that time the parchment was full. The deil looked along down the aisle, and saw a whole row of sleepers, and no room for their names; so he stretched it till it tore; and he laughed, and I couldn't help it but laugh, too --and that's my apology. Sing the Fiftieth Psalm."

A Good Judge of Accent

A Canadian bishop, well known for his broad Scotch accent as well as his belief that it was not perceptible, was called upon by a brother Scot one day, whom he had not seen for several years. Among other questions asked of him by the bishop was, "How long have you been in Canada?"

"About sax years," was the reply.

"Hoot, mon," says the bishop, "why hae ye na lost your accent, like mysel'?"

"Haudin' His Stick"

On my first visit to Edinburgh, having heard a great deal of the oratorical powers of some of the members of the General Assembly, I was anxious to hear and judge for myself. I accordingly paid an early visit to it. Seated next me I saw an elderly, hard-featured, sober-looking man, leaning with both hands on a stick and eyeing the stick with great earnestness, scarcely even moving his eyes to right or left.

My attention was soon directed to the speaker above me, who had opened the discourse of the day. The fervidness of his eloquence, his great command of language, and the strangeness of his manner excited my attention in an unusual degree. I wished to know who he was, and applied to my neighbor, the sober-looking, hard-featured man.

"Pray, sir, can you tell me who is speaking now?"

The man turned on me a defiant and contemptuous look for my ignorance, and answered, looking reverently at the cane on which his hands were imposed: "Sir, that's the great Docther Chawmers, and I'm haudin' his stick!" [16]

Indiscriminate Humor

The late Archibald Constable, the well-known Edinburgh publisher, was somewhat remarkable in his day for the caustic severity of his speech, which, however, was only a thin covering to a most amiable, if somewhat overbearing, disposition.

On one occasion a partner of the London publishing house of Longman, Hurst, Rees, Orme & Brown was dining with Mr. C——, at his country seat near the beautiful village of Lasswade. Looking out of the window, the Londoner remarked, "What a pretty lake, and what beautiful swans!"

"Lake, mon, and swans!—it's nae a lake, it's only a pond; and they're naething but geese. You'll maybe noteece that they are just five of them; and Baldy, that ne'er-do-weel bairn there, caws them Longman, Hurst, Rees, Orme and Brown!"

Sir Walter Scott, in telling the story, was wont to add: "That skit cost the 'crafty' many a guinea, for the cockney was deeply offended, as well he might be, not knowing the innocent intent with which his Scotch friend made such speeches."

Scotch Undergraduates and Funerals

The reported determination of a Scottish professor not to allow the students of his class more than one funeral in each family this session sounds like a grim joke; but it is fair to note that this gentleman, who has presumptively some experience of the ways of undergraduates, was lately reported to have come to the conclusion that the very high rate of mortality of late among the relatives of members of his class has been "artificially produced." Dark reminders of the hero of " Ruddigore," who was bound by the decrees of fate to commit one crime a day, have been heard in connection with this mysterious reference; but the *University Correspondent* has thrown a little light on the subject. The suggestion is that the northern undergraduate—not unlike his English brother—when he is feeling a little bored by his surroundings at the university, has a habit of producing a sad telegram informing him of the demise of a maiden aunt or second-cousin who never existed. [17]

Honest Johnny M'Cree

In one of his speeches Sheridan says : I remember a story told respecting Mr. Garrick, who was once applied to by an eccentric Scotchman to introduce a work of his on the stage. This Scotchman was such a good-humored fellow, that he was called " honest Johnny M'Cree."

Johnny wrote four acts of a tragedy which he showed to Mr. Garrick, who dissuaded him from finishing it, telling him that his talent did not lie that way; so Johnny abandoned the tragedy, and set about writing a comedy. When this was finished he showed it to Mr. Garrick, who found it to be still more exceptionable than the tragedy, and of course could not be persuaded to bring it forward on the stage.

This surprised poor Johnny, and he remonstrated. " Nay, now, David," said Johnny, " did you not tell me that my talents did not lie in tragedy ?"

" Yes," said Garrick, " but I did not tell you that they lay in comedy."

" Then," exclaimed Johnny, " gin they dinna lie there, where the deil dittha lie, mon ?"

Heaven Before it was Wanted

A Scotch newspaper relates that a beggar wife, on receiving a gratuity from the Rev. John Skinner, of Langside, author of "Tullochgorum," said to him by way of thanks, "Oh, sir, I houp that ye and a' your family will be in heaven the nicht."

"Well," said Skinner, "I am very much obliged to you; only you need not have just been so particular as to the time."

Curious Delusion Concerning Light

A hard-headed Scotchman, a first-rate sailor and navigator, he, like many other people, had his craze, which consisted in looking down with lofty contempt upon such deluded mortals as supposed that light was derived from the sun! Yet he gazed on that luminary day after day as he took its meridian altitude and was obliged to temper his vision with the usual piece of dark-colored glass.

"How," I asked him, "do you account for light if it is not derived from the sun?"

"Weel," he said, "it comes from the eer; but you will be knowing all about it some day."

He was of a taciturn nature, but of the few remarks which he did make the usual one was, "Weel, and so yer think that light comes from the sun, do yer? Weel! ha, ha!" and he would turn away with a contemptuous chuckle. [18]

Less Sense than a Sheep

Lord Cockburn, the proprietor of Bonally, was sitting on a hillside with a shepherd; and observing the sheep reposing in the coolest situation he observed to him, "John, if I were a sheep, I would lie on the other side of the hill." The shepherd answered, "Ay, my lord, but if ye had been a sheep, ye would hae mair sense."

Consoled by a Relative's Lameness

For authenticity of one remark made by the Rev. Walter Dunlop I can readily vouch. Some time previous to the death of his wife Mr. Dunlop had quar-

reled with that lady's brother—a gentleman who had
the misfortune to lose a leg, and propelled himself by
means of a stick substitute.

When engaged with two of the deacons of his
church, considering the names of those to whom
"bids" to the funeral should be sent, one observed,
"Mr. Dunlop, ye maun send ane to Mr.——" naming
the obnoxious relative.

"Ou, ay," returned the minister, striving that his
sense of duty should overcome his reluctance to the
proposal. "Ye can send *him* ane." Then immediately added, with much gravity, and in a tone that
told the vast relief which the reflection afforded,
"He'll no be able to come up the stairs." [4]

Curious Sentence

Some years ago the celebrated Edward Irving had
been lecturing at Dumfries, and a man who passed
as a wag in that locality had been to hear him.

He met Watty Dunlop the following day, who
said, "Weel, Willie, man, an' what do ye think of
Mr. Irving?"

"Oh," said Willie contemptuously, "the man's
crack't."

Dunlop patted him on the shoulder, with a quiet
remark, "Willie, ye'll aften see a light peeping
through a crack!" [7]

Too Canny to Admit Anything Particular

An elder of the parish kirk of Montrose was suspected of illegal practices, and the magistrates being
loth to prosecute him, privately requested the minister to warn the man that his evil doings were known,
and that if he did not desist he would be punished
and disgraced. The minister accordingly paid the
elder a visit, but could extort neither confession nor
promise of amendment from the delinquent.

"Well, Sandy," said the minister, as he rose to
retire from his fruitless mission, "you seem to think
your sins cannot be proved before an earthly tribunal,
but you may be assured that they will all come out in
the day of judgment."

"Verra true, sir," replied the elder, calmly. "An' it is to be hoped for the credit of the kirk that neither yours nor mine come oot afore then."

Mortifying Unanimity

I said, to one who picked me up,
Just slipping from a rock,
"I'm not much good at climbing, eh?"
"No, sirr, ye arrrn't," quoth Jock.

I showed him then a sketch I'd made,
Of rough hill-side and lock;
"I'm not an artist, mind," I said;
"No, sirr, ye arrrn't," quoth Jock.

A poem, next, I read aloud—
One of my num'rous stock;
"I'm no great poet," I remarked;
"No, sirr, ye arrrn't," said Jock.

Alas! I fear I well deserved
(Although it proved a shock),
In answer to each modest sham,
That plain retort from Jock.

A Consoling "If"

Bannockburn is always the set-off to Flodden in popular estimation, and without it Flodden would be a sore subject.

"So you are going to England to practice surgery," said a Scottish lawyer to a client, who had been a cow-doctor; "but have you skill enough for your new profession!"

"Hoots! ay! plenty o' skill!"

"But are you not afraid ye may sometimes kill your patients, if you do not study medicine for awhile as your proper profession?"

"Nae fear! and if I do kill a few o' the South-rons, it will take a great deal of killing to mak' up for Flodden!"

Happy Escape from an Angry Mob

The most famous surgeon in Edinburg, towards the

close of the last (the eighteenth) century, was certainly Mr. Alexander Wood, Member of the Incorporation of Chirurgeons, or what is now called the Royal
College of Surgeons.   In these days he was known by
no other name than Lang Sandy Wood (or "Wud,"
as it was pronounced).   He deserves to be remembered as the last man in Edinburgh who wore a cocked
hat and sword as part of his ordinary dress, and the
first who was known to carry an umbrella.

It is generally supposed that he was induced to
discontinue the wearing of the sword and cocked hat
by an unfortunate accident which very nearly happened to him about 1792.   At that time the then lord
provost, or chief magistrate of the city, a Mr. Stirling,
was very unpopular with the lower orders of society,
and one dark night, as Sandy was proceeding over the
North Bridge on some errand of mercy, he was met by
an infuriated mob on their way from the "closes" of
the old town to burn the provost's house in revenge
for some wrong—real or imaginary—supposed to be
inflicted by that functionary.   Catching sight of an
old gentleman in a cocked hat and sword, they
instantly concluded that this must be the provost—
these two articles of dress being then part of the
official attire of the Edinburgh chief magistrate.   Then
arose the cry of "Throw him over the bridge"—a
suggestion no sooner made than it was attempted to
be carried into execution.

The tall old surgeon was in mortal terror, and had
barely time to gasp out, just as he was carried to the
parapet of the bridge, "Gude folk, I'm no' the provost.   Carry me to a lamp post an' ye'll see I'm Lang
Sandy Wood!"

With considerable doubt whether or not the obnoxious magistrate was not trying to save his life by trad-
ing on the popularity of Sandy, they carried him to
one of the dim oil-lamps, with which the city was then
lit, and after scanning his face closely, satisfied themselves of the truth of their victim's assertion.   Then
came a revulsion of feeling, and amid shouts of
applause the popular surgeon was carried to his residence on the shoulders of the mob.

The End Justifying the Means

Sandy Wood had the most eccentric ways of curing people. One of his patients, the Hon. Mrs. ——, took it into her head that she was a hen, and that her mission in life was to hatch eggs. So firmly did this delusion take possession of her mind that, by-and-bye she found it impossible to rise off her seat, lest the eggs should get cold. Sandy encouraged the mania, and requested that he might have the pleasure of taking a "dish of tea" with her that evening, and that she would have the very best china on the table.

She cordially agreed to this, and when her guest arrived in the evening he found the tea-table covered with some very valuable crockery, which did not belie its name, for it had really been imported from China by a relative of the lady, an East Indian Nabob.

The surgeon made a few remarks about the closeness of the room, asked permission to raise the window, and then, watching an opportunity when the hostess' eye was upon him, he seized the trayful of fragile ware and feigned to throw them out of the window.

The lady screamed, and, forgetful in her fright of her supposed inability to rise, she rushed from her seat to arrest the arm of the vandal.

The task was not a hard one, for the eccentric old surgeon laughed as he replaced the tray on the table, and escorted his patient to her seat. The spell had been broken, and nothing more was ever heard of the egg-hatching mania.

———

Another lady patient of his had a tumor in her throat, which threatened her death if it did not burst. She entirely lost her voice, and all his efforts to reach the seat of the malady were unavailing. As a last resort, he quietly placed the poker in the fire; and after in vain attempting to get his patient to scream, so as to burst the tumor, he asked her to open her mouth, and seizing the then red-hot poker, he made a rush with it to her throat. The result was a yell of terror from the thoroughly frightened patient, which effected what he had long desired—the breaking of the tumor, and her recovery.

A Lecture on Baldness—Curious Results

Edinburgh laughed heartily, but was not at all scandalized, when one famous university professor kicked another famous professor in the same faculty, down before him from near the North Bridge to where the Register House now stands. The *causus belli* was simple, but, as reported, most irritating.

The offending professor was lecturing to his class one morning, and happened to say that baldness was no sign of age. " In fact, gentlemen," said the suave professor, " it's no sign at all, nor the converse. I was called in very early yesterday morning to see the wife of a distinguished colleague, a lady whose raven locks have long been the pride of rout and ball. It was in the morning, and I caught the lady in deshabille, and would you believe it, the raven locks were all fudge, and the lady was as bald as the palm of my hand."

The professor said nothing more, but no sooner was his lecture ended than the students casually inquired of the coachman whom the professor was called to see yesterday morning. The coachman, innocently enough, answered, " Oh, Mrs. Prof. ——."

This was enough, and so before four-and-twenty hours went round, the story came to Prof. A—— that Prof. B—— had said, in his class, that Mrs. Prof. A—— wore a wig. For two days they did not meet, and when they did, the offender was punished in the ignominious manner described.

A Miserly Professor

An Edinburgh professor was noted for his miserly habits, though, in reality, he was a rich man and the proprietor of several ancestral estates. He once observed a Highland student—proverbially a poor set—about to pick up a penny in the college quad, but just as he was about to pick it up, the learned professor gave him a push, which sent the poor fellow

right over, when Dr. —— cooly pocketed the coin and
walked on, amid the laughter of a crowd of students
who were watching the scene. He did not always
stick at trifles. Going down the crowded street he
saw a street boy pick up a shilling. Instantly the
professor chucked it out of the boy's hand, and then,
holding it between his thumb and forefinger, with his
gold-headed cane in the other, carefully guarding it,
he read out to the whimpering boy a long lecture on
honesty being the best policy; how the "coin" was
not his; how it might belong to some poor man whose
family might be suffering for the want of that coin,
and so on, concluding by pocketing the shilling, and
charging the finder that "if ever he heard of anybody
having lost that shilling, to say that Prof. —— had
got it. Everybody knows me. It is quite safe.
Honesty, my lad, is always the best policy. Remember that, and read your catechism well."

On one occasion he was called, in consultation with
Prof. Gregory, about a patient of his who happened
to be a student of medicine. The day previously,
however, Dr. Gregory had called alone, and on going
away was offered the customary guinea. This the
stately physician firmly refused; he never took fees
from students. The patient replied that Prof. ——
did. Immediately Gregory's face brightened up.
"I will be here to-morrow in consultation with him.
Be good enough to offer me a fee before him, sir."

To-morrow came, and the student did as he had
been requested.

"What is that, sir?" the professor answered, looking at his proffered guinea: "A fee, sir! Do you
mean to insult me, sir? What do you take us to be—
cannibals? Do we live on one another? No, sir. The
man who could take a fee from a student of his own
profession ought to be kicked—kicked, sir, out of the
faculty! Good morning!" and with that the celebrated physician walked to the door, in well-affected
displeasure. Next day to the astonishment of the
patient, Prof. —— sent a packet with all the fees
returned.

It is said that he once took a bag of potatoes for a fee, and ever after boasted of his generosity in the matter: " The man was a poor man, sir. We must be liberal, sir. Our Master enjoins it on us, and it is recommended in a fine passage in the admirable aphorisms of Hippocrates. The man had no money, sir, so I had to deal gently with him, and take what he had; though as a rule—as a rule—I prefer the modern to the ancient exchange, *pecunia* instead of *pecus.* Hah! hah!''

Silencing English Insolence

" There never was a Scotchman " said an insolent cockney, at Stirling, to a worthy Scot, who was acting as guide to the castle " who did not want to get out of Scotland almost as soon as he got into it.''

" That such may be the fack, I'll no' gainsay,'' replied the Scot. " There were about twenty thousand o' your countrymen, and mair, who wanted to get out of Scotland on the day of Bannockburn. But they could na' win. And they're laying at Bannockburn the noo; and have never been able to get out o' Scotland yet.''

———

It was Johnson's humor to be anti-Scottish. He objected theoretically to haggis, though he ate a good plateful of it.

" What do you think o' the haggis?'' asked the hospitable old lady, at whose table he was dining, seeing that he partook so plentifully of it.

"Humph!'' he replied, with his mouth full, " it's very good food for hogs!''

" Then let me help you to some mair o' 't,'' said the lady, helping him bountifully.

Helping Business

Prof. James Gregory, perhaps the most celebrated physician of his day, but who, in popular estimation, is dolefully remembered as the inventor of a nauseous compound known as Gregory's Mixture. He was a tall and very handsome man, and stately and grave in

all his manners, but, withal, with a touch of Scotch
humor in him. One evening, walking home from the
university, he came upon a street row or bicker, a sort
of town-and-gown-riot very common in those days.
Observing a boy systematically engaged in breaking
windows, he seized him, and inquired, in the sternest
voice, what he did that for.

"Oh," was the reply, "my master's a glazier, and
I'm trying to help business."

"Indeed. Very proper; very proper, my boy,"
Dr. Gregory answered, and, as he proceeded to maul
him well with his cane, "you see I must follow your
example. I'm a doctor, and must help business a
little." And with that, he gave a few finishing whacks
to the witty youth, and went off chuckling at having
turned the tables on the glazier's apprentice.

Sandy Wood's Proposal of Marriage

When proposing to his future wife's father for his
daughter, the old gentleman took a pinch of snuff and
said, "Weel, Sandy, lad, I've naething again' ye, but
what have ye to support a wife on?"

Sandy's reply was to pull a case of lancets out of
his pocket with the remark, "These!"

Rival Anatomists in Edinburgh University

Perhaps the most eminent teacher of anatomy in
Edinburgh, or in Britain, early in this century, was
Dr. Robert Knox. He was a man abounding in anything but the milk of human kindness towards his
professional brethren, and if people had cared in those
days to go to law about libels, it is to be feared Knox
would have been rarely out of a court of law. Per-
sonality and satirical allusions were ever at his
tongue's end. After attracting immense classes his
career came very suddenly to a close. Burke and
Hare, who committed such atrocious murders to supply the dissecting-room with "subjects" were finally
discovered, and one of them executed—the other turning king's evidence. Knox's name got mixed up with
the case, being supposed to be privy to these murders,
though many considered him innocent. The populace,

however, were of a different opinion. Knox's house
was mobbed, and though he braved it out, he never
after succeeded in regaining popular esteem. He was
a splendid lecturer, and a man, who, amid all his
self-conceit and malice, could occasionally say a
bitingly witty thing.

It is usual with lecturers at their opening lecture to
recommend text-books, and accordingly Knox would
commence as follows : " Gentlemen, there are no
text-books I can recommend. I wrote one myself,
but it is poor stuff. I can't recommend it. The man
who knows most about a subject writes worst on
it. If you want a good text-book on any subject,
recommend me to the man who knows nothing earthly
about the subject. The result is that we have no
good text-book on anatomy. We *will* have soon, however—Prof. Monro is going to write one."

That was the finale, and, of course, brought down
the house, when, with a sinister expression on his
face, partly due to long sarcasm, and partly to the
loss of an eye, he would bow himself out of the
lecture-room.

The Prof. Monro referred to by Knox was the professor of anatomy of Edinburgh University, and the
third of that name who had filled the chair for one
hundred and twenty years. He succeeded his father
and grandfather, as if by right of birth—and if it was
not by that right he had no other claim to fill that
chair.

Knox lectured at a different hour from Monro,
namely, exactly five minutes after the conclusion of
the latter's lecture. Accordingly the students tripped
over from Monro to Knox, greatly to the annoyance,
but in no way to the loss of the former. It may well
be supposed that during their forced attendance on
Monro's lectures they did not spend much time in
listening to what he had to say. In fact they used to
amuse themselves during the hour of his lecture, and
always used to organize some great field days during
the session. So lazy was Monro that he was in the
habit of using his grandfather's lectures, written more
than one hundred years before. They were—as was

the fashion then—written in Latin, but his grandson
gave a free translation as he proceeded, without, however, taking the trouble to alter the dates. Accordingly,
in 1820 or 1830, students used to be electrified to hear
him slowly drawling out, "When I was in Padua in
1694—" This was the signal for the fun to begin. On
the occasion when this famous speech was known to
be due, the room was always full, and no sooner was
it uttered than there descended showers of peas on
the head of the devoted professor, who, to the end
of his life could never understand what it was all
about. [19]

"Discretion—the Better Part of Valor"

A spirited ballad was written on the Jacobite vic-
tory at Prestonpans by a doughty Haddingtonshire
farmer of the name of Skirving, in which he dis-
tributed his praise and blame among the combatants
in the most impartial manner. Among others, he
accused one "Lieutenant Smith, of Irish birth," of
leaping over the head of "Major Bowle, that worthy
soul," when lying wounded on the ground, and
escaping from the field, instead of rendering the
assistance for which the sufferer called. Smith, being
aggrieved, sent the author a challenge to meet him at
Haddington. "Na, na," said the worthy farmer, who
was working in his field when the hostile message
reached him, "I have no time to gang to Haddington,
but tell Mr. Smith to come here, and I'll tak' a look
at him. If he's a man about my ain size, I'll ficht
him; but if he's muckle bigger and stronger, I'll do
just as he did—I'll run awa'!"

Losing His Senses

A census taker tells the following story: The first
difficulty I experienced was with Old Ronaldson. He
was always a little queer, as old bachelors often are.
As I left the census paper with him, he held the door
in one hand while he took the paper from me in the
other. I said I would call again for the paper. "Ye
needn't trouble yourself!" said he, in a very ill-
natured tone; "I'll not be bothered with your

papers.'' However, I did not mind him much; for I
thought when he discovered that the paper had
nothing to do with taxes he would feel more comfort-
able, and that he would fill it up properly.

The only person whom Old Ronaldson allowed
near him was Mrs. Birnie; she used to put his house
in order and arrange his washing: for Ronaldson was
an old soldier; and although he had a temper, he was
perfect in his dress and most orderly in all his household arrangements. When Mrs. Birnie went in her
usual way to his house on the morning referred to,
the old gentleman was up and dressed; but he was
in a terrible temper, flurried and greatly agitated.

" Good morning, sir,'' said Mrs. Birnie—I had the
particular words from her own lips—" Good morning,'' said she; but Old Ronaldson, who was as a rule
extremely polite to her, did not on this occasion
reply. His agitation increased. He fumbled in all
his pockets; pulled out and in all the drawers of his
desk; turned the contents of an old chest out on the
floor—all the time accompanying his search with
muttered imprecations, which at length broke into a
perfect storm.

Mrs. Birnie had often seen Mr. Ronaldson excited
before, but she had never seen him in such a state as
this. At length he approached an old bookcase and,
after looking earnestly about and behind it, he suddenly seized and pulled it toward him, when a lot of
old papers fell on the floor, and a perfect cloud of
dust filled the room. Mrs. Birnie stood dumbfounded.
At length the old gentleman, covered with dust and
perspiring with his violent exertions, sat down on the
corner of his bed, and in a most wretched tone of
voice said: " Oh, Mrs. Birnie, don't be alarmed, but
I've lost my *senses!* ''

" I was just thinking as much myself,'' said Mrs.
Birnie; and off she ran to my house at the top of her
speed. " Oh, Mr. M'Lauchlin,'' said she, " come
immediately—come this very minute; for Old Ronald-
ron's clean mad. He's tearing his hair, and cursing
in a manner most awful to hear; and worse than that
—he's begun to tear down the house about himself.

Oh, sir, come immediately, and get him put in a strait jacket."

Of course I at once sent for old Dr. Macnab, and asked him to fetch a certificate for an insane person with him. Now, old Dr. Macnab is a cautious and sensible man. His bald head and silvery hair, his beautiful white neck-cloth and shiny black coat, not to speak of his silver-headed cane and dignified manner, all combined to make our doctor an authority in the parish.

"Ay, ay," said the good doctor, when he met me; "I always feared the worst about Mr. Ronaldson. Not good for man to be alone, sir. I always advised him to take a wife. Never would take my advice. You see the result, Mr. M'Lauchlin. However, we must see the poor man."

When we arrived, we found all as Mrs. Birnie had said; indeed by this time matters had become worse and worse, and a goodly number of the neighbors were gathered. One old lady recommended that the barber should be sent for to shave Ronaldson's head. This was the least necessary, as his head, poor fellow, was already as bald and smooth as a ball of ivory. Another kind neighbor had brought in some brandy, and Old Ronaldson had taken several glasses, and pronounced it capital; which everyone said was a sure sign "he was coming to himself." One of his tender-hearted neighbors, who had helped herself to a break-fast cupful of this medicine, was shedding tears pro-fusely, and as she kept rocking from side to side, nursing her elbows, she cried bitterly: "Poor Mr. Ronaldson's lost his senses!"

The instant Dr. Macnab appeared, Old Ronaldson stepped forward, shook him warmly by the hand, and said: "I'm truly glad to see you, doctor You will soon put it all right. I have only lost my *senses*— that's all! That's what all these women are making this row about."

"Let me feel your pulse,' said the doctor gently.

"Oh, nonsense, doctor," cried Ronaldson—"non-sense; I've only lost my *senses*." And he made as if he would fly at the heap of drawers, dust, and rub-

bish which lay in the centre of the floor, and have it
all raked out again.

"Oh, lost your senses, have you?" said the doctor
with a bland smile. "You'll soon get over that—that's
a trifle." But he deliberately pulled out his big gold
repeater and held Ronaldson by the wrist. "Just as
I feared. Pulse ninety-five, eye troubled, face
flushed, muckle excitement," etc. So there and
then, Old Ronaldson was doomed. I did not wish a
painful scene; so, when I got my certificate signed by
the doctor, I quietly slipped out, got a pair of horses
and a close carriage, and asked Mr. Ronaldson to
meet me, if he felt able, at the inn in half an hour, as
I felt sure a walk in the open air would do him good.
He gladly fell in with this plan, and promised to be
with me at noon certain.

As I have said, he is an old soldier, was an officer's
servant in fact, and is a most tidy and punctual person. But old Mrs. Birnie had, with much thoughtful-
ness, the moment he began to make preparations for
this, put his razors out of the way. Hereupon he got
worse and worse, stamped and stormed, and at last
worked himself into a terrible passion. I grew tired
waiting at the inn, and so returned, and found him in
a sad state. When he saw me, he cried: "Oh, Mr.
M'Lauchlin, the deil's in this house this day."

"Very true," said Mrs. Birnie to me in an aside.
"You see, sir, he speaks sense—whiles."

"Everything has gone against me this day," he
went on; "but," said he, "I'll get out of this if my
beard never comes off. Hand me my Wellington
boots, Mrs. Birnie; I hope you have not swallowed
them, too!"

The moment Ronaldson began to draw on his boots,
affairs changed as if by magic. "There," cried he
triumphantly—"There is that confounded paper of
yours which has made all this row! See, Mrs. Birnie,"
he exclaimed, flourishing my census paper in his
hand; *I've found my senses!*"

"Oh," cried the much affected widow, "I am glad
to hear it," and in her ecstatic joy she rushed upon
the old soldier, took his head to her bosom, and wept

for joy. I seized the opportunity to beat a hasty
retreat, and left the pair to congratulate each other
upon the happy finding of Old Ronaldson's *senses*.

It's a Gran' Nicht

The following is a fine comic sketch of an interview between a Scotch peasant lover and "Kirsty,"
his sweetheart, who was only waiting for him to
speak. It is in fine contrast with the confident, rush-
ing away in which that sort of thing is done in other
countries.

The young lover stands by the cottage gable in the
fading light, declaring, "It's a gran' nicht!" Ever
so often he says it, yet he feels its grandeur not at
all, for the presence of something grander or better,
I suppose — the maiden, Kirsty Grant. Does he
whisper soft somethings of her betterness, I wonder,
while thus he lingers? His only communication is
the important fact, "It's a gran' nicht." He would
linger, blessed in her presence, but the closing day
warns him to be gone. It will be midnight before he can
reach his village home miles away. Yet was it sweet
to linger. "It's a very gran' nicht, but I maun haist
awa'. Mither 'ill be wunnerin'," said he.

"'Deed, ye'll hae tae draw yer feet gey fast tae
win hame afore the Sabbath; sae e'en be steppin',"
she answered, cooly.

"It's gran'!" said he; "I wish ilka Saiturday
nicht was lik' this ane."

"Wi' ye, Saiturday nicht shud maist be lik' Sunday
morn, if ye bevil it richt,' said she, with a toss of
her head, for she rightly guessed that somehow the
lad's pleasure was referable to herself. "I maun
shut up the coo."

"Good-nicht!" said he.

"Good-nicht!" said she, disappearing.

He stepped away in the muirland, making for home.
"Isn't she smairt?" said he to himself; "man, isn't
she smairt? Said she, 'Saiturday nicht shud aye be
wi' ye lik' Sunday morn, if ye beviled it richt!' Was
it na a hint for me? Man, I wish I daur spaik oot
to her!"

A Highlander on Bagpipes

Mr. Barclay, an eminent Scotch artist, was engaged in painting a Highland scene for Lord Breadalbane, in which his lordship's handsome piper was introduced. When the artist was instructing him as to attitude, and that he must maintain an appearance at once of animation and ease by keeping up a conversation, the latter replied that he would do his best, and commenced as follows :

" Maister Parclay, ye read yer Bible at times, I *suppone* (suppose), sir ? "

" Oh, yes."

" Weel, Maister Parclay, if ye do tat, sir, ten you've read te third and fifth verses of te third chapter of Daniel, when te princes, te governors, te captains, te judges, te treasurers, te counsellors, te sheriffs and all te rulers of te provinces were gathered together into te dedication of te image tat Nebuchadnezzar, te king, had set up, and tey were told tat whenever tey began to hear te sound of te cornet, flute, harp, sackbut, dulcimer, and all kinds of music, tey were to fall down and worship te golden image that Nebuchadnezzar, te king, had set up. I tell ye, Maister Parclay, if tey had a Hielandman, wi' his pipes tere, tat nonsense would not hae happened. Na, na, he would hae sent tem a' fleeing. It would hae been wi' tem as Bobby Burns said, ' Skirl up to Bangor, for ye maun a' come back to te bagpipe at last.' "

Wolloping Judas

The late Dr. Adamson, of Cupar-Fife, colleague to Dr. Campbell, father to the lord chancellor of that name, at a late Saturday night supper was about to depart, alleging that he must prepare for the Sunday service. For two previous Sundays he had been holding forth on Judas Iscariot, and a member of his congregation, who sat at the table detained him with : " Sit down, doctor, sit down ; there's nae need for ye to gang awa' ; just gie Judas another wallop in the tow."

" ' Alice ' Brown, the Jaud ! "

An old offender was, some years ago, brought up before a well-known Glasgow magistrate. The con-

stable, as a preliminary, informed his bailieship that
he had in custody John Anderson, *alias* Brown, *alias*
Smith. "Very weel," said the magistrate, with an
air of dignity, "I'll try the women first. Bring in
Alice Brown! what has she been about, the jaud?"

Earning His Dismissal

Dean Ramsay tells an amusing story of the cool
self-sufficiency of the young Scottish domestic—a boy
who, in a very quiet, determined way, made his exit
from a house into which he had lately been introduced. He had been told that he should be dismissed if he broke any of the china that was under
his charge.

On the morning of a great dinner party he was
entrusted (rather rashly) with a great load of
plates, which he was to carry upstairs from the kitchen
to the dining-room, and which were piled up and
rested upon his two hands.

In going upstairs his foot slipped, and the plates
were broken to atoms. He at once went up to the
drawing-room, put his head in at the door, and
shouted, "The plates are a' smashed, and I'm
awa'!" [7]

Paris and Peebles Contrasted

In the memoir of Robert Chambers, by his brother
William, allusion is made to the exceedingly quiet
town of Peebles, their birthplace, and the strong local
attachments of the Scottish people. An honest old
burgher of the town was enabled by some strange
chance to visit Paris, and was eagerly questioned,
when he came back, as to the character of that capital
of capitals; to which he answered that, "Paris, a'
things considered, was a wonderful place; but still,
Peebles for pleasure!"

Short Measure

An old woman who had made a great deal of money
by selling whiskey was visited when on her death-bed
by her minister, to whom she spake, as is usual on
such occasions, about her temporal as well as her

spiritual affairs. As to her temporalities, they seemed to be in a very flourishing condition, for she was dying worth a very large sum of money.

"And so, Molly," said the minister, "you tell me you are worth so much money?"

"Indeed, minister," replied Molly, "I am."

"And you tell me, too," continued the minister, "that you made all that money by filling the noggin?"

"'Na, na, minister," said the dying woman; "I didna tell you *that*. I made the maist of it by *not* filling the noggin."

Two Views of a Divine Call

Of Scotland's great preacher, the late Rev. Dr. Macleod, the following is told: In visiting his Dalkeith parishioners to say farewell, he called on one of those sharp-tongued old ladies whose privileged gibes have added so much to the treasury of Scottish humor.

To her he expressed his regret at leaving his friends at Dalkeith, but stated that he considered his invitation to Glasgow in the light of "a call from the Lord."

"Ay, ay," was the sharp response; "but if the Lord hadna called you to a better steepend, it might hae been lang gin ye had heard Him!"

A Scotch View of Shakespeare

A Scotchman was asserting that some of the most celebrated poets and brightest intellects the world ever produced were descendants of his race, and quoted Scott, Burns, and others as evidence.

An Englishman who was present retorted: "I suppose that you will claim next that even Shakespeare was a Scotchman."

"Weel," he replied, "I'm nae so sure o' that; but ane thing I do ken—*he had intellect eneuch for a Scotchman.*"

"As Guid Deid as Leevin!"

There was a mixture of shrewdness and simplicity

in the following : Shortly after the establishment of the Ministers' Widows' Fund, the minister of Cranshaws asked in marriage the daughter of a small farmer in the neighborhood.

The damsel asked her father whether she should accept the clergyman's offer. "Oh," said the sire, "tak' him, Jenny ; he's as gude deid as leevin." The farmer meant that his daughter would, owing to the new fund, be equally well off a widow as a wife.

The Mercy of Providence

An old minister was once visiting his hearers, and accosted a humble farmer who had been lazy with his crops in the wet season. "I hear, Jamie," said the minister, "that ye are behind with your harvest."

"Oh, sir," was the reply, "I hae got it all in except three wee stacks, and I leave them to the mercy of Providence."

A Scotch Curtain Lecture on Profit and Pain

The man who said this was not an athiest, but simply a druggist—a Scotch druggist—who was aroused by the ringing of his night-bell. He arose, went downstairs, and served a customer with a dose of salts.

His wife grumbled : "What profit do you get out of that penny ?"

"A ha'penny," was the reply.

"And for that ha'penny you'll be awake a long time," rejoined the wife.

"A-weel," replied the placid druggist, "the dose of salts will keep him awake much longer ; let us thank Heaven that we have the profit and not the pain of the transaction."

A Definition of " Fou "

A gentleman recently gave an entertainment in London on the peculiarities of Scotchmen, in the course of which he gave this definition of the national word *fou :* "Being gently excited by the moderate use of dangerous beverages."

The Journeyman Dog

A gentleman, staying in the family of a sheep-farmer, remarked that daily as the family sat down to dinner a shepherd's dog came in, received its portion, and soon after disappeared.

"I never see that dog except at dinner," said the visitor.

"The reason is," said the farmer, "we've lent him to oor neibor, Jamie Nicol, and we telt him to come hame ilka day to his dinner. When he gets his dinner, puir beast, he gaes awa' back till his wark."

Church Economy

A congregagtion was once looking out for a minister, and after hearing a host of candidates with more or less popular gifts, their choice fell upon a sticket probationer, whose election caused great surprise in the country.

One of the hearers was afterward asked by an eminent minister how the congregation could have brought themselves to select such a minister.

His reply was quite characteristic : " Weel, we had twa or three reasons — first, naebody recommended him ; then he was nae studier, and besides, he had money in the bank."

It appeared that of the two former ministers, who had not come up to expectation, one of them had brought flaming testimonials, and the other had buried himself among his books, so that the people never saw him but in the pulpit, while the third reason was, perhaps the most cogent of all, for the people did not care to burden themselves with a too generous support of their pastor.

In another case the minister usurped the functions of session and committee, an 1 ignored the office bearers altogether. One of the elders observed to another one Sunday morning, as the minister was trotting up to the meeting-house on his smart little pny, "It's so a fine wee powny the minister rides."

"Ay," said the other, "it's a gey strange ane ; it can carry minister, session, and committee without turnin' a hair."

Tired of Standing

A Paisley man, visiting Glasgow, much admired the statue of Sir John Moore, which is an erect figure. Soon afterwards he brought another Paisley man to see the statue, but not being topographically posted, he stared at the statue of James Watt, which is in a sitting attitude. Feeling somewhat puzzled as to the identity of what was before him with what he recollected to have seen, he disposed of the difficulty by exclaiming: "Odds, man, he's sat down since I last saw him!"

Religious Loneliness

"How is your church getting on?" asked a friend of a religious Scotchman, who had separated in turn from the Kirk, the Free Church, the United Presbyterian, and several lesser bodies.

"Pretty weel, pretty weel. There's naebody belongs to it now but my brither and mysel', and I am sure o' Sandy's soundness."

Prison Piety

Every place has its advantages, even the lock-up. A Scotch "gentleman," who had been guilty of some irregularity that demanded his compulsory withdrawal from polite society for sixty days, was asked, after his release, as to how he "got on."

"Weel," replied he, "ye see, a body canna hae everything in this life; and I'm no gaun to misca' the place, no' me. For a' the time I was there—just twa months, note, by-the-by—I was weel proteckit frae the wiles o' a wickit worl' outside, while my 'bread was aye gi'en me and my water sure.'"

A Successful Tradesman

One day, during a snow storm, the Rev. George More was riding from Aberdeen to a village in the vicinity of the town. He was enveloped in a Spanish cloak, and had a shawl tied round his neck and shoulders. These loose garments, covered with snow, and waving in the blast, startled the horse of a "bagman," who chanced to ride past. The alarmed steed plunged, and very nearly threw its rider, who exclaimed :

"Why, sir, you would frighten the very devil!" .

"I am glad to hear that," said Mr. More, "for it's just my trade."

Multum in Parvo

A Highland porter, observing a stranger looking intently on the Rev. Dr. Candlish, who was of small stature, said, "Ay, tak' a gude look—there's no muckle o' him, but there's a deal *in* him!"

When Asses May Not Be Parsons

In the pulpit one-half of Dr. Guthrie's rich nature was necessarily restrained. He could be pathetic there, but not humorous; though we did once hear him begin a sermon by saying that God on one occasion used an ass to preach to a sinner, but that He was not in the way of using asses when He could get better instruments!

A Scotch Version of the Lives of Esau and Jacob

Within the grounds of Hamilton Palace, in the west of Scotland, is a mausoleum. The walls are ornamented with bas-reliefs forming Bible illustrations. These have been paraphrased in verse by a local bard. One of the series is a history of Jacob, and from it the following extracts are taken. The br hers are thus introduced :

> When Esau and Jacob were boys,
>   A wild boy Esau was ;
> Jacob was a peaceable boy,
>   But Esau loved the chase.
> One day from hunting he came home,
>   A hungry man was he ;
> Jacob some famous pottage had,
>   Which soon caught Esau's e'e.

Rebekah instructs Jacob in the proposed deception of Isaac, but he is fearful of discovery. The former replies :

No fear of that, my darling son ;
    Just do as I direct—
I will you dress up for the scene,
    That he will ne'er suspect.

Jacob obeys :

Away he went as he was bid,
    And quickly he them slew ;
His mother straightway did them cook
    And made a fav'rite stew.

Isaac is suspicious of Jacob :

Then Isaac unto Jacob said,
    " Come near to me, I pray,
That I may *feel* it is the truth
    That unto me you say."
Then Jacob he went unto him,
    And he his hands did feel.
" The hands are Esau's hands, my son,
    But it's like Jacob's squeal."

Faint Heart Never Won Fair Lady

An anecdote is told of Professor Haldane, of
St. Andrews, one of the most estimable of men, yet,
in spite of a pleasing person, a genial manner, a good
house and a handsome competency, he was well-
advanced in life before he could make up his mind to
marry. When it was reported that he had fitted up
his house afresh, it was supposed that he was going
to change his state. On a given day, at an hour
unusually early for a call, the good doctor was seen
at the house of a lady for whom he had long been
supposed to have a predilection, and betraying much
excitement of manner till the door was opened.

As soon as he was shown in, and saw the fair one
whom he sought calmly engaged in knitting stock-
ings, and not at all disturbed by his entrance, his
courage, like that of Bob Acres, began to ooze out,
and he sat himself down on the edge of the chair in
such a state of pitiable confusion as to elicit the com-
passion of the lady in question. She could not under-

stand what ailed him, but felt instinctively that the
truest good breeding would be to take no notice
of his embarrassment, and lead the conversation
herself.

Thus, then, she opened fire: "Weel, doctor, hae
ye got through a' your papering and painting yet?"
(A clearing of the throat preparatory to speech, but
not a sound uttered.) "I'm told your new carpets
are just beautifu'." (A further effort to clear the
throat.) "They say the pattern o' the dining-room
chairs is something quite out o' the way. In short,
that everything aboot the house is perfect."

Here was a providential opening he was not such a
goose as to overlook. He screwed up his courage,
advanced his chair, sidled toward her, simpering the
while, raised his eyes furtively to her face, and said,
with a gentle inflection of his voice which no ear but
a wilfully deaf one could have misinterpreted: "Na,
na, Miss J——n, it's no' *quite* perfect; it canna be
quite that so lang as there's ae thing wanting!"

"And what can that be?" said the imperturbable
spinster.

Utterly discomfited by her wilful blindness to his
meaning, the poor man beat a hasty retreat, drew
back his chair from its dangerous proximity, caught
up his hat, and, in tones of blighted hope, gasped
forth his declaration in these words; "Eh, dear!
Well 'am sure! The thing wanted is a—a—a *side-
boord!*"

"Surely the Net is Spread in Vain in the Sight of any Bird"

Our May had an ee to a man,
  Nae less than the newly-placed preacher,
And we plotted a dainty bit plan
  For trappin' our spiritual teacher.

        Oh! but we were sly,
          We were sly an' sleekit;
        But, ne'er say a herrin' is dry—
   .   Until it's weel reestit an' reekit.

We treated young Mr. M'Gock,
　An' plied him wi' tea an' wi' toddy,
An' we praised every word that he spake,
　Till we put him maist out o' the body.

　　Oh ! but we were sly, etc.

Frae the kirk we were never awa',
　Except when frae home he was helpin'
An' then May,—an' aften us a'—
　Gaed far an' near after him skelpin'.

　　Oh ! but we were sly, etc.

We said aye what the neebors thocht droll,
　That to hear him gang through wi' a sermon
Was—though a wee dry on the whole—
　As refreshin's the dew on Mount Hermon.

　　Oh ! but we were sly, etc.

But to come to the heart o' the nit,
　The dainty bit plan that we plotted
Was to get a subscription afit,
　An' a watch to the minister voted.

　　Oh ! but we were sly, etc.

The young women folk o' the kirk
　By turns lent a han' in collectin',
But May took the feck o' the mark
　An' the trouble the rest o' directin'.

　　Oh ! but we were sly, etc.

A gran' watch was gotten belyve,
　An' May, wi' sma' " priggin," consentit
To be ane o' a party o' five
　To gang to the Manse an' present it.

　　Oh ! but we were sly, etc.

We a' gied a word o' advice
　To May in a deep consultation,
To hae something to say unco' nice,
　An' to speak for the hale deputation.

　　Oh ! but we were sly, etc.

Takin' present an' speech baith in han',
  May delivered a bonny palaver,
To let Mr. M'Gock understan'
  How zealous she was in his favor.
        Oh ! but we were sly, etc.

She said that the gift was to prove
  That his female friends valued him highly,
But it couldna express a' their love,
  An' she glinted her ee at him slyly.
        Oh ! but we were sly, etc.

He put the gowd watch in his fab,
  And proudly he said he wad wear it,
An' after some flatterin' gab,
  He tauld May he was goin' to be marriet.
        Oh ! but we were sly,
          We were sly and sleekit,
        But Mr. M'Gock was nae gowk,
          Wi' our dainty bit plan to be cheekit.

May came home wi' her heart in her mouth
  An' frae that hour she turned a Dissenter,
An' noo she's renewin' her youth
  Wi' some hopes o' the Burgher Precentor.
        Oh ! but she was sly,
          She was sly and sleekit,
        An' cleverly opens ae door
          As sune as anither is sleekit.

A Highland Outburst of Gratitude and an Inburst of Hurricane

" Ah, my friends, what causes have we for gratitude—oh, yes ;—for the deepest gratitude ! Look at
the place of our habitation. How grateful should we
be that we do not leeve in the far north—oh, no !—
amidst the frost and snaw, and the cauld and the
weet—oh, no !—where there's a long day tae half o'
the year—oh, yes !—and a lang nicht the tither—oh,
yes !—that we do not depend upon the aurawry bore-
awlis—oh, no !—that we do not gang shivering aboot
in skins—oh, no !—smoking amang the snow like
modiwarts—oh, no ! no !—And how grateful should we

be that we do not leeve in the far south, beneath the equawtor, and a sun aye burnin', burnin'; where the sky's het—ah, yes!—and yearth's het, and the water's het, and ye're brunt black as a smiddy—ah, yes!—where there's teegars—oh, yes!—and lions—oh, yes!—and crocodiles—oh, yes!—and fearsome beasts growlin' and girnin' at ye amang the woods; where the very air is a fever, like the burnin' breath o' a fiery drawgon; that we do not leeve in these places—oh, no! no! no! no!—but that we leeve in this blessit island of oors callit Great Britain—oh, yes! yes! and in that pairt of it named Scotland, and in that bit o' auld Scotland that looks up at Ben Nevis—oh, yes! yes! yes!—where there's neither frost, nor cauld, nor wund, nor weet, nor hail, nor rain, nor teegars, nor lions, nor burnin' suns, nor hurricanes, nor——''

Here a tremendous blast of wind and rain from Ben Nevis blew in the windows of the kirk, and brought the preacher's eloquence to an abrupt conclusion.

A Different Thing Entirely

While surveying the west coast of Scotland, Captain Robinson had received on board his ship the Grand Duke Constantine. As the duke could only remain a very short time, the captain resolved to show him as much as possible during his brief stay. Accordingly he steamed to Iona on a Sunday, believing that day especially suited for pointing out to his royal visitor remains associated with religion. Landing on the island he waited on the custodian of the ancient church with the request that he would open it.

'' Not so,'' said the keeper; '' not on Sunday.''

'' Do you know whom I have brought to the island ?'' said the captain.

'' He's the Emperor o' a' the Russias, I ken by the flag,'' responded the keeper; '' but had it been the Queen hersel' I wadna' gi'e up the keys on the Lord's day.''

'' Would you take a glass of whiskey on the Sabbath ?'' inquired the captain.

'' *That's a different thing entirely*,'' said the keeper.

Canny Dogs

The following is given by a Scotchman by way of illustrating the kindly consideration evinced by the Scottish peasantry towards the domestic animals—especially the shepherds to their dogs—which consequently become their attached companions. A minister calling to visit one of his flock found before the fireplace three dogs apparently asleep. At the sound of a whistle two rose up and walked out; the third remained still.

"It is odd," said the minister, "that this dog does not get up like the others."

"It's no astonishing ava," said the shepherd, "for it's no' his turn; he was oot i' the mornin'."

A Compliment by Return

The minister's man at Lintrathen, though sufficiently respectful, seldom indulges in the complimentary vein. On one occasion he handsomely acknowledged a compliment by returning another. The minister had got married, and was presented with a carriage, for which John was appointed to provide a horse. Driving out with his wife, the minister said to John in starting, "You've got us a capital horse."

"Weel, sir," said John, "it's just aboot as difficult as to choose a gude minister's wife, and we've been lucky wi' baith."

Curious Sentence

Lord Eskgrove is described by Lord Cockburn, in his "*Memorials*" as a most eccentric personage.

Cockburn heard him sentence a tailor for murdering a soldier, in these words: "And not only did you murder him, thereby he was berea-ved of his life, but you did thrust, or pierce, or push, or project, or propel the li-thall weapon through the belly band of his regimental breeches, which were his majesty's."

Advice to an M. P.

When Sir George Sinclair was chosen member of Parliament for his native county, a man came up to him and said: "Noo, Maister George, I'll gie ye some advice. They've made ye a Parliament man, and my advice to ye is, be ye aye tak-takin' what ye can get, and aye seek-seekin' until ye get mair."

Stretching It

Concerning the long-bow, no American effort can surpass one that comes to us from Scotland: It was told that Colonel M'Dowall, when he returned from the war, was one day walking along by The Nyroch, when he came on an old man sitting greetin' on a muckle stone at the roadside. When he came up, the old man rose and took off his bonnet, and said:

"Ye're welcome hame again, laird."

"Thank you," said the colonel; adding, after a pause, "I should surely know your face. Aren't you Nathan M'Culloch?"

"Ye're richt, 'deed," said Nathan, "it's just me, laird."

"You must be a good age, now, Nathan," says the colonel.

"I'm no verra aul' yet, laird," was the reply; "I'm just turnt a hunner."

"A hundred!" says the colonel, musing; "well, you must be all that. But the idea of a man of a hundred sitting blubbering that way! Whatever could *you* get to cry about?"

"It was my father lashed me, sir," said Nathan, blubbering again; "an' he put me oot, so he did."

"Your father!" said the colonel; "is your father alive yet?"

"Leevin! ay," replied Nathan; "I ken that the day tae my sorrow."

"Where is he?" says the colonel. "What an age he must be! I would like to see him."

"Oh, he's up in the barn there," says Nathan; "an no' in a horrid gude humor the noo, aither."

They went up to the barn together, and found the father busy threshing the barley with the big flail, and tearing on fearful. Seeing Nathan and the laird coming in, he stopped and saluted the colonel, who, after inquiring how he was, asked him why he had struck Nathan.

"The young rascal!" says the father, "there's nae dooin' wi' him; he's never oot o' mischief. I had to lick him this mornin' *for throwin' stanes at his grandfather!*"

Driving the Deevil Out

A Scotch minister, named Downes, settled in a rural district in the north of Ireland, where the people are more Scotch in language and manners than in the land o' cakes itself. One evening he and a brother divine set out together to take part in some religious service.

Meeting one of his parishioners on the way, the latter quaintly observed, "Weel, Mr. Downes, you clergymen 'ill drive the deevil oot o' the country the nicht!'

"Yes," replied the minister, "we will. *I see you are making your escape.*"

Tommy did not use the deevil's name in his pastor's presence again."

Mental Aberration

In Lanarkshire, Scotland, there lived, about fifty years ago, a poor crazy man, by name Will Shooler. Will was a regular attendant of the parish church in the town, on the ceiling of which there was, for ornament, a dove with outstretched wings. One Sabbath day, Will, grew rather tired of the sermon, and throwing his arms and head back, he saw the dove, and exclaimed, "O Lord! what a big hen!"

Sunday Shaving and Milking

On first going to Ross-shire to visit and preach for my friend Mr. Carment, I asked him on the Saturday evening before retiring to rest whether I would get warm water in the morning. Whereupon he held up a warning hand, saying: "Whist, whist!"

On my looking and expressing astonishment, he said, with a twinkle in his eye, "Speak of shaving on the Lord's day in Ross-shire, and you never need preach here more!"

In that same county Sir Kenneth Mackenzie directed my attention to a servant-girl, who, if not less scrupulous, was more logical in her practice. She astonished her master, one of Sir Kenneth's tenants, by refusing to feed the cows on the Sabbath. She was ready to milk, but by no means feed them—and her defence shows that though a fanatic, she was not a fool.

" The cows," she said—drawing a nice metaphysical distinction between what are not and what are works of necessity and mercy that would have done honor to a casuist—" the cows canna milk themselves ; so to milk them is clear work of necessity and mercy ; but let them out to the fields, and they'll feed themselves." Here certainly was *scrupulosity ;* but the error was one that leaned to the right side.   [15]

A Typical Quarrel

The story of the happy young couple who quarreled on the first day of their housekeeping life about the " rat " or the " mouse " which ran out of the fireplace, it seems, had its origin " long time ago " in the incident thus done into rhyme. The last verse explains the mysterious mistake :

John Davidson, and Tib his wife,
    Sat toastin' their taes ae nicht,
When something startit in the fluir
    And blinkit by their sicht.

" Guidwife," quoth John, " did you see that moose ?
    Whar sorra was the cat ? "
" A moose ? "—" Ay, a moose."—" Na, na, guidman,
    It wasna a moose ! 'twas a rat."

" Ow, ow, guidwife, to think ye've been
    Sae lang aboot the hoose,
An' no' to ken a moose frae a rat !
    Yan wasna a rat ! 'twas a moose ! "

" I've seen mair mice than you, guidman—
    An' what think ye o' that ?
Sae haud your tongue, an' say nae mair—
    I tell ye, *it* was a *rat*."

"*Me* haud my tongue for *you*, guidwife!
    I'll be mester o' this hoose—
I saw't as plain as een could see,
    An' I tell ye, *it* was a *moose*."

"If you're the mester of the hoose,
    It's I'm the mistress o't;
An' I ken best what's in the hoose—
    Sae I tell ye, *it* was a *rat*."

"Weel, weel, guidwife, gae mak' the brose,
    An' ca' it what ye please."
So up she rose and mad' the brose,
    While John sat toastin' his taes.

They supit, and supit, and supit the brose,
    And aye their lips played smack;
They supit, and supit, and supit the brose,
    Till their lugs began to crack.

"Sic fules we were to fa' out, guidwife,
    About a moose"—"A what?
It's a lee ye tell, an' I say again,
    It wasna a moose, 'twas a rat."

"Wad ye ca' me a leear to my very face?
    My faith, but ye craw crouse!
I tell you, Tib, I never will bear 't—
    "'Twas a moose" — "'Twas a rat" — "'Twas a
        moose."

Wi' that she struck him ower the pow—
    "Ye dour auld doit, tak' that—
Gae to your bed, ye canker'd sumph—
    'Twas a rat."—"'Twas a moose!"—"'Twas a rat!"

She sent the brose caup at his heels
    As he hirpled ben the hoose;
Yet he shoved out his head, as he steekit the door,
    And cried, "'Twas a moose, 'twas a moose!"

But when the carle fell asleep
    She paid him back for that,
And roared into his sleepin' lug,
    "'Twas a *rat*, 'twas a RAT, 'twas a RAT!"

The devil be wi' me if I think
  It was a beast, at all—
Next morning, when she swepit the fluir,
  She found wee Johnnie's ball!

A Ready Student

Dr. Richie, of Edinburgh, though a very clever man, once met his match. When examining a student as to the classes he attended, he said: "I understand you attend the class for mathematics?"

"Yes."

"How many sides has a circle?"

"Two," said the student.

"Indeed! What are they?"

"An inside and an outside."

A laugh among the students followed this answer.

The doctor next inquired: "And you attend the moral philosophy class, also?"

"Yes."

"Well, you doubtless heard lectures on various subjects. Did you ever hear one on 'Cause and Effect?'"

"Yes."

"Does an effect ever go before a cause?"

"Yes."

"Give me an instance."

"A barrow wheeled by a man."

The doctor hastily sat down and proposed no more questions.

Appearing "in Three Pieces"

Wilson, the celebrated vocalist, was upset one day in his carriage near Edinburgh. A Scotch paper, after recording the accident, said: "We are happy to state he was able to appear the following evening in three pieces."

"Every Man to His Own Trade"

A worthy old Scotch minister, who didn't object to put his hand to a bit of work when occasion required it, was one day forking sheaves in the stackyard to

his man John, who was "biggin'." One of the wheels
of the cart on which the minister was standing happened to be resting on a sheaf, and when the cart was
empty his reverence said: "That's them a' noo,
John, excep' ane 'at's aneath the wheel, an' ye'll hae
to come an' gie's a lift up wi' the wheel ere I get it
oot." "Oh," said John, "just drive forrit the cart a
bit." "Very true, very true," rejoined the minister;
"every man to his own trade."

From Different Points of View

The following anecdote is related of Sir James
Mackintosh, the Scotch philosopher and historian,
and the celebrated Dr. Parr: Sir James had invited
the reverend doctor to take a drive in his gig. The
horse became very restive and unmanageable. "Gently, gently, Jemmy," said the doctor, "pray don't
irritate him; always soothe your horse, whatever you
do, Jemmy! You'll do better without me, I am certain; so let me down, Jemmy—let me down." Once
on *terra firma*, the doctor's views of the case were
changed. "Now, Jemmy, touch him up," said he.
"Never let a horse get the better of you. Touch him
up, conquer him, don't spare him. And now I'll
leave you to manage him—I'll walk back."

Speaking from "Notes"

A porter at a Scotch railway station, who had grown
grey in the service, was one day superintending matters on the platform, when the parish minister stepped
up to him and asked when the next train arrived from
the south. The aged official took off his cap and
carefully read the hour and the minute of the train
from a document stuck in the crown.

Somewhat surprised at this, the minister said:
"Dear me, John, is your memory failing, or what is
up with you? You used to have all these matters
entirely by heart."

"Weel, sir," said John, "I dunna ken if my memory's failin', or fat's up; but the fac' is I'm growin'
like yersel'—I cunna manage without the paper."

"Consecrated" Ground

The Police Commissioners of Broughton Ferry, near Dundee, some time since compelled house proprietors to lay down concrete on the footpath in front of their properties. An old lady, residing in a cottage, proudly told a friend the other day that the front of her house had been "consecrated up to the vera doorstep."

Unanswerable

When a Scotchman answers a question, he settles the matter in dispute once for all. On a certain occasion the question was asked : " Why was Mary Queen of Scots born at Linlithgow ? " Sandy Kerr promptly answered : " Because her mither was staying there, sir ; " and there actually seemed to be nothing more to say on the subject.

Practical Thrift

An admirable humorous reply, says Dean Ramsay, is recorded by a Scotch officer, well known and esteemed in his day for mirth and humor. Captain Innes, of the Guards (usually called Jack Innes by his contemporaries), was, with others, getting ready for Flushing or some of those expeditions of the great war. His commanding officer, Lord Huntly, remonstrated about the badness of his hat, and recommended a new one. " Na, na, bide a wee," said Jack. " Where we're gain', faith, there'll soon be mair hats nor heads." [7]

Fool Finding

A Scotch student, supposed to be deficient in judgment, was asked by a professor, in the course of his examination, how he would discover a fool ? " By the questions he would ask," was the prompt and highly suggestive reply.

Robbing on Credit

A Scotch parson said recently, somewhat sarcastically, of a toper, that he put an enemy into his mouth to steal away his brains, but that the enemy, after a thorough search, returned without anything.

Going to the Doctor's and "Taking" Something

A Scotch lad was on one occasion accused of stealing some articles from a doctor's shop. The judge was much struck with his respectable appearance, and asked him why he was guilty of such a contemptible act.

"Weel, ye see," replied the prisoner, "I had a bit of pain in my side, and my mither tauld me tae gang tae the doctor's and tak' something."

"Oh, yes," said the judge, "but surely she didn't tell you to go and take an eight-day clock!"

The prisoner was evidently nonplused, but it was only for a moment. Turning to the judge, a bright smile of humor stealing over his countenance, he replied quietly:

"There's an auld proverb that says, 'Time an' the doctur cure a' diseases,' an' sae I thocht"—but the remainder was lost in the laughter of the court.

A Case in Which Comparisons Were Odious

The late Rev. Dr. John Hunter, the much-loved minister of the Tron Parish, Edinburgh, had a call one morning from one of his many poor parishioners, who said he had come to ask a favor. On the worthy minister's requesting him to specify its nature, he replied, "Weel, sir, it's to marry me."

"Very good, John," the minister said; "let me know the place, day and hour, and I shall be at your service."

"But, sir," the bridegroom answered, "it's the noo!" (The bride was waiting outside.)

"Filthy and untidy as you are! No, no; go home and wash, and dress yourself, and then I shall be prepared to perform the ceremony."

"Bless ye, sir, ye should see *her!*" was the response of the applicant.

Pulpit Aids

Young Minister: "I don't think I need put on the gown, John; it's only an encumbrance."

Beadle: "Ay, sir; it makes ye mair impressive—an' ye need it a', sir, ye need it a'."

Choosing a Minister

The parish kirk of Driechtor had been rather
unfortunate in its ministers, two of them having gone
off in a decline within a twelvemonth of their appointment, and now, after hearing a number of candidates,
for the vacancy, the members were looking forward
with keen interest to the meeting at which the election
takes place.

"Weel, Marget," asked one female parishioner of
another, as they foregathered on the road one day,
"wha are you gaun to vote for?"

"I'm just thinkin' I'll vote for nane o' them. I'm
no muckle o' a judge, an' it'll be the safest plan,"
was Marget's sagacious reply.

"Toots, woman, if that's the way o't, vote wi' me."

"An' hoo are you gaun to vote?"

"I'm gaun to vote for the soundest lungs, an'll no
bother us deein' again in a hurry."

Prince Albert and the Ship's Cook

During the earlier visits of the royal family to
Balmoral, Prince Albert, dressed in a very simple
manner, was crossing one of the Scotch lakes in a
steamer, and was curious to note everything relating
to the management of the vessel, and among other
things, the cooking. Approaching the galley, where
a brawny Highlander was attending the culinary
matters, he was attracted by the savory odors of a
compound known by Scotchmen as "hodge-podge,"
which the Highlander was preparing.

"What is that?" asked the prince, who was not
known to the cook.

"Hodge-podge, sir," was the reply.

"How is it made?" was the next question.

"Why, there's mutton intil't, and turnips intil't,
and carrots intil't and——

"Yes, yes," said the prince, who had not learned
that "intil't" meant "into it;" "but what is
intil't?"

"Why, there's mutton intil't, and turnips intil't,
and carrots intil't and——"

"Yes, I see, but what is intil't?"

The man looked at him, and seeing the prince was serious, he replied: "There's mutton intil't, and turnips intil't and——"

"Yes, certainly, I know," urged the inquirer; "but what is intil't—intil't?"

"Ye daft gowk," yelled the Highlander, brandishing a large spoon, "am I no' telling ye what's intil't! There's mutton intil't and——"

Here the interview was brought to a close by one of the prince's suite, who was fortunately passing, and stepped in to save his royal highness from being rapped over the head with the big spoon while in search of information from the cook.

"To Memory 'Dear'"

"Jeems," said the laird one day to his gardener, "there was something I was going to ask you, but man, for the life o' me I canna mind what it was." "Mebbe," said Jeems, who had received no pay for three weeks, "mebbe," said he, "it was to spier at me fat wey I was keepin' body and soul thegither on the wages I wasna gettin'."

Good "for Nothing"—not the Goodness Worth Having

It was a wet day and Jamie Stoddart could not go out to play; Mrs. Stoddart, who had just cleared away the breakfast things, and was about to commence a big heap of ironing, noticed sighs of incipient restlessness in the laddie, and said; "Now, I hope you'll be a good boy the day, Jamie; I've an awfu' lot o' work to dae, an' I can't have you bothering me." "Wull ye gie me a penny if I'm awfu' guid a' day lang?" asked her son. "Mebbe I will," was the reply; "but would it no' be better to be a guid laddie just to please me?" "I'm no' sae shuir o' that," answered the laddie, reflectively. "Ma teacher at the schule says it aye better to be good even for a little, than to be guid for naething." He got that penny.

"The Weaker Vessel"

The minister of a parish in Scotland was called in some time ago to effect a reconciliation between a fisherman of a certain vilage and his wife. After using all the arguments in his power to convince the offending husband that it was unmanly in him, to say the least of it, to strike Polly with his fist, the minister concluded: "David, you know that the wife is the weaker vessel, and you should have pity on her."

"Weel, then," said David, sulkily, "if she's the weaker vessel she should carry the less sail."

Minding His Business

An Englishman traveling in the north of Scotland, came up to a macadamizer of the roads, and while he was busy breaking the road metal, asked him if the direction in which he was going was the way to Aberdeen. The laborer, glad to rest himself a little, dropped his hammer, and said quietly to the stranger, "Now, where cam' ye from?" The traveler, nettled at not receiving a direct answer, asked him, "What business have you with where I came from?" The macadamizer, taking up his hammer and beginning to resume his occupation, said, "Oh, just as little business as where you are gauin to!"

"Married!"—Not "Living"

"Weel, Girzie, how are ye leevin'?" said one. "Me! I'm no leevin' at a'. I'm mairret!"

A Powerful Preacher

Shortly after a Congregational chapel had been planted in the small burgh of Bonnytown, an incident occurred which showed that the powers of its minister were appreciated in certain quarters. A boy, named Johnny Fordyce, had been indiscreet enough to put a sixpence in his mouth and accidently swallowed it. Mrs. Fordyce, concerned both for her boy and the sixpence, tried every means for its recovery, consulted her neighbors, and finally in despair called in a doctor, but without result. As a last resort, a woman present suggested that they should send for the Congregationalist "meenister." "The meenister," chorused mother and neighbors. "Ay, the meenister," rejoined the old dame; "od's, if there's ony money in him he'll sune draw it oot o' 'm!"

Lost Dogs

"What dogs are these, Jasper?" inquired a gentleman of a lad, who was dragging a couple of waspish-looking terriers along a street in Edinburgh. "I dinna ken, sir," replied the urchin; "they came wi' the railway, and they ate the direction, and dinna ken whar to gang."

Stratagem of a Scotch Pedlar

Early in the nineteenth century, Sandy Frazer, a native of the northern part of this island—who by vending of linen, which he carried around the country on his back, had acquired the sum of one hundred pieces of gold—resolving to extend his business by the addition of other wares, set out for London, in order to purchase them at the best advantage. When he had arrived within a few miles of the end of his journey, he was obliged to take shelter in a house of entertainment—which stood in a lonely part of the road—from a violent storm of wind and rain. He had not been there long, before he was joined by two horsemen of genteel appearance, who stopped on the same account. As he was in possession of the fire-side, they were under necessity of joining company with him, in order to dry themselves; which otherwise the meanness of his appearance would probably have prevented their doing.

The new companions had not sat long, before the cheerfulness of his temper, and something uncommonly droll in his conversation, made them invite him to sup with them at their expense; where they entertained him so generously, that, forgetting his national prudence, he could not forbear shewing his treasure, as a proof of not being unworthy of the honor they had done him.

The storm having obliged them to remain all night, they departed together the next morning; and as a farther mark of their regard they kept company with him, though he traveled on foot, till they came into a solitary part of the road, when, one of them, putting a pistol to his breast, took of him the earnings of his whole life, leaving him only a single piece of gold, which, by good fortune, he happened to have loose in his pocket. His distress at such a loss may be easily conceived : however, he sank not under it. A thought instantly occurred to him how it might possibly be retrieved, which he lost not a moment in proceeding to execute. He had observed that the master of the house, where he had met these two plunderers, seemed to be perfectly acquainted with them; he returned therefore thither directly, and feigned to have been taken suddenly ill on the road with a disorder of the bowels ; called for some wine, which he had heated, and rendered still stronger with spice. All the time he was drinking it, he did nothing but pray for his late companions ; who, he said, had not only advised him to take it, but had also been so generous as to give him a piece of gold (which he produced) to pay for it ; and then, seeming to be much relieved, he lamented most heavily his not knowing where to return thanks to his benefactors ; which he said, the violence of his pain had made him forget to inquire.

The master of the house, to whom his guests had not mentioned the man's having money, that he might not expect to share it with them, never suspected the truth of his story, informed him without scruple, who they were, and where they lived. This was directly what he had schemed for. He crawled away till he was out of sight of the house, in order to keep up the deceit, when he made all the haste he could to town ; and, inquiring for his spoilers, he had the satisfaction to hear they were people in trade, and of good repute for their wealth.

The next morning, therefore, as soon, as he thought they were stirring, he went to the house of one of them, whom he found in the room where his merchandise was exposed for sale. The merchant instantly knew him; but, imagining he came on some other business (for he did not think it possible that he could have traced him, or even that he could know him in his altered appearance) asked him in the usual way what he wanted.

"I want to speak wi' ye in private, sir," he answered, getting between him and the door; and then, on the merchant's affecting surprise— "In gude troth, sir," he continued, "I think it is somewhat strange that ye shud na ken Sandy, who supped with ye the neeght before the laust, after au the kindness ye shewed to him." Then lowering his voice, so as not to be overheard by the people present, he told him, with a determined accent, that if he did not instantly return him his money, he would apply to a magistrate for redress.

This was a demand which admitted not of dispute. The money was paid him, gratuity for having lent it, and his receipt taken to that effect; after which he went directly to the other, upon whom he made a like successful demand.

The Highlander and the Angels

A genuine Highlander was one day looking at a print from a picture by one of the old masters, in which angels were represented blowing trumpets. He inquired if the angels played on trumpets, and being answered in the affirmative, made the following pithy remark :

"Hech, sirs, but they maun be pleased wi' music. I wonder they dinna borrow a pair o' bagpipes!"

One Side of Scotch Humor

Charles Lamb was present at a party of North Britons, where a son of Burns was expected, and he happened to drop a remark that he wished it were the father instead of the son, when four of the Scotchmen started up at once, saying that it was impossible, because he (the father) was dead.

Reproving a Miser

Lord Braco was his own factor and collected his own rents, in which duties he is said to have been so rigorously exact that a farmer, being one rent-day deficient in a single farthing, he caused him to trudge to a considerable distance to procure that little sum before he would grant a discharge. When the business was adjusted, the countryman said to his lordship, " Now, Braco, I wad gie ye a shilling for a sight o' a' the gowd and siller ye hae." "Weel, man," answered the miser, " it's no cost ye ony mair " ; and he exhibited to the farmer several iron boxes full of gold and silver coin. " Now," said the farmer, " I'm as rich as yourself, Braco." " Ay, man," said his lordship, " how can that be ? " " Because I've seen it," replied the countryman, " and ye can do nae mair."

A Shrewd Reply

Sir Walter Scott says that the alleged origin of the invention of cards produced one of the shrewdest replies he had ever heard given in evidence. It was by the late Dr. Gregory, of Edinburgh, to a counsel of great eminence at the Scottish bar. The doctor's testimony went to prove the insanity of the party whose mental capacity was the point at issue. On a cross-interrogation he admitted that the person in question played admirably at whist. " And do you seriously say, doctor," said the learned counsel, " that a person having a superior capacity for a game so difficult, and which requires in a pre-eminent degree, memory, judgment and combination, can be at the same time deranged in his understanding ? " " I am no card player," said the doctor, with great address, " but I have read in history that cards were invented for the amusement of an insane king." The consequences of this reply were decisive.

Two Good Memories

A simple Highland girl, on her way home for the north, called as she passed by Crieff upon an old

master with whom she had formerly served. Being
kindly invited by him to share in the family dinner,
and the usual ceremony of asking a blessing having
been gone through, the poor girl, anxious to compliment, as she conceived, her ancient host, exclaimed :
" Ah, master, ye maun hae a grond memory, for that's
the grace ye had when I was wi' you seven years
ago."

Compensation

A venerable Scotch minister used to say to any of
his flock who were laboring under affliction : " Time
is short, and if your cross is heavy you have not far to
carry it."

Fowls and Ducks!

A Scotchman giving evidence at the bar of the
House of Lords in the affair of Captain Porteous, and
telling of the variety of shot which was fired upon that
unhappy occasion, was asked by the Duke of New-
castle what kind of shot it was? " Why," said the
man in his broad dialect, " sic as they shoot fools
(fowls) wi' an' the like." " What kind of fools?"
asked the duke, smiling at the word. " Why, my
lord, dukes (ducks) and sic' kin' o' fools."

Square-Headed

A learned Scottish lawyer being just called to the
Bench, sent for a new tie-wig. The peruquier, on
applying his apparatus in one direction was observed
to smile ; upon which the judge desired to know what
ludicrous circumstance gave rise to his mirth? The
barber replied that he could not but remark the
extreme *length* of his honor's head. " That's well,"
said Lord S——, " we lawyers have occasion for *long
heads!*" The barber, who by this time had completed the dimensions, now burst out into a fit of
laughter ; and an explanation being insisted on, at
last declared that he could not possibly contain himself when he discovered that " *his lordship's head was
just as thick as it was long!*"

Refusing Information

Two Scotchmen met the other day on one of the bridges of Glasgow, one of them having in his hand a very handsome fowling-piece, when the following dialogue ensued : " Ods, mon, but that's a bonny gun." " Ay, deed is it." " Whaur did you get it?" " Owre by there." " And wha's it for?" " D'ye ken the yeditor of the Glasgow *Herald?* " " Ou ay." " Weel, it's nae for him."

Sabbath Breaking

The following anecdote is told in illustration of the Scotch veneration for the Sabbath : A geologist, while in the country, and having his pocket hammer with him, took it out and was chipping the rock by the wayside for examination. His proceedings did not escape the quick eye and ready tongue of an old Scotchwoman. " What are you doing there, man?" " Don't you see? I'm breaking a stone." " Y'are doing mair than that ; y'are breaking the Sabbath."

Highland Simplicity

On one occasion a young girl fresh from the West Highlands came on a visit to a sister she had residing in Glasgow. At the outskirts of the town she stopped at a toll-bar, and began to rap smartly with her knuckles on the gate. The keeper, amused at the girl's action, and curious to know what she wanted, came out, when she very demurely interrogated him as follows :

" Is this Glasco? "

" Yes."

" Is Peggy in? "

The Fall of Adam and Its Consequences

As might have been expected, perhaps, Dean Ramsay is especially copious in clerical stories and those trenching on theological topics. He tells us how a man who was asked what Adam was like, first described our general forefather somewhat vaguely as " just like ither fouk." Being pressed for a more special description, he likened him to a horse-couper known to himself and the minister. "Why was Adam like that horse-couper?" "Weel," replied the catechumen, "naebody got onything by him, and mony lost."

Remarkable Presence of Mind

A well-known parsimonious Scottish professor was working one day in his garden in his ordinary beggar-like attire, and was alarmed to see the carriage of the great man of the parish whirling rapidly along the road to his house. It was too late to attempt a retreat, and get himself put in order to receive "my lord." To retreat was impossible; to remain there and as he was, to be shamed and disgraced. With a promptitude seldom or never surpassed, he struck his battered hat down on his shoulders, drew up his hands into the sleeves of his ragged coat, stuck out his arms at an acute angle, planted his legs far apart, and throwing rigidity into all his form, stood thus in the potato ground, the very beau-ideal of what in England is called a "scarecrow," in Scotland "a potato-bogle," never suspected by the visitors as they drove up to the front entrance, while he made for the back door to don his best suit.

Beginning Life Where He Ought to Have Ended, and Vice Versa

A worthy Scotch couple, when asked how their son had broken down so early in life, gave the following explanation: "When we began life together we worked hard and lived on porridge, and such like; gradually adding to our comforts as our means improved, until we were able to dine off a bit of roast beef, and sometimes a boiled chickie (chicken); but Jack, our son, he worked backwards and began with the chickie first."

How to Exterminate Old Thieves

The humorous, but stern criminal judge, Lord Braxfield, had a favorite maxim which he used frequently to repeat: "Hang a thief when he's young, and he'll no steal when he's auld."

A Sympathetic Hearer

An old minister in the Cheviots used, when excited in the pulpit, to raise his voice to a loud half-whimper, half-whine. One day a shepherd had brought with him a young collie, who became so thrilled by the high note of the preacher that he also broke out into a quaver so like the other that the minister stopped short. "Put out that collie," he said, angrily. The shepherd, equally angry, seized the animal by the neck, and as he dragged him down the aisle, sent back the growling retort at the pulpit, " It was yersel' begond it !''

Ginger Ale

A short time since, a bailie of Glasgow invited some of his electioneering friends to a dinner, during which the champagne circulated freely, and was much relished by the honest bodies; when one of them, more fond of it than the rest, bawled out to the servant who waited, " I say, Jock, gie us some mair o' that *ginger yill*, will ye ? ''

A Conditional Promise

At Hawick, the people used to wear wooden clogs, which made a *clanking* noise on the pavement. A dying old woman had some friends by her bedside, who said to her : " Weel, Jenny, ye are gaun to heaven, and gin ye should see our folk, ye can tell them that we're all weel." To which Jenny replied : " Weel, gin I should see them, I'se tell 'em. But you maun.a expect that I'se to gang clank, clanking thro heaven looking for your folk."

Scripture Examination

An old schoolmaster, who usually heard his pupils once a week through Watts' Scripture History, and afterwards asked them promiscuously such questions as suggested themselves to his mind, one day desired a young urchin to tell him who Jesse was ; when the boy briskly replied, " The Flower of Dunblane, sir.''

A Minor Major

Lord Annandale, one of the Scotch judges, had a son, who, at the age of eleven or twelve, rose to the rank of a major. One morning his lady mother, hearing a noise in the *nursery*, rang to know the cause of it. "It's only," said the servant, "the major greetin' (crying) for his porridge!"

A Cute Way of Getting an Old Account

An old Scotch grave-digger was remonstrated with one day at a funeral for making a serious over-charge for digging a grave. "Weel, ye see, sir," said the old man, in explanation, making a motion with his thumb towards the grave, "him and me had a bit o' a tift twa-three years syne owre the head of a watch I selt him, an' I've never been able to get the money oot o' him yet. 'Now,' says I to myself, 'this is my last chance, an' I'll better tak' it.'"

"Hearers Only—Not Doers"

Could anything be better than the improvement of a minister of Arran, who was discoursing on the carelessness of his flock? "Brethren, when you leave the church, just look down at the duke's swans; they are vera bonny swans, an' they'll be sooming about an' dooking doon their heads and laving theirsels wi' the clean water till they're a' drookit; then you'll see them sooming to the shore, an' they'll gie their wings a bit flap an' they're dry again. Now, my friends, you come here every Sabbath, an' I lave you a' ower wi' the Gospel till you are fairly drookit wi't. But you just gang awa ham·, an' sit doon by your fireside, gie your wings a bit flap, an' ye're as dry as ever again."

The Chieftain and the Cabby

The following story illustrates the disadvantage of having an article in common use called after one's own name. The chief of the clan McIntosh once had a dispute with a cabman about his fare. "Do you

know who I am?" indignantly exclaimed the Highlander; "I am the McIntosh."

"I don't care if you are an umbrella," replied the
cabby; "I'll have my rights."

Not All Profit

A humorous minister of Stirling, hearing that one
of his hearers was about to be married for the third
time, said to him: "They tell me, John, you are getting money wi' her; you did so on the last two occasions; you'll get quite rich by your wives."

"'Deed, sir," quietly replied John, "what wi'
bringin' them in and puttin' them out, there's nae
muckle be made of them."

Pie, or Patience?

A little Scotch boy, aged five, was taking dinner
at his grandfather's and had reached the dessert. "I
want some pie," said young Angus.

"Have patience," said his grandmother.

"Which would you rather have, Angus," said
grandfather; "patience or pie?"

"Pie," replied Angus, emphatically.

"But then," said his grandfather, "there might not
be any left for me."

"Well," said Angus, "you have some of patience."

How to Treat a Surplus

In a school in Aberdeenshire, one day, a dull boy was
making his way to his master for the third time with an
arithmetical question. The teacher, a little annoyed,
exclaimed, "Come, come, John, what's the matter now?"

"I canna get ma question richt," replied the boy.

"What's wrong with it, this time?"

"I've gotten auchteenpence ower muckle."

"Never mind," said a smart boy, 'in a loud
whisper, with a sly glance at the master, "keep it tae
yersel', Jock."

Landseer's Deadly Influence

An amusing incident took place during one of
Landseer's early visits to Scotland. In the course of
his journey he stopped at a village, and as his habit

was, took great notice of the many dogs, jotting down
sketches of such as took his fancy most. On the next
day he continued his journey. As he passed through
the village, Landseer was surprised and horrified to
see dogs of all kinds, some of which he recognized,
hanging dead from trees or railings on every side.
Presently he saw a boy, who, with tears in his eyes,
was hurrying a young pup towards the river to drown
it. He questioned the urchin, and to his surprise
found that the villagers looked upon him as an excise-
officer, who was taking notes of the dogs with a view to
prosecute the owners of such as had not paid their tax.

Trying One Grave First

An old shoemaker in Glasgow was sitting by the
bedside of his wife who was dying. She took him
by the hand and said: "Weel, John, we're gowin' to
part. I have been a gude wife to you, John." "Oh,
just middling, Jenny, just middlin'," said John, not
disposed to commit himself. "John," says she, "ye
maun promise to bury me in the auld kirkyard at
Str'avon, beside my mither. I could'na rest in peace
among unco' folk, in the dirt and smoke o' Glasgow."
"Weel, weel, Jenny, my woman," said John, sooth-
ingly, "we'll just try ye in Glasgow first, an' gin ye
dinna lie quiet, we'll try you in Str'avon." [S]

"Capital Punishment"—Modified

Two Scotchmen, turning the corner of a street
rather sharply, come into collision. The shock was
stunning to one of them. He pulled off his hat, and,
laying his hand on his forehead, said: "Sic a blow!
My heed's a' ringin' again!"

"Nae wonder," said his companion; "your head was
aye empty—that makes it ring. My heed disna ring
a bit."

"How could it ring" said the other, "seeing it was
crackit?"

Matter More Than Manner

Norman M'Leod was once preaching in a district in
Ayrshire, where the reading of a sermon is regarded
as the greatest fault of which the minister can be

guilty. When the congregation dispersed an old woman, overflowing with enthusiasm, addressed her neighbor. "Did ye ever hear onything sae gran'? Wasna that a sermon?" But all her expressions of admiration being met by a stolid glance, she shouted: "Speak, woman! Wasna that a sermon?" "Ou ay," replied her friend sulkily; "but he read it." "Read it!" said the other, with indignant emphasis. "I wadna care if he had whistled it."

Curious Use of a Word

The word "honest" has in Scotland a peculiar application, irrespective of any integrity of moral character. It is a kindly mode of referring to an individual, as we would say to a stranger: "Honest man, would you tell me the way to——?" or as Lord Hermand, when about to sentence a woman for stealing, began remonstratively; "Honest woman, what gav'd ye steal your neighbor's tub?"

Finding Work for His Class, While He Dined

A clergyman in Scotland, who had appointed a day for the catechising of some of his congregation, happened to receive an invitation to dinner for the same day, and having forgotten his previous engagement, he accepted it. Just as he was mounting his gig to depart, he perceived the first of his class entering his garden, and the remainder coming over the hill, and at once became aware of the mistake he had made. Here was a fix. But the minister's ready wit soon came to his assistance.

"What have you come for, John?" he asked, addressing the first comer.

"An' dee ye no' remember, sir, ye bade us come to be catecheesed?"

"Ou, ay; weel, no' to keep ye going further, John, was it a hoorned coo or a hemmel that Noah took into the ark?"

"'Deed, sir, I canna tell."

"Weel, turn back and ask the ither folk the same question, and if they canna answer it, bid them go home and find oot."

The Value of a Laugh in Sickness

Dr. Patrick Scougal, a Scottish bishop, in the seventeenth century, being earnestly sought by an old woman to visit her sick cow, the prelate, after many remonstrances, reluctantly consented, and, walking round the beast, said gravely, " If she live, she live ; and if she die, she die ; and I can do nae mair for her." Not long afterwards, he was dangerously afflicted with a quinsy in the throat ; hereupon the old woman, having got access to his chamber, walked round his bed repeating the same words which the bishop had pronounced when walking round the cow, and which she believed had cured the animal. At this extraordinary sight the bishop was seized with a fit of laughter, which burst the quinsy, and saved his life.

Why Israel Made a Golden Calf

The following answer from a little girl was shrewd and reflective. The question was : " Why did the Israelites make a golden calf ? "

" They hadna as muckle siller as would mak' a *coo*'." [9]

An Economical Preacher's Bad Memory

A parochial incumbent, whose scene of labor some years ago bordered on the Strath of Blain, was blamed for having an erroneous opinion of the memories of his hearers, insomuch as he frequently entertained them with " could kail hot again," in the shape of sermons that he had previously given. On one occasion his own memory allowed him to make a slip, and only one Sabbath elapsed between the giving of the sermon the second time. After the dismissal of the congregation, the beadle remarked to him, " I hae often heard ye blamed, sir, for gein' us auld sermons ; but they'll surely no' say that o' the ane ye gi'ed them this afternoon, for its just a fortnicht sin' they heard it afore in the same place." [8]

Sharpening His Teeth

An English gentleman, traveling in the Highlands, being rather late in coming down to dinner, Donald was sent upstairs to intimate all was ready. He speedily returned, nodding significantly, as much as to say it was all right.

"But, Donald," said his master, after some further trial of a hungry man's patience, "are ye sure ye made the gentleman understand?"

"*Understand!*" retorted Donald (who had peeped into the room and found the guest engaged at his toilet); "I'se warrant ye he understands; he's *sharpening* his teeth—" not supposing the toothbrush could be of any other use.

Droll Solemnity

An old maid of Scotland, after reading aloud to her two sisters, also unmarried, the births, marriages, and deaths, in the ladies' corner of a newspaper, thus moralized: "Weel, weel, these are solemn events, death and marriage: but ye ken they're what we must a' come to."

"Eh, Miss Jenny, but ye have been lang spared!" was the reply of the youngest sister.

Matrimony a Cure for Blindness

An example of this truth is given in the case of a sly old Scotchman who, on marrying a very young wife, was rallied by his friends on the inequality of their ages.

"She will be near me," he replied, "to close my een."

"Weel," remarked another party, "I've had twa wives, and they *opened* my een."

Plain Speaking

"I was at the manse the ither day," said the precentor to an old crony, "an' the minister and me got on the crack. He says to me: 'Jim,' says he, 'I'm very sorry to tell you that I must advise you to give up your post, for there are several people complaining that you cannot sing!'

"'Weel, sir,' said I, 'I dinna think you should be in sic a hurry to advise me. I've been telt a dizzen times ye canna preach, but I never advised ye to gie up your place.'

"I saw he was vexed, so I jist said : 'Ne'er heed, sir; the fules 'll hae to hear us till we think fit to stop.' "

Trying to Shift the Job

A country laird, at his death, left his property in equal shares to his two sons, who continued to live very amicably together for many years. At length one said to the other : "Sam, we're getting auld now; you'll tak' a wife, and when I dee ye'll get my share o' the grund."

"Na, John; you're the youngest and maist active; you'll tak' a wife, and when I dee you'll get my share."

"Od ! " says John ; "Sam, that's just the way with you when there's any *fash or trouble.* There's naething you'll do at a'."

A New Explanation of an Extra Charge

The following story is told of a distinguished Edinburgh professor : Desiring to go to church one wet Sunday, he hired a cab. On reaching the church door he tendered a shilling—the legal fare—to cabby, and was somewhat surprised to hear the cabman say : "Twa shillin', sir." The professor, fixing his eye on the extortioner, demanded why he charged two shillings, upon which the cabman dryly answered : "We wish to discourage traveling on the Sabbath as much as possible, sir."

National Thrift Exemplified

Nowadays, when we hear that patients are beginning to question whether they are bound to pay their doctors or not unless a cure has been effected, the following anecdote of a cautious Scotchman may serve as a useful hint : A poor old man had been some time ill, but refused to have advice, dreading the doctor's bill. At last he gave in to the repeated requests of his family, and sent for the doctor. On his arrival, the old man greeted him with : " Noo, doctor, if ye dinna think I am worth repairing, dinna put much expense on me." The doctor, finding him worth repairing, soon set him on his legs again, and the old man considered his bargain a good one.

New Use for a "Cosy"

A newly-married lady, displaying her wedding presents to an old Highland servant-maid, shows a fancy tea-cosy."

Servant Maid: "That'll be a bonny present."

Lady: "It is, indeed."

Servant Maid: "Ay, an' you'll pe shurely wear this at a crand party?"

Mending Matters

"Had you the audacity, John," said a Scottish laird to his servant, "to go and tell some people that I was a mean fellow, and no gentleman?" "Na, na," was the candid answer; "you'll no catch me at the like o' that. I aye keep my thoughts to mysel'."

Degrees of Capacity

Francis Jeffrey was an example of a man who had acquired an artificial style and language, suitable only for printed books and a small circle of friends and associates in Edinburgh. His diction and pronunciation were unintelligible to the bulk of his countrymen, and offensive and ridiculous in the House of Commons. His weight in his party, his great intelligence, and the affection of his friends, could not prevent him from failing in Parliament. An amusing illustration is given by an acquaintance of the contrast between him and his friend Henry Cockburn, in the examination of a witness. The trial turned upon the intellectual competency of a testator. Jeffrey asked a witness, a plain countryman, whether the testator was a man of "intellectual capacity?—an intellectual, shrewd man?—a man of capacity?—had he ordinary mental endowments?"

"What d'ye mean, sir?"

"I mean," replied Jeffrey, testily, "was the man

of sufficient ordinary intelligence to qualify him to manage his own affairs?"

"I dinna ken," replied the chafed and mystified witness; "Wad ye say the question ower again, sir?"

Jeffrey being baffled, Cockburn took up the examination. He said: "Ye kenned Tammas——?"

"Ou, ay; I kenned Tammas weel; me and him herded together when we were laddies."

"Was there onything in the cretur?"

"Deil a thing but what the spune put in him."

"Would you have trusted him to sell a cow for you?"

"A cow! I wadna lippened him to sell a calf."

Francis Jeffrey could not, if he had devoted an article in the *Edinburgh Review* to the subject, have given a more exact measurement than was presented in few words of the capacity of the testator to manage his own affairs.

"Invisible and Incomprehensible"

First Scot: "Fat sort o' minister hae ye gotten, Geordie?"

Second Scot: "Oh, weel; he's no muckle worth. We seldom get a glint o' him; six days o' th' week he's envees'ble, and on the seventh he's encomprehens'ble."

Fetching His "Character"

At a Scotch fair a farmer was trying to engage a lad to assist on the farm, but would not finish the bargain until he brought a character from the last place, so he said: "Run and get it, and meet me at the cross, at four o'clock."

The youth was up to time, and the farmer said, "Well, have you got your character with you?"

"Na," replied the youth; "but I've got yours, an' I'm no comin'."

Scottish Negativeness

If you remark to an old Scotchman that "It's a good day," his usual reply is, "Aweel, sir, I've seen waur." Such a man does not say his wife is an excellent woman. He says, "Ses's no' a bad body."

A buxom lass, smartly dressed, is "No' sae vera unpurposelike." The richest and rarest viands are "No' sae bad." The best acting and the best singing are designated as "No' bad." A man noted for his benevolence is "No' the warst man in the worilt." A Scotchman is always afraid of expressing unqualified praise. He suspects if he did so it would tend to spoil the object of his laudations, if a person, male or female, old or young; or, if that object were a song, a picture, a piece of work, a landscape, or such, that those who heard him speak so highly of it would think he had never in his life seen or heard anything better, which would be an imputation on his knowledge of things. "*Nil Admirari*" is not exactly the motto of the normal Scotchman. He is quite ready to admire admirable things, but yet loath to admit it, only by inference, that he had never witnessed or experienced anything better. Indeed, he has always something of the like kind which he can quote to show that the person, place or thing in question is only comparatively good, great, clever, beautiful, or grand. Then, when anybody makes a remark, however novel, that squares with a Scotchman's ideas, he will say, "That's just what I've offen thoucht!" "That's exactly ma way of thinking!" "That's just what I aye say!" "That's just what I was actually on the point o' saying!"

Either Too Fast or Too Slow

An artist, returning from a sketching tour in Arran, was crossing the mountains on his way back to catch the early steamer for Brodick. His watch had stopped, so he could not form an idea of the time of day. To his joy he met a shepherd, of whom he inquired the hour. The native, pulling out his watch, replied: "Sir, it will shoost pe five o'clock on my wee watchy; but whether she'll be two oors too slow, or two oors too fast, I dinna ken."

A Highland Servant Girl and the Kitchen Bell

Some years ago a lady engaged a domestic servant from the Highlands. In the evening the lady wanted

supper brought in, so she rang the bell. Not getting
any answer, she repeated the summons, but with the
same effect. She then proceeded to the kitchen,
where to her amazement she found the servant
almost convulsed with laughter. She pointed to the
bell and exclaimed: "As sure's I leeve I never touched
it, an' its waggin' yet!'

Not Necessarily Out of His Depth

In Scotland the topic of a sermon, or discourse is
called by old-fashioned folk "its ground," or, as they
would say, "its grund." An old woman, bustling
into kirk rather late, found the preacher had commenced, and opening her Bible, nudged her next
neighbor, with the inquiry: "What's the grund?"

"Oh," rejoined the other, who happened to be a
brother minister, and therefore a privileged critic,
"he's lost his grund long since, and he's just
swimming."

Scotch Literalness

"You must beware," says Charles Lamb, "of indi-
rect expressions before a Caledonian. I have a print,
a graceful female, after Leonardo da Vinci, which I
was showing off to Mr. ——. After he had examined
it, I asked him how he liked 'my beauty' (a name it
goes by among my friends), when he very gravely
assured me that he "had very considerable respect
for my character and talents'—so he was pleased
to say—'but had not given himself much thought
for the degree of my personal pretensions.'"

A Scotch "Native"

"Are you a native of this parish?" asked a Scotch
sheriff of a witness who was summoned to testify in a
case of illicit distilling.

"Maistly, yer honor," was the reply.

"I mean, were you born in this parish?"

"Na, yer honor; I wasna born in this parish, but
I'm maist a native for a' that."

" You come here when you were a child, I suppose you mean?" said the sheriff.

" Na, sir, I'm just here about sax year, noo."

" Then how do you come to be nearly a native of this parish?"

" Weel, ye see, whan I cam' here, sax year sin', I jist weighed eight stane, an' I'm fully seventeen stane noo ; sae ye see that about nine stane a' me belangs to this parish an' the ither eight comes frae Camlachie."

"A Call to a Wider Sphere"

An old Highland clergyman, who had received several calls to parishes, asked his servant where he should go. His servant said : "Go where there is most sin, sir."

The preacher concluded that good advice, and went where there was most money.

Why Janet Slept During Her Pastor's Sermon

Dean Ramsay tells the following quaint story of Scotch life :

There was a worthy old woman at Cults, whose place in church was what is commonly called the lateran —a kind of senate gallery at the top of the pulpit stairs. She was a most regular attendant, but as regularly fell asleep during the sermon, of which fault the preacher had sometimes audible intimation.

It was observed, however, that though Janet slept during her own pastor's discourse, she could be attentive enough when she pleased, and especially was she alert when some young preacher occupied the pulpit. A little piqued at this, Mr. Gillespie said to her one day: "Janet, I think you hardly behave respectfully to your own minister in one matter."

" Me, sir?" exclaimed Janet ; " I would like to see ony mon, no' to say woman, but yoursel', say that o' me ! What can you mean, sir?"

" Weel, Janet, ye ken when I preach you're almost always fast asleep before I've given out my text, but when any of these young men from St. Andrew's preach for me, I see you never sleep a wink. Now, that's what I call no' using me as you should do."

"Hoot, sir," was the reply, "is that a'? I'll soon tell you the reason of that. When you preach, we a' ken the word o' God's safe in your hands; but when they young birkies tak it in haun, my certie, but it tak's us a' to look after them." [7]

Spinning it Out

As a verbose preacher was addressing the congregation on a certain occasion, one by one of his officials dropped out of the church into the vestry. As the last one who left put his head into the vestry, those who had preceded him inquired if the prolix speaker had not finished his address. "Well," said he, "his tow's dune lang syne, but he's aye spinnin' awa' yet."

A Wife's Protection

"Wake up, wake up; there's a man in the house!" cried Mrs. Macdougal to her husband the other night. Mac rolled out of bed and grasped his revolver, and opened the door to sally forth for the robber. Then, turning to his wife, he said: "Come, Maggie, and lead the way. It's a cowardly man that would hurt a woman."

Scotch Provincialism

A gentleman from Aberdeen was awoke one night lately in an hotel in Princes Street by an alarm of fire. Upon going to the window, he called out, "Watchman, far eist?" (Where is it?). The watchman thanked him and went to the Register Office, where he found he was going in the wrong direction and returned. On repassing the hotel, he was again called to by the Aberdonian, who bawled out, "Watchman, far was't?" (Where was it?) On looking up to him, the watchman replied, "Ye're a leein' scoonril; ye first tell'd me it was far east, an' noo ye say it's far west; but I tell ye it's neither e' tane or e' tither, cause it's ower i' e' Coogate."

More Polite than Some Smokers

The other day a man who indulged in "the weed,"

took a seat in a carriage set apart for smokers on the
Tynemouth line. He lost no time in getting up a
cloud, and whilst puffing away he was accosted by a
decent elderly female sitting in an opposite corner.

" Is this a smokin' carriage, sor ? "

" Yes, good woman," he replied ; " but if my pipe
annoys you " (obligingly taking it from his lips), " I'll
put it out."

" No, hinny," said she, drawing a well-used
" cutty " from beneath her shawl ; " aa's gawin' to
hev a pipe mesel'! "

The Fly-fisher and the Highland Lassie

An English tourist visited Arran, and being a keen
disciple of Isaac Walton, was arranging to have a
good day's sport. Being told that the horse-fly would
suit his purpose admirably for bait, he addressed
himself to Christy, the Highland servant-maid. " I
say, my girl, can you get me some horse-flies ? "

Christy looked stupid, and he repeated his question. Finding that she did not yet comprehend him,
he exclaimed : " Why, girl, did you never see a
horse-fly ? "

" Naa, sir," said the girl ; " but a wanse saw a
coo jump over a preshipice."

Not at Home

One evening, John Clerk (Lord Eldon) had been
dipping rather too freely in the convivial bowl with a
friend in Queen Street, and on emerging into the
open air, his intellect became to a considerable extent
confused, and not being able to distinguish objects
with any degree of minuteness or certainty, he thought
himself in a fair way of losing the road to his own
house in Picardy Place. In this perplexity he espied
some one coming towards him. whom he stopped with
this query : " D'ye ken whaur John Clerk bides ? "

" What's the use o' your speerin' that question ? "
said the man ; " you're John Clerk himsel'."

" I ken that," said John ; " but it's no himsel' that's
wanted—it's his house."

Faring Alike

First Scotch Boatman : " Weel, Geordie, how got
ye on the day ?"

*Second Ditto (droughty—he had been out with a
Free Kirk minister, a strict abstainer)* : " Nae ava.
The auld carle had nae whusky, sae I took him where
there was nae fush ! "

" Saddling the Ass "

Dr. Guthrie, in the course of an address in the New
Free College, remarked that he was often annoyed
and vexed beyond measure to find discourses of the
ablest character murdered and massacred by a
wretched delivery. Some ministers appeared to have
a habit of emphasizing every third word or so ; and
he would tell them an anecdote which he had heard
to illustrate the importance of correct reading. A
minister once reading 1 Kings xiii : 13, read it thus :
" And the prophet said unto his sons, *Saddle me the
ass.* So they saddled *him*, the ass."

An Open Question

A Scottish minister, being one day engaged in
visiting some members of his flock, came to the door
of a house where his gentle tapping could not be
heard for the noise of contention within. After waiting a little he opened the door and walked in, saying
with an authoritative voice, " I should like to know
who is head of this house?" " Weel, sir," said the
husband and father, " if ye sit down a wee, we'll
maybe be able to tell ye, for we're just trying to settle
that point."

Domestics in By-gone Days

Dean Ramsay records the following anecdote in his
" Reminiscences of Scottish Life and Character " :
The charge these old domestics used to take in the
interests of the family, and the cool way in which they
took upon them to protect those interests, sometimes
led to very provoking and sometimes to a very ludi-

crous exhibition of importance. A friend told me of
a dinner scene illustrative of this sort of interference
which had happened at Airth in the last generation.
Mrs. Murry, of Abercairney, had been amongst the
guests, and at dinner one of the family noticed that
she was looking about for the proper spoon to help
herself to salt. The old servant, Thomas, was
appealed to, that the want might be supplied. He
did not notice the appeal. It was repeated in a more
peremptory manner : " Thomas, Mrs. Murry has not
a salt-spoon "; to which he replied most emphatically, " Last time Mrs. Murry dined here we *lost* a
salt-spoon." [7]

A Misdeal

A celebrated Scotch divine had just risen up to the
pulpit to lead the congregation in prayer, when a
gentlemen in front of the gallery took out his handkerchief to wipe the dust from his brow, forgetting
that a pack of cards was wrapped up in it; the
whole pack was scattered over the breast of the gallery. The minister could not resist a sarcasm, solemn
as the act was in which he was about to engage.
" O man, man! surely your psalm-book has been
ill-bund."

" A Sign of Grace "

A good story is told by Mr. Aird, Moderator of the
Free Church of Scotland, respecting a minister who
in the old days of patronage was forced upon a congregation at Alness. He was coldly received, but
calling one day upon an old elder, he took a chair in
spite of his gruff reception. In order to meet an
awkward pause, he took out his snuff-box. " Oh,"
said the elder, " ye tak' snuff, dae ye? "

" Oh, yes," was the reply.

" Weel," said the elder, " that's the fust sign of
grace I've seen in ye."

" How's that ? "

" Dae we nae read o' Solomon's temple," replied
the elder, " that a' the snuffers were of pure gold?"

Extraordinary Absence of Mind

A certain Scottish professor was not more remarkable for his writings on political economy, than for his frequent unconsciousness of what passed before him. His absence of mind was so remarkable, that his wife once wagered that she would accost him in the street, inquire after the health of herself and family, and that he would not recognize her. She actually won the wager.

The professor was once taking a solitary walk on the banks of the canal, into which in his abstraction, he walked. When within a yard of the centre, an honest woman washing clothes behind him, brawled out, "Come oot, come oot, fule body, or ye'll be droon't."

These warning sounds invading the tympanum of the professorial ear, had the effect of making him turn right about and forthwith recover the dry ground. The good woman, concluding him to be an idiot, sympathetically exclaimed, "Puir body! a weel, they hae muckle to answer for that lets ye gang yer lane!"

Salmon or Sermon

A clergyman in Perthshire, who was more skilful as an angler than popular as a preacher, having fallen into conversation with some of his parishioners on the benefits of early rising, mentioned as an instance, that he had that very morning, before breakfast, composed a sermon, and killed a salmon—an achievement on which he plumed himself greatly. "Aweel, sir," observed one of the company, "I would rather have your salmon than your sermon."

"Bock Again!"—A Prompt Answer

A countryman in Scotland, who was very fond of apples, especially if they came cheap, was one day getting over the hedge into his neighbor's orchard, who, happening to be walking towards the spot at the time, cried out, "Hoot, hoot, Sandy, where are thee ganging?"

"Bock again, now you are there," replied the thief, with the utmost *sang froid*.

A "Kippered" Divine

It is said that Dr. Chalmers once entertained a distinguished guest from Switzerland, whom he asked if he would be helped to kippered salmon. The foreign divine asked the meaning of the uncouth word "kippered," and was told that it meant "preserved." The poor man, in public prayer, soon after, offered a petition that the distinguished divine might long be "kippered to the Free Church of Scotland."

Scotch Caution versus Suretiship

The old Jews and the old Scotch Highlanders had one feeling in common—a dread of suretiship. The Book of Proverbs contains several warnings of the danger that lurks in a surety bond, but none are more admonishing than one uttered by an Highlander. Donald had been tried for his life, and narrowly escaped conviction. In discharging him the judge thought it proper to say : "Prisoner, before you leave the bar, I'll give you a piece of advice. You have got off this time, but if you ever come before me, again, I'll be caution (surety) you'll be hanged."

"Thank you, my lord," said Donald, "for your good advice, and as I'm no' ungratefu', I beg to gie your lordship a piece of advice in turn. Never be ' caution ' for anybody, for the cautioner has often to pay the penalty."

A Descendant of the Stuarts

A gentleman from the north, being of a genealogical turn of mind, believed that he had discovered in his pedigree some remote connection with the royal Stuart blood. Going south, he made much of his presumed relationship, until he was generally spoken of in bated breath by his innocent English friends, "as a descendant of the Stuarts." At a public gathering he was thus mentioned, and the description instantly engaged the rapt attention of a new arrival from Caledonia.

"A descendant o' the Stuarts !" he cried; "eh, sirs, I'd like feine to see ane o' the royal race."

"Then there he is," answered the interlocutor, pointing him out—"there—the gentleman standing in front of the fireplace."

" Gude sakes !" said the astonished Scot; " that's just my ain brither Jack."

" Law " Set Aside by " Gospel "

It is related that a Scotch minister chanced to meet two of his parishioners in the office of a lawyer, whom he regarded as being too sharp.

The lawyer jocularly and not very graciously put the question : " Doctor, these are members of your flock ; may I ask, do you look upon them as black or white sheep?"

"I don't know," answered the divine drily, " whether they are black or white sheep , but I know if they are here long they are pretty sure to be well fleeced."

" Knowledge—It Shall Vanish Away "

A gentleman was once riding in Scotland by a bleaching ground, where a woman was at work watering her webs of linen-cloth. He asked her where she went to church, what she heard, and how much she remembered of the preceding day's sermon. She could not even remember the text.

"And what good can the preaching do you," said he, " if you forget it all?"

"Ah, sir," replied the woman, "if you look at this web on the grass, you will see that as fast as ever I put the water on it the sun dries it all up ; and yet, see, it grows whiter and whiter."

A Harmless Joke

Sandy Merton was a half-witted fellow who lived in a small town in the west of Scotland. One day Sandy entered the doctor's shop, carrying under his arm a rusty gun.

"Well, Alexander," said the doctor, "who gave you the gun?"

" Maister Tamson, the publican, gied me it, an' he said the only kind o' poother it wud shoot wi' was Seidlitz poother ; sae gie I tuppence worth."

Looking before Leaping

A bluff, consequential gentleman from the South, with more beef on his bones than brains in his head, riding along the Hamilton road, near to Blantyre, asked a herdboy on the roadside, in a tone and manner evidently meant to quiz, if he were " half way to Hamilton?" "Man," replied the boy, " I wad need to ken where ye hae come frae afore I could answer that question."

"Lichts Oot!"

An old Highland sergeant in one of the Scottish regiments, was going his round one night to see that all the lights were out in the barrack rooms. Coming to a room where he thought he saw a light shining, he roared out : " Put oot that licht there !"

One of the men shouted back : "Man, it's the mune, sergeant."

Not hearing very well, the sergeant cried in return : "I dinna care a tacket what it is—pit it oot !"

A Teetotal Preacher Asks for "a Glass," and Gets it

A teetotal minister, who was very particular about his toilet, went to preach one Sunday for a brother minister in a parish in Kinross-shire. On entering the vestry he looked around in search of a mirror, to see that his appearance was all right before entering the pulpit , but, failing to find one, he said to the beadle : " John, can I have a glass before entering the pulpit ?"

" Certainly, sir !" replied John. " Just bide a wee, and I'll get ane for ye immediately " ; and he left the vestry at once.

On his return the minister said : " Well, John, have you succeeded ?"

" Yes, sir," replied John ; " I've brocht a gill. That'll be a glass for the forenoon, and anither for the afternoon."

"Old Bags"

Lord Eldon, who was well known by the nick-name " Old Bags," in one of his sporting excursions, unex-

pectedly came across a person who was sporting over
his land without leave. His lordship inquired if the
stranger was aware he was trespassing, or if he knew
to whom the estate belonged? "What's that to do
with you?" was the reply. "I suppose you are one
of Old Bags' keepers." "No," replied his lordship,
"I am Old Bags himself."

A Poem for the Future

The late Dr. Jamieson, the Scottish lexicographer,
was vain of his literary reputation, and, like many
others who knew not where their great strength lies,
thought himself gifted with a kind of intellectual
able-to-do-everything. The doctor published a poem,
entitled "Eternity."

This poem became the subject of conversational
remark, soon after publication, at a party where the
doctor was present, and a lady was asked her opinion
of it. "It's a bonny poem," said she, "and it's weel
named Eternity, for it will ne'er be read in time."

A Badly Arranged Prayer

A Presbyterian minister in the reign of King William III, performing public worship in the Tron
Church at Edinburgh, used this remarkable expression
in his prayer: "Lord, have mercy upon all fools and
idiots, and particularly upon the Town Council of
Edinburgh." [9]

Simplicity of a Collier's Wife

A clergyman in a mining village not far from Ric-
carton, in the course of his pastoral visits, called at
the domicile of a collier in his parish. Inquiring of a
woman he saw, and whom he presumed to be his wife,
if her husband was at home, she said: "Deed, na,
sir; he's at his work."

"Is your husband, my good woman, a communicant?"

"A communicant! He's naething o' the kind. He's
just a collier."

Astonished at the ignorance displayed, the clergyman could not help ejaculating: "Oh, what darkness!"

The collier's wife understanding the language literally, not figuratively, was also astonished.

"Darkness! Little ye ken o't. Had you been here before we got the extra window in the gable ye would scarcely been able to see your finger afore you."

The pastor sighed.

"I must, my dear woman, put up a petition for you here."

"Petition—petition! Bide a wee. Nae petition (partition) will ye put up here sae lang as I am in the house; but at the term we're going ower to New-diggings, and then ye may put as many o' them as ye like."

A Scotch "Supply"

Many good stories have been told of the beadles of the Scottish churches. The latest is as good as any: One Sabbath morning when a minister of an Ayrshire Established Church was about to enter the pulpit, he found that John, the precentor, had not arrived. He instructed the beadle, who was also bellman, to ring for five minutes longer while they waited to see if John came.

When he returned, the minister inquired: "Has John come yet?"

"No, sir," answered the beadle.

"Most extraordinary! What are we to do? I see no help for it, but you must take John's place yourself for a day."

"Ah, no, sir," replied the beadle, "I couldna dae that. Aiblins I could tak' *your* place, but I couldna tak' John's."

Praying for Wind

Dean Ramsay relates this incident: In one of our northern counties, a rural district had its harvest operations seriously affected by continuous rains. The crops being much laid, wind was desired in order to restore them to a condition fit for the sickle. A minister in his Sabbath services, expressed their wants in prayer as follows: "O Lord, we pray thee to send

us wind, no' a rantin' tantin' wind; but a noohin'
(noughin?) soughin', winnin' wind."

Disturbed Devotions

The Rev. Dr. Alexander relates that there lived in
Peebleshire a half-witted man, who was in the habit
of saying his prayers in a field behind a turf-dyke.
One day he was followed to this spot by some wags,
who secreted themselves on the opposite side listening to the man, who expressed his conviction that he
was a very great sinner, and that even were the turf-
dyke at that moment to fall upon him it would be no
more than he deserved. No sooner had he said this,
than the persons on the opposite side pushed the
dyke over him, when, scrambling out, he was heard
to say: "Hech, sirs, it's an awfu' world this; a
body canna say a thing in a joke, but it's ta'en in
earnest." [9]

The "Tables" of "The Law"

When catechizing by the Scottish clergy was customary, the minister of Coldingham, in Berwickshire,
asked a simple country wife, who resided at the farm
of Coldingham Law, which was always styled "The
Law" for brevity's sake: "How many tables, Janet,
are there in the law?"

"Indeed, sir, I canna just be certain," was the
simple reply; "but I think there's ane in the fore
room, ane in the back room, an' anither upstairs."

"Eating Among the Brutes"

The Rev. Dr. M'C——, minister of Douglas, in
Clydesdale, was one day dining with a large party
where the Hon. Henry Erskine and some lawyers
were present. A great dish of water-cresses being,
according to the fashion of the period, handed round
after dinner, Dr. M'C——, who was extravagantly
fond of vegetables, helped himself much more largely
than any other person, and, as he ate with his fingers
with a peculiar voracity of manner, Mr. Erskine was
struck with the idea that he resembled Nebuchadnez-

zar in his state of condemnation. Resolved to give
the minister a hit for the grossness of his taste and
manner of eating, the wit addressed him with : " Dr.
M'C——, ye bring me in mind of the great king
Nebuchadnezzar" ; and the company were beginning
to titter at the ludicrous allusion, when the reverend
devourer of cresses replied : " Ay, do I mind ye o'
Nebuchadnezzar? That'll be because I'm eating
among the brutes, then."

An Angry Preacher

" I know what sort o' heaven you'd pe wanting,"
shouted an earnest and excited Highland minister in
the ears of an apathetic congregation, to whom he
had delivered, without any apparent effect, a vivid
and impressive address on the glory of heaven ; " I
know what sort o' heaven you'd pe wantin'. You'd
pe wantin' that all the seas would pe hot water, that
all the rivers would pe rivers of whiskey, and that all
the hills and mountains would be loaves o' sugar.
That's the sort o' heaven you'd pe wantin' ; more-
over," he added, warming to his work, "you'd pe
wantin' that all the corn-stooks would pe pipe staples
and tobaccos, and sweeshin'—that's the sort o' heaven
you'd pe wantin'."

A Comfortable Preacher

One Sunday, as a certain Scottish minister was
returning homewards, he was accosted by an old
woman who said : " Oh, sir, well do I like the day
when you preach ! "

The minister was aware that he was not very popular, and he answered : " My good woman, I am glad
to hear it ! There are too few like you. And why
do you like when I preach ? "

" Oh, sir," she replied, " when you preach I always
get a good seat ! "

" Haste " and " Leisure "

A clergyman in the north of Scotland, very homely
in his address, chose for his text a passage in the
Psalms, " I said in my haste all men are liars." "Ay,"

premised the minister by way of introduction, "ye
said in your haste, David, did ye?—gin ye had been
here, ye micht hae said it at your leisure, my man."

"Making Hay While the Sun Shines"

An anecdote is told of a certain Highland hotel-
keeper, who was one day bickering with an Englishman in the lobby of the inn regarding the bill.   The
stranger said it was a gross imposition, and that he
could live cheaper in the best hotel in London; to
which the landlord with nonchalance replied, "Oh,
nae doot, sir, nae doot; but do ye no' ken the reason?"   "No, not a bit of it," said the stranger
hastily.   "Weel, then," replied the host, "as ye
seem to be a sensible callant, I'll tell ye; there's 365
days in the Lonnun hotel-keeper's calendar, but we
have only three months in ours!   Do ye understand
me noo, frien'?   We maun mak' hay in the Hielans
when the sun shines, for it's unco seldom he dis't!"

Speaking Figuratively

A preacher of the name of Ker, on being inducted
into a church in Teviotdale, told the people the
relation there was to be between him and them in the
following words: "Sirs, I am come to be your
shepherd, and you must be my sheep, and the Bible
will be my tar bottle, for I will mark you with it";
and laying his hand on the clerk or precentor's head,
he said: "Andrew, you shall be my dog."   "The
sorra bit of your dog will I be," said Andrew.   "O,
Andrew, you don't understand me; I speak mysti-
cally," said the preacher.   "Yes, but you speak mis-
chievously," said Andrew.   [9]

A Canny Witness

During a trial in Scotland, a barrister was examining an old woman, and trying to persuade her to his
view by some "leading questions."   After several
attempts to induce her memory to recur to a particular circumstance, the barrister angrily observed,
"Surely you must remember this fact—surely you can
call to mind such and such a circumstance."   The

witness answered, " I ha' tauld ye I can't tell ; but if ye know so much mair about it than I do (pointing to the judge), do'e tell maister yerself."

A Mother's Confidence in Her Son

Mrs. Baird received the news from India of the gallant but unfortunate action of '84 against Hyder Ali, in which her son (then Captain Baird, afterwards Sir David Baird) was engaged ; it was stated that he and other officers had been taken prisoners and chained together two and two. The friends were careful in breaking such sad intelligence to the mother of Captain Baird. When, however, she was made fully to understand the position of her son and his gallant companions, disdaining all weak and useless expressions of her own grief, and knowing well the restless and athletic habits of her son, all she said was, " Lord, pity the chiel that's chained to our Davy ! " [7]

Lord Clancarty and the Roman Catholic Chaplain

When Lord Clancarty was captain of a man-of-war in 1724, and was cruising off the coast of Guinea, his lieutenant, a Scotch Presbyterian, came hastily into the cabin, and told his lordship that the chaplain was dead, and what was worse, he died a Roman Catholic. Lord Clancarty replied that he was very glad of it. " Hoot fie, my lord," said the officer, " what, are ye glad that yer chaplain died a pawpish ? " " Yes," answered his lordship, " for he is the first sea-parson I ever knew that had any religion at all." [9]

An Idiot's Views of Insanity

A clergyman in the north of Scotland, on coming into church one Sunday morning, found the pulpit occupied by the parish idiot (a thing which often happens in some English parishes—with this difference, that instead of the minister finding the idiot in the pulpit, it is the *people* who find him). The authorities had been unable to remove him without more violence than was seemly, and therefore waited for the minister to dispossess Sam of the place he had

assumed. "Come down, sir, immediately," was the
peremptory and indignant call ; and on Sam remain-
ing unmoved, it was repeated with still greater
energy. Sam, however, very confidentially replied,
looking down from his elevation, "Na, na, meenister,
just ye come up wi' me. This is a perverse generation, and faith, they need us baith." [7]

Lord Mansfield and a Scotch Barrister on Pronunciation

A man who knows the world, will not only make
the most of everything he does know, but of
many things he does not know, and will gain more
credit by his adroit mode of hiding his ignorance,
than the pedant by his awkward attempt to exhibit
his erudition. In Scotland, the *"jus et norma
loquendi"* has made it the fashion to pronounce the
law term curător curător. Lord Mansfield gravely
corrected a certain Scotch barrister when in court,
reprehending what appeared to English usage a false
quantity, by repeating—"Curător, sir, if you please."
The barrister immediately replied, "I am happy to
be corrected by so great an orător as your lordship."

Satisfactory Security

Patrick Forbes, Bishop of Aberdeen, had lent an
unlucky brother money, until he was tired out, but
the borrower renewed his application, and promised
security. The bishop on that condition consented to
the loan : "But where is your security?" said he,
when the poor fellow replied : "God Almighty is my
bondsman in providence ; he is the only security I
have to offer." So singular a reply of a despair-
ing man smote the feelings of the bishop, and he thus
replied : "It is the first time certainly that such a
security was ever offered to me ; and since it is so,
take the money, and may Almighty God, your bondsman, see that it does you good." [9]

Better than a Countess

Mrs. Coutts, wife of the eminent banker, and previously Miss Mellon, the celebrated actress, made her

appearance one day at one of the principal prome-
nades in Edinburgh, dressed in a most magnificent
style, so as to quite overawe our northern neighbors.
"Hoot, mon," said a gentleman standing by, who
did not know who she was, "yon's a braw lady;
she'll be a countess, I'm thinking." "No," replied
an eminent banker, "not just a *countess*, but what's
better, a *dis-countess*."

Remembering Each Other

Mr. Miller, of Ballumbie, had occasion to find fault
with one of his laborers, who had been improvident,
and known better days. He was digging a drain,
and he told him if he did not make better work he
should turn him off. The man was very angry, and
throwing down his spade, called out in a tone of
resentment, "Ye are ower pridefeu', Davie Miller. I
mind ye i' the warld when ye had neither cow nor
ewe." "Very well," replied Mr. Miller, mildly, "I
remember you when you had both."

Marriages Which are Made in Heaven—How Revealed

Archbishop Leighton never was married. While
he held the See of Dumblane, he was of course a subject of considerable interest to the celibate ladies in
the neighborhood. One day he received a visit from
one of them who had reached the age of desperation.
Her manner was solemn though somewhat embarrassed; it was evident from the first that there was
something very particular on her mind. The good
bishop spoke with his usual kindness, encouraged
her to be communicative, and by and by drew from
her that she had had a very strange dream, or rather,
as she thought, a revelation from heaven. On further
questioning, she confessed that it had been intimated
to her that she was to be united in marriage to the
bishop. One may imagine what a start this gave to
the quiet scholar, who had long ago married his
books, and never thought of any other bride. He
recovered, however, and very gently addressing her,
said that "Doubtless these intimations were not to be

despised. As yet, however, the designs of heaven were but imperfectly explained, as they had been revealed to only one of the parties. He would wait to see if any similar communication should be made to himself, and whenever it happened he would be sure to let her know." Nothing could be more admirable than this humor, except perhaps the benevolence shown in so bringing an estimable woman off from a false position. [9]

Not Up to Sample

"How did it happen," asked a lady of a very silly Scotch nobleman, "that the Scots who came out of their own country were, generally speaking, men of more ability than those who remained at home?"

"Oh, madam," said he, "the reason is obvious. At every outlet there are persons stationed to examine all who pass, that for the honor of the country, no one be permitted to leave it who is not a man of understanding."

"Then," said she, "I suppose your lordship was smuggled."

The Queen's Daughters—or "Appearances Were Against Them"

A good many years ago, when her majesty was spending a short time in the neighborhood of the Trossachs, the Princesses Louise and Beatrice paid an unexpected visit to an old female cottager on the slopes of Glenfinlas, who, knowing that they had some connection with the royal household, bluntly ejaculated: "Ye'll be the Queen's servants, I'm thinkin'?"

"No," they quietly rejoined; "we are the Queen's daughters."

"Ye dinna look like it," was the immediate reply of the unusually outspoken Celt, "as ye hae neither a ring on your fingers, nor a bit gowd i' your lugs!"

"OO"—with Variations

The following is a dialogue between a Scotch shopman and a customer, relating to a plaid hanging at the shop door:

Customer (inquiring the material) : "Oo" (Wool)?
Shopman : "Ay, oo" (Yes, wool).
Customer : "A' oo" (All wool)?
Shopman : "Ay, a' oo" (Yes, all wool).
Customer : "A' ae oo" (All same wool)?
Shopman : "Ay, a' *ae* oo" (Yes, all the same wool). [7]

A Widow's Promise

The clerk of a large parish, not five miles from Bridgenorth, Scotland, perceiving a female crossing a churchyard in a widow's garb with a watering can and bundle, had the curiosity to follow her, and he discovered her to be Mrs. Smith, whose husband had not long been interred.

The following conversation took place :

"Ah, Mrs. Smith, "what are you doing with your watering can?"

"Why, Mr. Prince, I have begged a few hay-seeds, which I have in a bundle, and am going to sow them upon my husband's grave, and have brought a little water with me to make 'em spring."

"You have no occasion to do that, as the grass will soon grow upon it," replied the clerk.

"Ah, Mr. Prince, that may be ; but, do you know, my husband, who now lives there, made me promise him on his death-bed I would never marry again till the grass grew over his grave, and having a good offer made me, I dinna wish to break my word, or be kept as I am."

Drunken Wit

The late Rev. Mr. Neal, one of the ministers of the West Church, when taking a walk in the afternoon, saw an old woman sitting by the roadside evidently much intoxicated, with her bundle lying before her in the mud. He immediately recognized her to be one of his parishioners.

"Will you just help me with my bundle, gudeman?" said she, as he stopped.

"Fie, fie, Janet," said the pastor, "to see the like

o' you in such a plight. Do you not know where all
drunkards go to?"

"Ah, sure," said Janet, "they just go whaur a
drap o' gude drink is to be got."

Popularity Tested by the Collection

The late Dr. Cook, of Addington, after assisting the
late Dr. Forsyth, of Morham, at a communion service,
repaired as usual to the manse. While in the enjoy-
ment of a little social intercourse, the minister of
Morham—which, by the way, is one of the smallest
parishes in Scotland—quietly remarked to his brother
divine : "Doctor, you must be a very popular man in
the parish."   "Ay," replied the doctor, "how's
that?"   "Why," rejoined the other, "our usual collection is threepence, but to-day it is ninepence!"
"Eh, is that all?" said Dr. Cook, "then wae's me
for my popularity, for I put in the extra sixpence
myself!"

An "Exceptional" Prayer

A minister in the North, returning thanks in his
prayers one Sabbath for the excellent harvest, began
as usual, "O Lord, we thank Thee," etc., and went
on to mention the abundance of the harvest and its
safe ingathering ; but feeling anxious to be quite candid and scrupulously truthful, added, "all except a
few fields between this and Stonehaven *not worth
mentioning.*"

"Verra Weel Pitched"

A Scotchman was riding a donkey one day across a
sheep pasture, but when the animal came to a sheep
drain he would not go over. So the man rode back a
short distance, turned, and applied the whip, thinking, of course, that the donkey, when at the top of his
speed, would jump the drain. But when the donkey
got to the drain he stopped sharply and the man went
over his head and cleared the drain. No sooner had
he touched the ground than he got up, and, looking
the beast straight in the face, said: "Verra weel
pitched, but, then, hoo are ye goin' to get ower
yersel'?"

An Out-of-the-Way Reproof

King James I, being one day in the North, a violent tempest burst loose and a church being the nearest building, his majesty took shelter there, and sat down in an obscure and low seat. The minister had just mounted the pulpit and soon recognized the king, notwithstanding his plain costume. He commenced his sermon, however, and went on with it logically and quietly, but at last, suddenly starting off at a tangent, he commenced to inveigh most violently against the habit of swearing, and expatiated on this subject till the end of his discourse.

After the sermon was ended the king had his dinner, to which he invited the minister, and when the bottle had circulated for a while : " Parson," says the king, " why didst thou flee so from thy text ? "

" If it please your majesty," was the reply, " when you took the pains to come so far out of your way to hear me, I thought it very good manners for me to step a little way out of my text to meet with your majesty."

" By my saul, mon," exclaimed James, " and thou hast met with me so as never mon did."

It will be remembered that James I was notorious for cursing and swearing, in a manner almost verging on blasphemy. [9]

A Castle Stor(e)y

A Glasgow antiquary recently visited an old castle, and asked one of the villagers if he knew anything of an old story about the building.

" Ay," said the rustic, " there was another auld storey, but it fell down lang since."

A Satisfactory Explanation

A trial took place before a bailie, who excelled more as a citizen than as a scholar. A witness had occasion to refer to the testimony of a man who had died recently, and he spoke of him frequently as the defunct.

Amazed at the constant repetition of a word he did not understand, the bailie petulantly said : " What's

the use o' yer talkin' sae muckle aboot the man
Defunct? Canna ye bring him here and let him
speak for himsel'?"

"The defunct's dead, my lord," replied the witness.

"Oh, puir man, that alters the case," said the
sapient administrator of the law.

Sandy's Reply to the Sheriff

Sandy Gibb, master-blacksmith in a certain town
in Scotland, was summoned as a witness to the
Sheriff-Court in a case of two of his workmen. The
sheriff, after hearing the testimony, asked Sandy why
he did not advise them to settle, seeing the costs had
already amounted to three times the disputed claim.
Sandy's reply was, "I advised the fules to settle, for
I saw that the shirra-officer wad tak' their coates, the
lawwers their sarks, an' gif they got to your lordship's
haunds ye'd tear the skin aff them." Sandy was
ordered to stand down.

A Grammatical Beggar

A beggar some time ago applied for alms at the
door of a partisan of the Anti-begging Society. After
in vain detailing his manifold sorrows, the inexorable
gentleman peremtorily dismissed him: "Go away,"
said he, "go, we canna gie ye naething."

"You might at least," replied the mendicant, with
an air of arch dignity, "have refused me grammati-
cally."

Good Enough to Give Away

A woman entered a provision shop and asked for
a pound of butter, "an' look ye here, guidman," she
exclaimed, "see an' gie me it guid, for the last pound
was that bad I had to gie't awa' to the wifie next
door."

A Dry Preacher

On one occasion when coming to church, Dr. Macknight, who was a much better commentator than
preacher, having been caught in a shower of rain,
entered the vestry, soaked through. Every means
were used to relieve him from his discomfort; but as

the time drew on for divine service, he became very querulous, and ejaculated over and over again : " Oh ! I wish that I was dry ! Do you think that I am dry ? Do you think that I am dry eneuch noo?" Tired by these endless complaints, his jocose colleague, Dr. Henry, the historian, at last replied : " Bide a wee, doctor, and ye'se be dry eneuch, gin ye once get into the pu'pit." [9]

A Poetical Question and Answer

Mr. Dewar, a shop-keeper at Edinburgh, being in want of silver for a bank note, went into the shop of a neighbor of the name of Scott, whom he thus addressed :

> " Master Scott,
> Can you change me a note? "

Mr. Scott's reply was :

> " I'm not very sure, but I'll see."

Then going into his back room he immediately returned and added :

> " Indeed, Mr. Dewar,
> It's out of my power,
> For my wife's away with the key."

Drinking by Candle Light

The taverns to which Edinburgh lawyers of a hundred years ago resorted were generally very obscure and mean—at least they would appear such now ; and many of them were situated in the profound recesses of the old town, where there was no light from the sun, the inmates having to use candles continually.

A small party of legal gentlemen happened one day to drop into one of these dens ; and as they sat a good while drinking, they at last forgot the time of day. Taking their impressions from the candles, they just supposed that they were enjoying an ordinary evening debauch.

" Sirs," said one of them at last, " it's time to rise ; ye ken I'm a married man, and should be early at home." And so they all rose, and prepared to stag-

ger home through the streets, which at night were but
dimly lighted with oil ; when, lo and behold ! on their
emerging from the tavern, they suddenly found themselves projected into the blaze of a summer afternoon,
and at the same time, under the gaze of a thousand
curious eyes, which were directed to their tipsy and
negligent figures.

Disqualified to be a Country Preacher

The gentleman who has been rendered famous by
the pen of Burns, under the epithet of *Rumble John*,
was one Sunday invited to preach in a parish church
in the Carse of Stirling, where, as there had been a
long course of dry weather, the farmers were beginning to wish for a gentle shower; for the sake of their
crops then on the eve of being ripe. Aware of this
Mr. Russell introduced a petition, according to
custom, into his last prayer, for a change of weather.
He prayed, it is said, that the windows of heaven
might be opened, and a flood fall to fatten the ground
and fulfill the hopes of the husbandmen. This was
asking too much ; for, in reality, nothing was wanting
but a series of very gentle showers. As if to show
how bad a farmer he was, a thunder storm immediately came on, of so severe a character, that before
the congregation was dismissed, there was not an
upright bean-stalk in the whole of the Carse. The
farmers, on seeing their crops so much injured, and
that apparently by the ignorance of the clergyman,
shook their heads to one another as they afterwards
clustered about the churchyard ; and one old man was
heard to remark to his wife, as he trudged indignantly
out, " That lad may be very gude for the town, as
they say he is, but I'm clear that he disna understan'
the kintra."

Grim Humor

An English traveler was taking a walk through a
Scotch fishing village, and being surprised at the
temerity of the children playing about the pier, he said
to a woman who stood by : " Do not the children frequently drop in ? "

"Ay, ay, the fule things, they often fa' ower the pier," she answered coolly.

"God bless me! Lost of course?"

"Na, na," was the reply; "noo and then, to be sure, a bairn's drooned, but unfortunately there's maistly some idle body in the way to fish oot the deevils!"

Sabbath Zeal

The reverence for the Sabbath in Scotland sometimes takes a form one would have hardly anticipated. An old Highland man said to an English tourist: "They're a God-fearin' set o' folks here, 'deed they are, an' I'll give ye an instance o't. Last Sabbath, just as the kirk was skalin', there was a drover chiel frae Dumfries along the road, whistlin' and lookin' as happy as if it was ta middle o' ta week. Weel, sir, our laads is a God-fearin' set o' laads, and they yokit upon him an' a'most killed him."

At the End of His Tether

An old Scotch lady was told that her minister used notes. She disbelieved it. Said one: "Go into the gallery and see!"

She did so, and saw the written sermon. After the luckless preacher had concluded his reading on the last page, he said: "But I will not enlarge."

The old woman cried out from her lofty position: "Ye canna! ye canna, for yer paper's give oot!"

A Thrifty Proposal

It is said that before the opening of the Glasgow Exhibition the laying out of the garden and grounds were under discussion, and it was suggested that a gondola would look ornamental on the water.

"Well," said a member of the town council, "I think we may as well have a *pair*, and they might *breed*."

Was He a Liberal or a Tory?

A keen politician, in the City of Glasgow, heard one day of the death of a party opponent, who in a fit of a mental aberration, had shot himself. "Ah," said he, "gane awa' that way by himsel', has he? I wish that he had ta'en twa or three days' shooting among his friends before he went!"

Advice on Nursing

A bachelor of seventy and upwards came one day to Bishop Alexander, of Dunkeld, and said he wished to marry a girl of the neighborhood whom he named. The bishop, a non-juring Scottish Episcopalian of the middle of last century, and himself an old bachelor, inquired into the motive of this strange proceeding, and soon drew from the old man the awkward apology, that he married to have a nurse. Too knowing to believe such a statement, the good bishop quietly replied, "See, John, then, and make her ane."

A Critic on His Own Criticism

Lord Eldon, so remarkable for his naïf expression, being reminded, of a criticism which he had formerly made upon a picture which he himself had forgotten, inquired, "Did I say that?" "Yes." "Then if I said that," quoth the self-satisfied wit, "it was *deevilish gude.*"

Holding A Candle to the Sun

A wet and witty barrister, one Saturday encountered an equally Bacchanalian senatorial friend, in the course of a walk to Leith. Remembering that he had a good joint of mutton roasting for dinner, he invited his friend to accompany him home; and they accordingly dined together, *secundum morem solitum.* After dinner was over, wine and cards commenced; and, as they were each fond of both, neither thought of reminding the other of the advance of time, till the church bell next day disturbed them in their darkened room about a quarter before eleven o'clock. The judge then rising to depart, Mr. —— walked behind him to the outer door, with a candle in each hand, by way of showing him out. Tak' care, my lord, tak' care," cried the kind host most anxiously, holding the candles out of the door into the sunny street, along which the people were pouring churchwards; "Tak' care; there's twa steps."

A False Deal

A gentleman was one night engaged with a judge in a tremendous drinking bout which lasted all night, and till within a single hour of the time when the court was to open next morning. The two cronies had little more than time to wash themselves in their respective houses when they had to meet again, in their professional capacities of judge and pleader, in the Parliament House. Mr. Clerk (afterwards Lord Eldon), it appears, had, in the hurry of his toilet, thrust the pack of cards he had been using over night into the pocket of his gown ; and thus as he was going to open up the pleading, in pulling out his handkerchief, he also pulled out fifty-two witnesses of his last night's debauch, which fell scattered within the bar. "Mr. Clerk," said his judicial associate in guilt, with the utmost coolness, "before ye begin, I think ye had better take up your hand."

A Scotch Matrimonial Jubilee

Two fishwives in London were talking about the Queen's jubilee. "Eh, wumman," said one to the other, "can ye tell me what a jubilee is, for I hear a' the folks spakin' aboot it ? "

"Ou, ay," replied the other, "I can tell ye that. Ye see when a man and a wumman has been marrit for five-and-twenty years, that's a silver waddin ; and when they've been marrit for fifty years, that's a gouden waddin ; but when the man's deed, that's a jubilee ! "

A Drunkard's Thoughts

An inebriate, some time back, got into a tramcar in Glasgow, and became very troublesome to the other passengers ; so much so that it was proposed to eject him. A genial and right reverend doctor, who was also a passenger took him in hand, however, and soothed him into good behavior for the rest of the journey. Before leaving, the man shook hands warmly with the doctor, after scowling at the other occupants of the car, and said : "Good-day, my freen', I see ye ken what it is to be foo'."

A Lofty "Style"

The late Mr. Andrew Balfour, one of the judges in
the Commissary Court of Edinburgh, used to talk in
in a very pompous and inflated style of language.
Having made an appointment with the late Honorable
Henry Erskine, on some particular business, and failing to attend, he apologized for it, by telling the learned
barrister that his brother, the Laird of Balbirnie, in
passing from one of his enclosures to another, had
fallen down from the stile and sprained his ankle.
This trifling accident he related in language highly
pedantic and bombastical.   The witty advocate, with
his usual vivacity, replied, " It was very fortunate for
your brother, Andrew, that it was not from *your* style
he fell, or he had broken his neck, instead of sprain-
ing his ankle ! "

During the time the above-named gentleman pre-
sided in court, his sister, Miss Balfour, happened to
be examined as a witness in a cause then before the
court.   Andrew began in his pompous way, by asking, " Woman, what is thy name? what is thy age?
and where is thy usual place of residence ? "   To
which interrogatories Miss Balfour only replied, by
staring him broad in the face, when the questions
were again repeated, with all the grimace and
pedantry he was master of, which the lady, observing, said, " Dear me, Andrew, do ye no ken yer ain
sister ? "   To which the judge answered, " Woman,
when I sit in court I administer justice ; I know no
one, neither father or mother, sister or brother ! "

Depression—Delight—Despair

Three boys at school, learning their catechism, the
one asked the other how far he had got.   To this he
answered, " I'm at ' A State o' Sin and Misery.' "
He then asked another what length he was, to which
he replied, " I'm just at ' Effectual Calling.' "   They
were both anxious, of course, to learn how far he was
himself, and having asked him, he answered, " Past
Redemption."

An Earl's Pride and Parsimony

A late nobleman, in whose character vanity and parsimony were the most remarkable features, was, for a long time before he died, in the habit of retailing the produce of his dairy and his orchard to the children and poor people of the neighborhood. It is told, that one day observing a pretty little girl tripping through his grounds with a milk pipkin, he stooped to kiss her; after which he said, in a pompous tone, "Now, my dear, you may tell your grandchildren, and tell them in their turn to tell their grandchildren, that you had once the honor of receiving a kiss from the Right Hon—the Earl of ——." The girl looked up in his face, and, with a strange mixture of simplicity and archness, remarked, "But ye took the penny for the milk, though!"

Question and Answer

At a church in Scotland, where there was a popular call, two candidates offered to preach of the names of Adam and Low. The last preached in the morning, and took for his text, "Adam, where art thou?" He made a most excellent discourse, and the congregation were much edified. In the evening Mr. Adam preached, and took for his text, "Lo, here am I!" The *impromptu* and his sermon gained him the church.

Robbing "On Credit"

Soon after the battle of Preston, two Highlanders, in roaming through the south of Mid-Lothian, entered the farm-house of Swanston, near the Pentland Hills, where they found no one at home but an old woman. They immediately proceeded to search the house, and soon, finding a web of coarse home-spun cloth, made no scruple to unroll and cut off as much as they thought would make a coat for each. The woman was exceedingly incensed at their rapacity, and even had the hardihood to invoke divine vengence upon their heads. "Ye villains!" she cried, "ye'll ha'e to account for this yet!"

"And when will we pe account for't?"

"At the last day, ye blackguards!" exclaimed the woman.

"Ta last tay!" replied the Highlander; "tat pe cood long credit—we'll e'en pe tak' a waistcoat, too!" at the same time cutting off a few additional yards of the cloth.

Taking a Light Supper

A poet being at supper where the fare was very scanty, and not of first-rate quality, said the following grace:

"O Thou, who blessed the loaves and fishes,
Look down upon these two poor dishes;
And though the 'taties be but sma',
Lord, make them large enough for a';
For if they do our bellies fill,
'Twill be a wondrous miracle!"

Rustic Notion of the Resurrection

It is the custom in Scotland for the elders to assist the minister in visiting the sick; and on such occasions they give the patient and the surrounding gossips the benefit of prayers. Being generally well acquainted in the different families, they often sit an hour or two after the sacred rites, to chat with those who are in health, and to receive the benefit of a dram. On one of these occasions in the house of Donald M'Intyre, whose wife had been confined to her fireside and armchair for many years, the elder and Donald grew *unco' gracious*. Glass after glass was filled from the bottle, and the elder entered into a number of metaphysical discussions, which he had heard from the minister. Among other topics was the resurrection. The elder was strenuous in support of the rising of the same body; but Donald could not comprehend how a body once dissolved in the dust could be reanimated. At last, catching what he thought a glimpse of the subject, he exclaimed, "Weel, weel, Sandy, ye're richt sae far; you and me, that are strong, healthy folk, *may* rise again; but that *puir* thing there, *far* she sits" (that poor thing, where she sits) "she'll ne'er rise again."

A Definition of Baptism

A Scotch clergyman, one day catechising his flock in the church, the beadle, or church officer, being somewhat ill-read in the catechism, thought it best to keep a modest place near the door, in the hope of escaping the inquisition. But the clergyman observed and called him forward. "John," said he, "what is baptism?" "Ou, sir," answered John, scratching his head, "ye ken, it's just saxpence to me, and fifteenpence to the precentor."

No End to His Wit

A gentleman in the west of Scotland, celebrated for his wit, was conversing with a lady, who, at last, overpowered by the brilliance and frequency of his *bon mots*, exclaimed, "Stop, sir; there is really no end to your wit." "God forbid, madam," replied the humorist, "that I should ever be at my wit's end."

Leaving the Lawyers a Margin

A man from the country applied lately to a respectable solicitor in this town for legal advice. After detailing the circumstances of the case, he was asked if he had stated the facts exactly as they occurred. "Ou, ay, sir," rejoined the applicant, "I thought it best to tell you the plain truth; ye can put the *lees* till't yoursel'."

A Lunatic's Advice to Money Lenders

The following curious conversation actually occurred in a garden attached to a lunatic asylum, near Dumfries. The interlocutors were the keeper, a very respectable man, and one of the most manageable of his patients:

"Tak' it easy, tak' it easy, Jamie; ye're no working against time, man; and when you come near the border, be sure and keep your feet aff the flowers."

"The flowers! hurt the bonnie sweet flowers!" said Jamie; "Na, na, I'm no sae daft as that comes to, neither; I wad as soon chap off my ain fingers as crush ane o' them   There's the summer snaw-drap

9

already keeking through its green sheath; as weel as
daisies and primroses, an' the thing they ca' rocket;
although it would mak' but a puir cracker on the
king's birthday—He! he! he!   Ay, there's hearts-
ease and rowantree, sprigs o' which I aye wear next
my skin; the tane to fleg awa' the witches, an' the
tither to keep my heart frae beating.   An' there's the
ginty wee flower that I gied a bit o' to Tibby Dalrym-
ple, wha tint her wits for love, an' wha said sae muckle
to me through the grating o' her cell, about the gude
that the smell o' the flower wad do her, that I couldna
find i' my heart to deny her, puir thing.''

"Very weel, Jamie," replied the keeper, "be a
guid lad, an' continue to dress that little corner until
I come back frae the sands."

"Ou, ay!" rejoined Jamie, "this is Wednesday,
an' you'll be gaun down to meet wi' some o' your
country friends.   It's changed time wi' them, I
jalous; whaur the public-house used to sell a gal-
lon o' whiskey, they dinna sell a mutchkin noo, I
hear; but that's naething, their customers will get
sooner hame to their families; an' then they'll be
fewer bane broken riding fule races.   But tak' care
o' yoursel', Mr.——, tak' care that some o' them dinna
come Yorkshire ower you.   They'll be inviting you
in to tak' a dram, nae doubt, an' making a puir
mouth about the badness o' times, trying to borrow a
little siller frae you. But if I was you, I'll tell ye what
I wad dae.   I wad get twa purses made, and ca' ane
o' them '*Somebody*,' and the ither '*A' the World*';
an' next I wad pit a' my siller in the first, and no' a
bawbee in the second; and then, when any o' them
spak' o' borrowing, I wad whup out the toom purse,
and shaking't before the chiel's een, swear that I
hadna a ha'penny in '*A' the World*,' until I gat it
frae' '*Somebody!*'''

Prophesying

A country clergyman, who, on Sundays, is more
indebted to his manuscript than to his memory, called
unceremoniously at a cottage while its possessor, a
pious parishioner, was engaged (a daily exercise) in

perusing a paragraph of the writing of an inspired prophet. "Weel, John," familiarly inquired the clerical visitant, "what's this you are about?" "I am prophesying," was the prompt reply. "Prophesying!" exclaimed the astonished divine ; "I doubt you are only reading a prophesy." "Weel," argued the religious rustic, "gif reading a preachin' be preachin', is na reading a prophecy prophesying?"

Definition of Metaphysics

A Scotch blacksmith being asked the meaning of "Metaphysics," explained it as follows : "When the party who listens dinna ken what the party who speaks means, and when the party who speaks dinna ken what he means himself—that is 'metaphysics.'"

His Word and His Bond Equally Binding

A crusty tenant of the late Laird D——, pressing him to complete some piece of work which had long stood over, the laird craved further delay, adding that he would give his word of honor—nay, his written bond, to have the thing done before a certain day. "Your word!" exclaimed the tenant, "it's weel kenn'd *that* will do me little guid ; and as for your writing, naebody can read it."

Bad Arithmeticians often Good Book-Keepers

Sir Walter Scott, in lending a book one day to a friend, cautioned him to be punctual in returning it. "This is really necessary," said the poet in apology ; "for though many of my friends are bad *arithmeticians*, I observe almost all of them to be good *book-keepers.*"

Curious Misunderstanding

An itinerant vendor of wood in Aberdeen having been asked how his wife was, replied, "O she's fine, I hae ta'en her to Banchory" ; and on it being innocently remarked that the change of air would do her good, he looked up and with a half-smile said, "Hoot, she's i' the kirkyard."

" Terms—' Cash Down '"

A story is told of a member of the Scotch Faculty
of Advocates, distinguished for his literary attain-
ments. One day, presenting himself on horseback
at a toll, he found, on searching his pockets, that
he had not a farthing about him wherewith to purchase a right of passage. He disclosed his circumstances to the man who kept the bar, and requested
that he might have credit till he came back ; but the
fellow was deaf to all entreaties, representing how
often he had been bilked by persons promising the
same thing. The advocate was offended at this
insinuation, and, drawing himself up in the saddle,
exclaimed : " Look at my face, sir, and say if you
think I am likely to cheat you? " The man looked
as he was desired, but answered, with a shake of his
head, " I'll thank you for the twapence, sir." Mr.
—— was obliged to turn back.

Forcing a Judge to Obey the Law

The Lord Justice-Clerk is the chief judge of the
Scottish Criminal Court, in addition to which dignity
he sits at the head of one division of the great Civil
Court of the country. It will thus be understood by
a southern reader that he is a personage of no small
local dignity. A bearer of this office was once shooting over the grounds of a friend in Ayrshire by himself, when a game-keeper, who was unacquainted
with his person, came up and demanded to see his
license, or card of permission. His lordship had,
unfortunately nothing of the sort about his person ;
but, secure in his high character and dignity, he made
very light of the omission, and was preparing to
renew his sport. The man, however, was zealous in
his trust, and sternly forbad him to proceed any further over the fields. " What, sirrah," cries his lordship, " do you know whom you are speaking to? I
am the Lord Justice-Clerk ! " " I dinna care," replied
the man, " whase clerk ye are ; but ye maun shank aff
these grounds, or, by my saul, I'll lay your feet fast."
The reader is left to conceive the astonishment of the
unfortunate judge at finding himself treated in a style
so different from his wont.

"Nothing," and How to See It

An Irish priest, proceeding to chapel, observed several girls seated on a tombstone, and asked them what they were doing there? "Nothing at all, please your riverence," was the reply of one of them. " Nothing?" said the priest; "what is nothing?"

"Shut your eyes, your riverence," retorted the girl, " and you'll see it."

Why Not?

A gentleman the other day, visiting a school at Edinburgh, had a book put in his hand for the purpose of examining a class. The word "inheritance" occurring in the verse, the querist interrogated the youngest as follows:

"What is inheritance?"
"Patrimony."
"What is patrimony?"
"Something left by a father."
"What would you call it if left by a mother?"
"Matrimony."

True (perhaps) of Other Places than Dundee

In the committee on the factory bill, the following sensible question was put to a witness named Peter Stuart, the overseer of the factory at Dundee. Question: "When do your girls marry?" "*Whenever they can meet with men!*"

Pretending to Make a Will

An old gentleman was one evening amusing the junior members of his family, and a number of their acquaintances, by making up a sort of imaginary will, in which he destined so much to one and so much to another; the eight-day clock to his niece or nephew, the bed to that, the table to a third, and so on. "But what will you leave to me, Mr. K.——?" said a lady, who felt impatient to know what was to be her lot. "I leave you *out*," replied the testator.

Unusual for a Scotchman

A countryman having read in the newspapers accounts of different bank failures, and having a hundred pounds deposited in a respectable banking company in Aberdeen, he became alarmed for its safety, hastened to town, and, calling at the bank, presented his deposit receipt, and, on demanding his money was paid, as is customary, with notes of the bank ; he grasped them in his hand, and having got within reach of the door turned round, and exclaimed, " Noo, sir, ye may braik when ye like."

An Author and His Printer

It is well known to literary people, that, in preparing works for the printer, after the proof sheets have been seen by the author, to go over them again, and clear them of what are called typographical errors—such as wrong spellings, inaccuracies of punctuation, and similiar imperfections. In performing this office for a celebrated northern critic and editor, a printer, now dead, was in the habit of introducing a much greater number of commas than it appeared to the author the sense required. The case was provoking, but did not produce a formal remonstrance, until Mr. W——n himself accidentally afforded the learned editor an opportunity of signifying his dissatisfaction with the plethora of punctuation under which his compositions were made to labor. The worthy printer coming to a passage one day which he did not understand, very naturally took it into his head that it was unintelligible, and transmitted it to his employer, with a remark on the margin, that there appeared some "obscurity in it."

The sheet was immediately returned, with the reply, which we give *verbatim :* " Mr. J—— sees no obscurity here, except such as arises from the quantity of·commas, which Mr. W——n seems to keep in a pepper-box beside him, for the purpose of dusting all his proofs with."

A Keen Reproof

A certain person, to show his detestation of Hume's infidel opinions always left any company where he

happened to be, if Hume joined it. The latter,
observing this, took occasion one day to reprehend it
as follows: " Friend," said he, " I am surprised to
find you display such a pointed aversion to me; I
would wish to be upon good terms with you here, as,
upon your own system, it seems very probable we
shall be doomed to tne same place hereafter. You
think I shall be dammed for want of faith, and I fear
you will have the same fate for want of charity."

The Scotch Mason and the Angel

The late Mr. Douglas, of Cavers, in Roxburghshire,
one day walked into Cavers churchyard, where he
saw a stonemason busily engaged in carving an angel
upon a gravestone. Observing that the man was
adorning the heavenly spirit, according to the custom
of the age, with a grand flowing periwig, Mr. Douglas
exclaimed to him, " in the name of wonder, who ever
saw an angel with a wig?" " And in the name of
wonder," answered the sculptor, " wha ever saw an
angel *without* ane?"

A Whole-witted Sermon from a Half-Witted Preacher

A half-witted itinerant preacher, well-known in the
county of Ayr, was stopped one evening on the road
to Stewarton, by a band of shearers, who insisted on
his retiring to a neighboring field to give them a sermon. After many attempts on his part to get off, and
threats on theirs if he did not comply, the honest
man was compelled to consent; and, from the back
of his shaggy haired sheltie, he delivered to his bare-
footed audience the following extemporaneous effu-
sion, taking for his text these words: " Naked came
I out of my mother's womb, and naked shall I return
thither." (Job 1 : v. 21.) " In discoursing from
these words," said the preacher, " I shall observe the
three following things: (1) Man's ingress into the
world; (2) His progress through the world; and (3)
His egress out of the world. First, man's ingress
into the world is naked and bare; secondly, his progress through the world is trouble and care; thirdly,

his egress out of the world is nobody knows where.
To conclude: If we do well here, we shall do well
there. And I could tell you no more were I to preach
a whole year."

More Witty Than True

There lived about the beginning of last century an
Episcopalian clergyman of the name of Robert Calder,
who was considered an extraordinary wit, and, who,
at least, must be allowed to have used very extraordinary expressions. He published a *jeu d' esprit*
under the form of a catechism, in which a person is
made to ask: "Who was the first Presbyterian?"
The answer is "Jonah." "How do ye make Jonah
out to be the first Presbyterian?" is again asked.
"Why," answers the other, "because the Lord
wanted him to gang east and he gaed wast!" (The
same might be said of Adam and all who preceded or
succeeded Jonah—not excepting Robert Calder.—ED.)

The Parson and His " Thirdly "

A certain minister had a custom of writing the
heads of his discourse on small slips of paper, which
he placed on the Bible before him to be used in succession. One day when he was explaining the second
head, he got so excited in his discourse, that he caused
the ensuing slip to fall over the side of the pulpit,
though unperceived by himself. On reaching the end
of the second head, he looked down for the third slip;
but alas! it was not to be found. "Thirdly," he
cried looking around him with great anxiety. After a
little pause, "Thirdly," again he exclaimed; but still
no thirdly appeared. "Thirdly, I say, my brethren,"
pursued the bewildered clergyman; but not another
word could he utter. At this point, while the congregation were partly sympathizing, and partly rejoicing
at this decisive instance of the impropriety of using
notes in preaching—which has always been an unpopular thing in Scotland, an old woman rose up and thus
addressed the preacher: "If I'm no' mista'en, sir, I
saw thirdly flee out at the east window, a quarter of
an hour syne."

Scotch Ingenuity

The Jacobite lairds of Fife were once, on the occasion of an election, induced to sign the oath of abjuration in great numbers, in order to vote for a friend of their party. It was much against their conscience; but the case was such as to make them wink pretty hard. During the carousal which followed, Mr. Balfour, of Forrat, a Jacobite of the old stamp, began, to their surprise, to inveigh against them as a set of perjured rascals, not remembering apparently, that he had signed as well as the rest. They burst out with one universal question: "How can you speak this way, Forrat, since you are just as guilty as ony o' us?" "That am I no'," said Forrat, with a triumphant air of innocence and waggery; look ye at the list of names, and ye'll see the word *witness* at the end of mine. I just signed as witness to your perjury!"

Bolder Than Charles the Bold

Joannes Scotus, the early Scotch philosopher, being in company with Charles the Bold, King of France, that monarch asked him good humoredly, what was the difference between a Scot and a sot. Scotus, who sat opposite the king, answered, "Only the breadth of the table."

"Short Commons"

A Mid-Lothian farmer, observed to his ploughboy that there was a fly in his milk.

"Oh, never mind, sir," said the boy; "it winna droon; there's nae meikle o't."

"Gudewife," said the farmer, "Jock says he has ower little milk."

"There's milk enough for a' my bread," said the sly rogue.

The Shoemaker and Small Feet

A lady, who seemed rather vain, entered a bootmaker's shop one day with the usual complaint: "Why, Mr. S——, these boots you last made for me are much too big; I really can't understand how you always make that mistake. Can you not make small boots?"

"Ou, ay," quickly responded the man; "I can mak' sma' buits, but I'm sorry I canna mak' sma' feet."

Pleasant Prospect Beyond the Grave

An elderly lady, intending to purchase the upper flat of a house in Prince's Street, opposite the West Church Burying-ground, Edinburgh, from which the chain of Pentland Hills formed a beautiful background, after having been made acquainted with all its conveniences, and the beauty of its situation, elegantly enumerated by the builder, he requested her to cast her eye on the romantic hills at a distance, on the other side of the church-yard. The lady admitted that she had "certainly a most pleasant prospect *beyond the grave.*"

Pulpit Foolery

The Rev. Hamilton Paul, a Scotch clergyman, is said to have been a reviver of Dean Swift's walk of wit in choice of texts. For example, when he left the town of Ayr, where he was understood to have been a great favorite with the fair sex, he preached his valedictory sermon from this passage, "And they all fell upon Paul's neck and kissed him." Another time, when he was called on to preach before a military company in green uniforms, he preached from the words, "And I beheld men like trees walking." Paul was always ready to have a gibe at the damsels. Near Portobello, there is a sea-bathing place named Joppa, and Paul's congregation was once thinned by the number of his female votaries who went thither. On the Sabbath after their wending he preached from the text, "Send men to Joppa." In a similar manner he improved the occasion of the mysterious disappearance of one of his parishioners, Moses Marshall, by selecting for his text the passage from Exodus xxii, "As for this Moses, we wot not what is become of him." He once made serious proposals to a young lady whose Christian name was Lydia. On this occasion the clerical wit took for his text : "And a certain woman, named Lydia, heard us; whose heart the Lord opened, that she attended unto the things which were spoken of Paul." [9]

A Restful Preacher

Dean Ramsay relates that the Earl of Lauderdale was alarmingly ill, one distressing symptom being a total absence of sleep, without which the medical man declared he could not recover. His son, who was somewhat simple, was seated under the table, and cried out, " Sen' for that preaching man frae Livingstone, for fayther aye sleeps in the kirk." One of the doctors thought the hint worth attending to, and the experiment of " getting a minister till him " succeeded, for sleep came on and the earl recovered. [7]

Why the Bishops Disliked the Bible

A Bishop of Dunkeld, in Scotland, before the Reformation, thanked God that he never knew what the Old and New Testaments were, affirming that he cared to know no more than his Portius and Pontifical. At a diet in Germany, one Bishop Albertus, lighting by chance upon a Bible, commenced reading ; one of his colleagues asked him what book it was. " I know not," was the reply, " but this I find, that whatever I read in it, is utterly against our religion." [9]

The Same with a Difference

A young wit asked a man who rode about on a wretched horse : " Is that the same horse you had last year?" " Na," said the man, brandishing his whip in the interrogator's face in so emphatic a manner as to preclude further questioning ; " na, but it's the same *whup.*" [7]

Official Consolation and Callousness

A friend has told me of a characteristic answer given by a driver to a traveler who complained of an inconvenience. A gentleman sitting opposite my friend in the stage-coach at Berwick, complained bitterly that the cushion on which he sat was quite wet. On looking up to the roof he saw a hole through which the rain descended copiously, and at once accounted for the mischief. He called for the coachman, and in great wrath reproached him with the evil under which he suffered, and pointed to the hole which was the cause

of it. All the satisfaction, however, that he got was
the quiet unmoved reply, "Ay, mony a ane has complained o' *that* hole." [7]

Objecting to Scotch "Tarmes"

In early times a Scotch laird had much difficulty
(as many worthy lairds have still) in meeting the
claims of those two woful periods of the year called in
Scotland the "tarmes." He had been employing for
some time, as workman, a stranger from the south,
on some house repairs. The workman rejoiced in the
not uncommon name in England of "Christmas."
The laird's servant, early one morning, called out at
his bedroom door, in great excitement, that "Christmas had run away, and nobody knew where he had
gone." He turned in his bed with the earnest ejacu-
lation, "I only wish he had taken Whitsunday and
Martinmas along with him."

A Patient Lady

The Rev. John Brown, of Haddington, the well-known
author of the "Self-Interpreting Bible," was a man of
singular bashfulness. In proof of the truth of this statement I need only state that his courtship lasted seven
years. Six years and a half had passed away, and
the reverend gentleman had got no further than he
had been the first six days. This state of things
became intolerable, a step in advance must be made,
and Mr. Brown summoned all his courage for the deed.
"Janet," said he one day, as they sat in solemn
silence, "we've been acquainted now six years an'
mair, and I've ne'er gotten a kiss yet. D'ye think I
might take one, my bonny lass?" "Just as you like,
John; only be becoming and proper wi' it." "Surely,
Janet; we'll ask a blessing." The blessing was
asked, the kiss was taken, and the worthy divine, perfectly overpowered with the blissful sensation, most
rapturously exclaimed, "Heigh! lass, but it is *gude*.
We'll return thanks." Six months after, the pious
pair were made one flesh, and, added his descendant,
who "humorously told the tale, "a happier couple
never spent a long and useful life together." [9]

Curious Pulpit Notice

John Brown, Burgher minister at Whitburn (son of the commentator, and father of the late Rev. Dr. John Brown, of Edinburgh, and grandfather of the accomplished M. D. of the same name), in the early part of the century was traveling on a small sheltie (a Shetland pony) to attend the summer sacrament at Haddington. Between Musselburgh and Tranent he overtook one of his own people.

"What are ye daein' here, Janet, and whaur ye gaun in this warm weather?"

"'Deed, sir," quoth Janet, "I'm gaun to Haddington for the occasion (the Lord's Supper), an' expeck to hear ye preach this afternoon."

"Very weel, Janet, but whaur ye gaun to sleep?"

"I dinna ken, sir, but providence is aye kind, an'll provide a bed."

On Mr. Brown jogged, but kindly thought of his humble follower; accordingly, after service in the afternoon, before pronouncing the blessing, he said from the pulpit, "Whaur's the auld wife that followed me frae Whitburn?"

"Here I'm, sir," uttered a shrill voice from a back seat.

"Aweel," said Mr. Brown; "I have faud ye a bed; ye're to sleep wi' Johnnie Fife's lass."

"Wishes Never Filled the Bag"

There are always pointed anecdotes against houses wanting in a liberal and hospitable expenditure in Scotland. Thus, we have heard of a master leaving such a mansion, and taxing his servant with being drunk, which he had too often been after country visits. On this occasion, however, he was innocent of the charge, for he had not the *opportunity* to transgress. So, when his master asserted, "Jemmy, you are drunk!" Jemmy very quietly answered, "Indeed, sir, I wish I wur."

Not Used to It

On one occasion an eccentric Scotchman, having business with the late Duke of Hamilton at Hamilton

Palace, the Duke politely asked him to lunch. A liveried servant waited upon them, and was most assiduous in his attentions to the duke and his guest. At last our eccentric friend lost patience, and looking at the servant, addressed him thus : "What the deil for are ye dance, dance, dancing about the room that gait; can ye no' draw in your chair and sit down? I'm sure there's *plenty on the table for three.*"   [7]

"Effectual Calling"

Maitland, the Jacobite historian of Edinburgh, relates with infinite zest the following anecdote of the Rev. Robert Bruce, the zealous Presbyterian minister who boldly bearded King James I: "1589, August 15.—Robert Bruce, one of the four ministers of Edinburgh, threatening to leave the town" (the reason from what follows, may be easily guessed at), "great endeavors were used to prevent his going; but none, it seems, so prevalent as that of the increase of his stipend to one thousand merks, which the good man was graciously pleased to accept, though it only amounted to one hundred and forty merks more than all the stipends of the other three ministers."

Motive for Church-Going

An old man, who for years walked every Sunday from Newhaven to Edinburgh to attend the late Dr. Jones' church, was one day complimented by that venerable clergyman for the regularity of his appearance in church. The old man unconsciously evinced how little he deserved the compliment by this reply : "'Deed, sir, its very true; but I like to hear the jingling o' the bells and see a' the braw folk."   [9]

"Grace" with No Meat After

A little girl of eight years of age was taken by her grandmother to church. The parish minister was not only a long preacher, but, as the custom was, delivered two sermons on the Sabbath day without any interval, and thus save the parishioners the two journeys to church. Elizabeth was sufficiently wearied before the close of the first discourse; but when, after singing and prayer, the good minister opened the Bible, read a second text, and prepared to give a second sermon, the young girl being both tired and hungry, lost all patience, and cried out to her grandmother, to the no small amusement of those who were so near as to hear her, "Come awa', Granny, and gang home; this is a lang grace, and nae meat." [7]

"No Better than Pharaoh"

In a town of one of the central counties a Mr. J—— carried on, about a century ago, a very extensive business in the linen manufacture. Although *strikes* were then unknown among the laboring classes, the spirit from which these take their rise has no doubt at all times existed. Among Mr. J——'s many workmen, one had given him constant annoyance for years, from his argumentative spirit. Insisting one day on getting something or other which his master thought most unreasonable, and refused to give in to, he at last submitted, with a bad grace, saying, "You're nae better than *Pharaoh*, sir, forcin' puir folks to mak' bricks without straw." "Well, Saunders," quietly rejoined his master, "if I'm nae better than Pharaoh, in one respect, I'll be better in another, for *I'll no' hinder ye going to the wilderness whenever ye choose.*"

Not One of "The Establishment"

At an hotel in Glasgow, a gentleman, finding that the person who acted as a waiter could not give him certain information which he wanted, put the question, "Do you belong to the establishment?" to which James replied, "No, sir; I belong to the Free Kirk."

A Board-School Examiner Floored

The parish minister in a town not a hundred miles from Dumfermline, Fifeshire, was recently going his round of all the board schools in the course of systematic examination. The day was warm, and the minister, feeling exhausted on reaching the school, took a seat for a few minutes to cool down and

recover his breath; but even while doing so he
thought he might as well utilize the time in a con-
genial sort of way, being naturally a bit of a wag.
So he addressed the boys thus : " Well, lads, can any
of you tell me why black sheep eat less than white
sheep ? "

There was no answer to this question, and the
minister, after telling them it was because there
were fewer of them, with pretended severity said he
was sorry to see them in such a state of ignorance as
not to be able to answer such a simple question, but
he would give them another.

" Can any of you lads tell me what bishop of the
Church of England has the largest hat ? "

Here the children were again cornered for a
solution.

" What ! don't you know," said the minister,
" that the bishop with the largest hat is the bishop
with the largest head ? But seeing I have been
giving you some puzzling questions, I will now
allow you to have your turn and put some questions
to me, to see if I can answer them."

Silence fell upon the whole school. No one was
apparently bold enough to tackle the minister. At
length, from the far corner of the room, a little chap
of about seven years got to his feet, and with an
audacity that actually appalled the master, cried out
in a loud, shrill, piping voice, with the utmost *sang
froid* :

" Can you tell me why millers wear white caps ? "

The minister was perfectly astounded, and for the
life of him could find no solution of the problem.

He began to feel somewhat uncomfortable, while
the master frowned with awful threatening in his
glance at the undaunted young culprit, who stood
calmly waiting a reply to his poser.

" No, my boy," said the minister at length; " I
cannot tell why millers wear white caps. What is
the reason ? "

" Weel, sir," replied the young shaver, " millers
wear white caps just to cover their heads."

It is needless to remark that the roar which followed rather disconcerted the minister, and he had some difficulty afterwards in proceeding with his official examination.

Keeping His Threat—at His Own Expense

An examiner at the Edinburgh University had made himself obnoxious by warning the students against putting hats on the desk.   The university in the Scottish capital is (or was) remarkable for a scarcity of cloak rooms, and in the excitement of examination hats are, or used to be, flung down anywhere.   The examiner announced one day that if he found another hat on his desk he would " rip it up."

The next day no hats were laid there when the students assembled. Presently, however, the examiner was called out of the room.   Then some naughty undergraduate slipped from his seat, got the examiner's hat, and placed it on the desk.   When the examiner re-entered the hall every eye was fixed upon him.   He observed the hat, and a gleam of triumph shot across his face.

" Gentlemen," he continued, " I told you what would happen if this occurred again."

Then he took his penknife from his pocket, opened it, and blandly cut the hat in pieces amidst prolonged applause.

New Style of Riding in a Funeral Procession

The following anecdote is an amusing illustration of the working of a defective brain, in a half-witted carle, who used to range the county of Galloway, armed with a huge pike-staff, and who one day met a funeral procession a few miles from Wigtown.

A long train of carriages, and farmers on horseback, suggested the propriety of his bestriding his staff, and following after the funeral.   The procession marched at a brisk pace, and on reaching the kirkyard stile, as each rider dismounted, " Daft Jock " descended from his wooden steed, besmeared with mire and perspiration, exclaiming, " Heck, sirs, had it no' been for the fashion o' the thing, I micht as well hae been on my ain feet."   [7]

Absence of Humor—Illustrated

Few amusements in the world are funnier than the play of different ideas under similar sounds, and it would be hard to find a thing more universally understood and caught at than a pun ; but there really are individuals so made that a word can mean but one thing to them, and even metaphors must go on all-fours. Lord Morpeth used to tell of a Scotch friend of his who, to the remark that some people could not feel a jest unless it was fired at them with a cannon, replied : " Weel, but how can ye fire a jest out of a cannon, man ? "

The Best Time to Quarrel

In Lanarkshire, there lived a sma' laird named Hamilton, who was noted for his eccentricity. On one occasion, a neighbor waited on him, and requested his name as an accommodation to a bill for twenty pounds at three months date, which led to the following characteristic and truly Scottish colloquy :

" Na, na, I canna do that."

" What for no', laird ? Ye hae dune the same thing for ithers."

" Ay, ay, Tammas, but there's wheels within wheels ye ken naething about ; I canna do't."

" It's a sma' affair to refuse me, laird."

" Weel, ye see, Tammas, if I was to pit my name till't ye wad get the siller frae the bank, and when the time came round, ye wadna be ready, and I wad hae to pay't ; sae then you and me wad quarrel ; sae we mae just as weel quarrel *the noo*, as lang's the siller's in ma pouch."

The Horse That Kept His Promise

A laird sold a horse to an Englishman, saying, " You buy him as you see him ; but he's an *honest beast.*" The purchaser took him home. In a few days he stumbled and fell, to the damage of his own knees and his rider's head. On this the angry purchaser remonstrated with the laird, whose reply was, " Weel, sir, I told ye he was an honest beast ; many a time has he threatened to come down with me, and I kenned he would keep his word some day."

A "Grand" Piano

At Glasgow, in a private house, Dr. Von Bülow, having been asked by his hostess what he thought of her piano, replied in these words : "Madam, your piano leaves something to be desired. It needs new strings," he added, in answer to the lady's inquiries as to what it really required. "The hammers, too, want new leather," he continued ; "and, while you are about it, with the new leather, you may as well have new wood. Then, when the inside of your piano has been completely renovated," he concluded, having now worked himself into a rage, "call in two strong men, throw it out of the window, and burn it in the street."

Scottish Patriotism

It is more common in Scotland than in England to find national feeling breaking out in national humor upon great events connected with national *history*. The following is perhaps as good as any : The Rev. Robert Scott, a Scotchman, who forgot not Scotland in his southern vicarage, tells me that at Inverary, some thirty years ago, he could not help overhearing the conversation of some Lowland cattle-dealers in the public room in which he was. The subject of the bravery of our navy being started, one of the interlocutors expressed his surprise that Nelson should have issued his signal at Trafalgar in the terms, "*England expects*," etc. He was met with the answer (which seemed highly satisfactory to the rest), "Ay, Nelson only said '*expects*' of the English ; he said nothing of Scotland, for he *kent* the *Scotch* would do theirs."

"Purpose"—not "Performance"—Heaven's Standard

The following occurred between a laird and an elder : A certain laird in Fife, well known for his parsimonious habits, whilst his substance largely increased did not increase his liberality, and his weekly contribution to the church collection never exceeded the sum of one penny. One day, however, by mistake he dropped into the plate at the door a five-shilling **piece,** but discovering his error before he was seated in his pew, hurried back, and was about to replace the crown by his customary penny, when the elder in attendance cried out, " Stop, laird ; ye may put *in* what ye like, but ye maun tak' naething *out !* ' The laird, finding his explanations went for nothing, at last said, " Aweel, I suppose I'll get credit for it in heaven." " Na, na, laird," said the elder, " ye'll only get credit for a penny."

The Book Worms

Robert Burns once met with a copy of Shakespeare in a nobleman's library, the text of which had been neglected and had become worm-eaten. It was beautifully bound. Burns at once wrote the following lines :

> Through and through the inspired leaves,
> Ye maggots, make your windings ;
> But oh ! respect his lordship's tastes,
> And spare his golden bindings. [2]

"Uncertainty of Life" from Two Good Points of View

"Ah, sir," said a gloomy-looking minister of the Scotch Kirk, addressing a stranger who was standing on the bridge of the *Lord of the Isles*, as she steamed through the Kyles of Bute, "does the thought ever occur to ye of the great oncertainty of life ? "

" Indeed it does," returned the stranger, briskly, " many times a day."

"And have you ever reflected, sir," went on the minister, "that we may be launched into eternity at any instant ? "

"Yes," returned the stranger, "I have thought of that, and said it, too, thousands of times."

" Indeed," ejaculated the parson ; " then it is possible I am speaking to a brother meenister ? "

"Well, no," answered the other promptly, "you are not. If you must know, I am traveling agent of the Royal Lynx Life Assurance Association ; and, if you are not assured, I can strongly recommend you to give our office a turn. You will find special terms for ministers in Table K of our prospectus"; and handing the astonished divine a printed leaflet from his satchel, he left him without another word.

Providing a Mouthful for the Cow

Old Maggie Dee had fully her share of Scotch prudence and economy. One bonnet had served her turn for upwards of a dozen years, and some young ladies who lived in the neighborhood, in offering to make and present her with a new one, asked whether she would prefer silk or straw as material.

"Weel, my lassies," said Maggie, after mature deliberation, "since ye insist on giein' me a bonnet, I think I'll tak' a strae ane; it will, maybe, juist be a mou'fu' to the coo when I'm through wi't."

A Poor Place for a Cadger

An English traveler had gone on a fine Highland road so long, without having seen an indication of fellow-travelers, that he became astonished at the solitude of the country; and no doubt before the Highlands were so much frequented as they are in our time, the roads had a very striking aspect of solitariness. Our traveler at last coming up to an old man breaking stones, he asked him if there was any traffic on this road—was it at *all* frequented?

"Ay," he said, "it's no' ill at that; there was a cadger body yestreen, and there's yoursell the day."

The Kirk of Lamington

As cauld a wind as ever blew,
    A caulder kirk, and in't but few;
As cauld a minister's e'er spak',
    Ye'se a' be het ere I come back. [2]

"Lost Labor"

One of Dr. Macknight's parishioners, a humorous blacksmith, who thought his pastor's writing of learned books was a sad waste of time, being asked if the doctor was at home, answered: "Na, na; he's awa to Edinbro' on a foolish job."

The doctor had gone off to the printer's with his laborious and valuable work, " The Harmony of the Four Gospels." On being further asked what this useless work might be which engaged a minister's time and attention, the blacksmith replied: " He's gane to mak' four men agree wha never cast (fell) out."

A New Story Book—at the Time

Sir Walter Scott once stated that he kept a Low-land laird waiting for him in the library at Abbots-ford, and that when he came in he found the laird deep in a book which Sir Walter perceived to be Johnson's Dictionary.

" Well, Mr. ——," said Sir Walter, " how do you like your book ?"

" They're vera pretty stories, Sir Walter," replied the laird, " but they're unco' short."

Will Any Gentleman Oblige "a Lady"?

In a tramway car at Glasgow, one wet afternoon, a woman of fifty—made up to look as nearly like twenty-five as possible—got on board at a crossing, to find every seat occupied. She stood for a moment, and then selecting a poorly dressed man of about forty years of age, she observed: "Are there no gentlemen on the car?"

" I dinna ken," he replied, as he looked up and down. " If there's nane, I'll hunt up one for you at the end of the line."

There was an embarrasing silence for a moment, and then a light broke in on him all of a sudden, and he rose and said: " But ye can hae this seat: I'm aye wellin' to stan' and gi'e my seat to an *auld* bodie."

That decided her. She gave him a look which he will not forget till his dying day, and grasping the strap she refused to sit down, even when five seats had become vacant.

Ham and Cheese

On one occasion the late Rev. Walter Dunlop, of the U. P. Church, Dumfries, after a hard day's labor, and while at "denner-tea," as he called it, kept

Incessantly praising the "haam," and stating that "Mrs. Dunlop at hame was as fond o' haam like that as he was," when the mistress kindly offered to send her the present of a ham.

"It's unco' kin' o' ye, unco' kin'—but I'll no' pit ye to the trouble; I'll just tak' it hame on the horse afore me."

When, on leaving, he mounted, and the ham was put into the sack, some difficulty was experienced in getting it to lie properly. His inventive genius soon cut the Gordian-knot.

"I think, mistress, a cheese in the ither en' would mak' a gran' balance."

The hint was immediately acted on, and, like another John Gilpin, he moved away with his "balance true." [7]

"A Reduction on a Series"

When the son of a certain London banker had eloped to Scotland with a great heiress whom he married, still retaining a paternal taste for parsimony, he objected to the demand of two guineas made by the "priest" at Gretna Green, stating that Captain —— had reported the canonical charge to be only five shillings. "True," replied Vulcan, "but Captain —— is an Irishman, and I've married him five times; so I consider him a regular customer; whereas, I may never see your face again."

The Selkirk Grace *

Some hae meat, and canna eat,
    And some wad eat that want it;
But we hae meat and we can eat,
    And sae the Lord be thankit. [2]

Inconsistencies of "God's People"

An entertaining anecdote, illustrative of life in the Scotch Highlands, is told by a border minister who once found himself a guest at a Presbytery meeting.

"After dinner, though there was no wine, there was no lack of whiskey. This, each made into toddy,

---

* Said by Burns, at the request of the Earl of Selkirk.

weak or strong, just as he liked it. No set speeches
were made or toasts proposed. After each had drunk
two or three tumblers, and no voice was heard above
the hum of conversation, the stranger got to his feet,
and craving the leave of the company, begged to
propose a toast. All were silent, until the moderator,
with solemn voice, told him that God's people in that
part of the country were not in the habit of drinking toasts. He felt himself rebuked, yet rejoined,
that he had been in a good many places, but had
never before seen God's people drink so much
toddy."

Sending Him to Sleep

"Sleepin, Tonald?" said a Highlander to a drowsy
acquaintance, whom he found ruminating on the
grass in a horizontal position.

"No, Tuncan," was the ready answer.

"Then, Tonald, would you'll no' lend me ten and
twenty shillings?" was the next question.

"Ough, ough!" was the response with a heavy
snore; "I'm sleepin' now, Tuncan, my lad."

How convenient it would be if we could always
evade troublesome requests, like our Highlander
here, by feigning ourselves in the land of dreams!

Wiser Than Solomon

Two Scotch lairds conversing, one said to the other
that he thought they were wiser than Solomon.
"How's that?" said the other. "Why," said the
first, "he did not know whether his son might not be
a fool, and we know that ours are sure to be."

Modern Improvements

Sir Alexander Ramsay had been constructing, upon
his estate in Scotland, a piece of machinery, which
was driven by a stream of water running through the
home farmyard. There was a threshing machine, a
winnowing machine, a circular saw for splitting trees,
and other contrivances.

Observing an old man, who had been long about
the place, looking very attentively at all that was going
on, Sir Alexander said:

" Wonderful things people can do now, Robby?''
" Ay, indeed, Sir Alexander,'' said Robby ; " I'm
thinking that if Solomon was alive now, he'd be
thought naething o' ! ''   [7]

Knox and Claverhouse

The shortest chronicle of the Reformation, by
Knox, and of the wars of Claverhouse (Claver'se) in
Scotland, which we know of, is that of an old lady
who, in speaking of those troublous times remarked :
" Scotland had a sair time o't.   First we had Knox
deavin'us wi' his clavers, and syne we've had
Claver'se deavin' us wi' his knocks.''

A Scotch Fair Proclamation of Olden Days

" Oh, yes !—an' that's e'e time. Oh, yes !—an' that's
twa times. Oh, yes !—an that's the third and last time.
All manner of person or persons whatsover let 'em
draw near, an' I shall let 'em ken that there is a fair
to be held at the muckle town of Langholm, for the
space of aught days, wherein any hustrin, custrin,
land-hopper dub-shouper, or gent-the-gate-swinger,
shall breed any hurdam, durdam, rabble-ment, babble-
ment or squabble-ment, he shall have his lugs tacked
to the muckle throne with a nail of twa-a-penny, until
he's down on his bodshanks, and up with his muckle
doup, and pray to ha'en nine times, ' God bless the
King,' and thrice the muckle Laird of Reltown, pay-
ing a goat to me, Jemmy Ferguson, baillie to the afore-
said manor. So you've heard my proclamation, and
I'll gang hame to my dinner.''

" Though Lost to Sight—to Memory Dear ! "

Some time ago a good wife, residing in the neighborhood of Perth, went to town to purchase some little
necessaries, and to visit several of her old acquaintances. In the course of her peregrinations she had
the misfortune to lose a one-pound note. Returning
home with a saddened heart she encountered her
husband, employed in the cottage garden, to whom
she communicated at great length all her transactions
in town, concluding with the question : " But man you
canna guess what's befaun me?"

"Deed, I canna guess," said the husband, resting musingly on his spade.

"Aweel," rejoined his helpmate, "I hae lost a note ; but dinna be angry—for we ought to be mair than thankfu' that we had ane to lose !"

The Philosophy of Battle and Victory

During the long French war two old ladies in Scotland were going to the kirk. The one said to the other : "Was it no' a wonderful thing that Breetish were aye victorious in battle ?"

"Not a bit," said the other lady ; "dinna ye ken the Breetish aye say their prayers before gaun into battle ?"

The other replied : "But canna the French say their prayers as weel ?"

The reply was most characteristic. "Hoot ! sic jabberin' bodies ; wha could understand them if thae did ?"

Patriotism and Economy

When Sir John Carr was at Glasgow, in the year 1807, he was asked by the magistrates to give his advice concerning the inscription to be placed on Nelson's monument, then just completed. The knight recommended this brief record : "Glasgow to Nelson."

"True," said the baillies, "and as there is the town of Nelson near us, we might add, ' Glasgow to Nelson nine miles,' so that the column might serve for the milestone and a monument."

Husband! Husband! Cease Your Strife!

"Husband, husband, cease your strife,
　Nor longer idly rave, sir !
Tho' I am your wedded wife,
　Yet, I'm not your slave, sir !"

　　"*One of two must still obey,*
　　　Nancy, Nancy ;
　　Is it man, or woman, say,
　　　My spouse, Nancy ?"

" If 'tis still the lordly word—
'Service' and 'obedience,'
I'll desert my sov'reign lord,
And so, good-by, allegiance!"

" *Sad will I be, so bereft,*
Nancy, Nancy!
Yet, I'll try to make a shift,
My spouse, Nancy."

" My poor heart, then break it must,
My last hour, I'm near it;
When you lay me in the dust,
Think, think how you'll bear it."

" *I will hope and trust in heaven,*
Nancy, Nancy;
Strength to bear it will be given,
My spouse, Nancy."

" Well, sir, from the silent dead
Still I'll try to daunt you,
Ever round your midnight bed
Horrid sprites shall haunt you."

" *I'll wed another,* LIKE MY DEAR
NANCY, NANCY;
Then, all hell will fly for fear
My spouse, Nancy." [2]

A Scathing Scottish Preacher in Finsbury Park

People in Finsbury Park, one Sunday in August,
1890, were much edified by the drily humorous
remarks of a canny Scotchman who was holding a
religious service. The "eternal feminine" came in
for severe strictures, this man from auld Reekie
speaking of woman as "a calamity on two legs." He
had also a word or two to say on government meanness, of which this is an illustration. An old friend
of his who had been through Waterloo, retired from
the army on the munificent pension of 13½d. per day.
When he died the government claimed his wooden
leg! [3]

A Saving Clause

A Scotch teetotal society has been formed among farmers. There is a clause in one of the rules that permits the use of whiskey at sheep-dipping time. One worthy member keeps a sheep which he dips every day.

The Man at the Wheel

Dr. Adam, in the intervals of his labors as rector of the High School of Edinburgh, was accustomed to spend many hours in the shop of his friend Booge, the famous cutler, sometimes grinding knives and scissors, at other times driving the wheel. One day two English gentlemen, attending the university, called upon Booge (for he was an excellent Greek and Latin scholar), in order that he might construe for them some passage in Greek which they could not understand. On looking at it, Booge found that the passage "feckled" him; but, being a wag, he said to the students, "Oh, it's quite simple. My laboring man at the wheel will translate it for you. John!" calling to the old man, "come here a moment, will you?"

The apparent laborer came forward, when Booge showed him the passage in Greek, which the students wished to have translated. The old man put on his spectacles, examined the passage, and proceeded to give a learned exposition, in the course of which he cited several scholastic authors in support of his views as to its proper translation. Having done so, he returned to his cutler's wheel.

Of course the students were amazed at the learning of the laboring man. They said they had heard much of the erudition of the Edinburgh tradesmen, but what they had listened to was beyond anything they could have imagined. [1]

Spiking an Old Gun

When Mr. Shirra was parish minister of St. Miriam's, one of the members of the church was John Henderson, or Anderson—a very decent douce shoemaker— and who left the church and joined the Independents, who had a meeting in Stirling. Some time afterwards,

when Mr. Shirra met John on the road, he said, "And
so, John, I understand you have become an Inde-
pendent?"

"'Deed, sir," replied John, "that's true."

"Oh, John," said the minister, "I'm sure you ken
that a rowin' (rolling) stane gathers nae fog" (moss).

"Ay," said John, "that's true, too; but can ye tell
me what guid the fog does to the stane?"   [7]

Playing at Ghosts

Some boys boarded with a teacher in Scotland,
whose house was not very far from a country churchyard. They determined to alarm the old grave-digger,
who was in the habit of reaching his cottage, often
late at night, by a short cut through the burying-
ground. One boy, named Warren, who was especially mischievous, and had often teased old Andrew,
dressed himself up in a white sheet, and, with his
companions, hid behind the graves.

After waiting patiently, but not without some
anxiety and fear, for Andrew, he was at last seen
approaching the memorial-stone behind which Warren
was esconced. Soon a number of low moans were
heard coming from among the graves.

"Ah, keep us a'!" exclaimed Andrew. "What's
that?"

And as he approached slowly and cautiously
towards the tombstones, a white figure arose, and got
taller and taller before his eyes.

"What's that?" asked Andrew, with a voice which
seemed to tremble with fear, although, if anyone had
seen how he grasped his stick, he would not have
seen his hand tremble.

"It's the resurrection!" exclaimed the irreverent
Bully Warren.

"The resurrection!" replied Andrew. "May I tak'
the leeberty o' askin'," he continued slowly, approaching the ghost, "if it's the general ane, or are ye jist
takin' a quiet daunder by yersel'?"

So saying, Andrew rushed at the ghost, and seizing
it—while a number of smaller ghosts rose, and ran in
terror to the schoolhouse—he exclaimed, "Come awa'

wi' me! I think I surely haena buried ye deep
eneuch, when ye can rise so easy. But I hae dug a
fine deep grave this morning, and I'll put ye in't, and
cover ye up wi' sae muckle yirth, that, my werd, ye'll
no' get out for another daunder."

So saying, Andrew, by way of carrying out his
threats, dragged Master Bully Warren towards his
newly-made grave.

The boy's horror may be imagined, as Andrew was
too powerful to permit of his escape. He assailed the
old man with agonized petitions for mercy, for he was
a great coward.

"I'm not a ghost! Oh, Andrew, I'm Peter Warren!
Andrew! Don't burry me! I'll never again annoy
you! Oh—o—o—o—o!"

Andrew, after he had administered what he considered due punishment, let Warren off with the admonition: "Never daur to speak o' gude things in yon
way. Never play at ghaists again, or leevin' folk like
me may grup you, an' mak' a ghaist o' ye. Aff wi ye!"

"Two Blacks Don't Make a White"

The family of a certain Scotch nobleman having
become rather irregular in their attendance at church,
the fact was observed and commented on by their
neighbors. A lady, anxious to defend them and to
prove that the family pew was not so often vacant as
was supposed, said that his lordship's two black servants were there every Sunday. "Ay," said a gentleman present, but two blacks don't mak' a white."

From Pugilism to Pulpit

Fuller was in early life, when a farmer lad at Soham,
famous as a boxer; not quarrelsome, but not without
"the stern delight" a man of strength and courage
feels in his exercise. Dr. Charles Stewart, of Dun-
earn, whose rare gifts and graces as a physician, a
divine, a scholar, and a gentleman, live only in the
memory of those few who knew and survive him, liked
to tell how Mr. Fuller used to say, that when he was
in the pulpit, and saw a *buirdly* man come along the
passage, he would instinctively draw himself up,

measure his imaginary antagonist, and forecast how
he would deal with him, his hands meanwhile con-
densing into fists, and tending to "square." He
must have been a hard hitter if he boxed as he
preached—what "the fancy" would call "an ugly
customer." [4]

A Consistent Seceder

A worthy old seceder used to ride from Gargren-
nock to Bucklyvie every Sabbath to attend the
Burgher Kirk. One day, as he rode past the parish
kirk of Kippen, the elder of the place accosted him,
"I'm sure, John, it's no' like the thing to see you
ridin' in sic' a downpour o' rain sae far by to thae
seceders. Ye ken the mercifu' man is mercifu' to his
beast. Could ye no step in by?"

"Weel," said John, "I wadna care sae muckle
about stablin' my beast inside, but it's anither thing
mysel' gain' in." [7]

"No Road this Way!"

The following anecdote is told regarding the late
Lord Dundrennan : "A half-silly basket-woman passing down his avenue at Compstone one day, he met
her, and said, "My good woman, there's no road this
way."

"Na, sir," she said, "I think ye're wrang there;
I think it's a most beautifu' road." [7]

Shakespeare—Nowhere !

It is related, as characteristic of the ardor of
Scottish nationality, that, at a representation of
Home's *Douglas*, at Glasgow or Edinburgh, a Scotchman turned, at some striking passage in the drama,
and said to a Southron at his elbow : "And wher's
your Wully Shakespeare noo?"

Steeple or People ?

Shortly after the disruption of the Free Church of
Scotland from the church paid by the State, a farmer
going to church met another going in the opposite
direction.

"Whaur are ye gaen?" said he. "To the Free Kirk?"

"Ou, ay, to the Free Kirk," cried the other in derision:

> "The Free Kirk—
> The wee kirk—
> The kirk wi'out the steeple!"

"Ay, ay," replied the first, "an' ye'll be gaen till

> "The auld kird—
> The cauld kirk—
> The kirk wi'out the people!"

This ended the colloquy for that occasion.

Hume Canonized

Hume's house in Edinburgh stood at the corner of a new street which had not yet received any name. A witty young lady, a daughter of Baron Ord, chalked on the wall of the house the words, "St. David's Street." Hume's maid-servant read them, and apprehensive that some joke was intended against her master, went in great alarm to report the matter to him. "Never mind, my lass," said the philosopher; "many a better man has been made a saint of before."

Two Ways of Mending Ways

The Rev. Mr. M——, of Bathgate, came up to a street pavior one day, and addressed him: "Eh, John, what's this you're at?"

"Oh! I'm mending the ways of Bathgate!"

"Ah, John, I've long been tryin' to mend the ways o' Bathgate, an' they're no' weel yet."

"Weel, Mr. M——, if you had tried my plan, and come doon to your *knees*, ye wad maybe hae come maar speed!"

The Prophet's Chamber

A Scotch preacher, being sent to officiate one Sunday at a country parish, was accommodated at night in the manse in a very diminutive closet, instead of the usual best bedroom appropriated to strangers.

"Is this the bedroom?" he said, starting back in amazement.

" 'Deed, ay, sir ; this is the prophet's chamber."

"It must be for the *minor* prophets, then," said the discomfited parson.

Objecting to Long Sermons

A minister in the north was taking to task one of his hearers who was a frequent defaulter, and was reproaching him as an habitual absentee from public worship. The accused vindicated himself on the plea of a dislike to long sermons.

" 'Deed, man," said his reverend minister, a little nettled at the insinuation thrown out against himself, "if ye dinna mend, ye may land yerself where ye'll no' be troubled wi' mony sermons, either lang or short."

"Weel, aiblins sae," retorted John, "but it mayna be for want o' ministers."

A Serious Dog and for a Serious Reason

A Highland gamekeeper, when asked why a certain terrier, of singular pluck, was so much more solemn than the other dogs, said : "Oh, sir, life's full o' sairiousness to him—he first can never get enuff o' fechtin'."

A Clever "Turn"

Lord Elibank, the Scotch peer, was told that Dr. Johnson, in his dictionary, had defined oats to be food for horses in England and for men in Scotland. "Ay," said his lordship, "and where else can you find such horses and such men?"

Entrace Free, and "Everything Found"

A member of the Scottish bar, when a youth, was somewhat of a dandy, and was still more remarkable for the shortness of his temper. One day, being about to pay a visit to the country, he made a great fuss in packing up his clothes for the journey, and his old aunt, annoyed at the bustle, said : "Whaur's this you're gaun, Robby, that you mak' sic a grand ware about your claes ?"

The young man lost his temper, and pettishly replied, "I am going to the devil."

"'Deed, Robby, then," was the quiet answer, "ye need na be sae nice, for he'll just tak' ye as ye are."

Two Questions on the Fall of Man

The Rev. Ralph Erskine, one of the fathers of the secession from the Kirk of Scotland, on a certain occasion paid a visit to his venerable brother, Ebenezer, at Abernethy.

"Oh, man!" said the latter, "but ye come in a gude time. I've a diet of examination to-day, and ye maun tak' it, as I have matters o' life and death to settle at Perth."

"With all my heart," quoth Ralph.

"Noo, my Billy," says Ebenezer, "ye'll find a' my folk easy to examine but ane, and him I reckon ye had better no' meddle wi'. He has our old-fashioned Scotch way of answering a question by putting another, and maybe he'll affront ye."

"Affront me!" quoth the indignant theologian; "do ye think he can foil me wi' my ain natural toils?"

"Aweel," says his brother, "I'se gie ye fair warning, ye had better no' ca' him up."

The recusant was one Walter Simpson, the Vulcan of the parish. Ralph, indignant at the bare idea of such an illiterate clown chopping divinity with him, determined to pose him at once with a grand leading unanswerable question. Accordingly, after putting some questions to some of the people present, he all at once, with a loud voice, cried out, "Walter Simpson!"

"Here, sir," says Walter, "are ye wanting me?"

"Attention, sir! Now Walter, can you tell me how long Adam stood in a state of innocence?"

"Ay, till he got a wife," instantly cried the blacksmith. "But," added he, "can you tell me hoo lang he stood after?"

"Sit doon, Walter," said the discomfited divine.

The Speech of a Cannibal

"Poor-man-of-mutton" is a term applied to a shoulder-of-mutton in Scotland after it has been served as a roast at dinner, and appears as a broiled bone at supper, or at the dinner next day. The Scotch Earl of B——, popularly known as Old Rag, being at an hotel in London, the landlord came in one morning to enumerate the good things in the larder. " Landlord," said the Earl of B——, " I think I *could* eat a morsel of poor man." This strange announcement, coupled with the extreme ugliness of his lordship, so terrified Boniface that he fled from the room and tumbled down the stairs. He supposed that the Earl, when at home, was in the habit of eating a joint of a vassal, or tenant, when his appetite was dainty.

Not "in Chains"

A Londoner was traveling on one of the Clyde steamers, and as it was passing the beautiful town of Largs, then little larger than a village, and unnoticed in his guide-book, he asked a Highland countryman, a fellow passenger, its name.

" Oh, that's Largs, sir."

" Is it incorporated ? "

" Chwat's your wull , sir ? "

" Is it incorporated ? "

" Chwat's your wull, sir ? "

" Dear me ! Is it a borough? Has it magistrates ? "

" Oh, yess, sir. Largs has a provost and bailies."

Anxious to have the question of incorporation settled, and aware that Scotch civic magistrates are invested with golden chains of office, which they usually wear round their necks, our London friend put his next question thus : " Do the magistrates wear chains ? "

The countryman very indignantly replied, " Na, na, sir ; the provost and bailies o' Largs aye gang loose."

A Piper's Opinion of a Lord—and Himself

" The stately step of a piper " is a proverb in Scotland, which reminds us of an anecdote of a certain noble lord, when in attendance upon the Queen at Balmoral, a few years ago. Having been commissioned by a friend to procure a performer on the pipes—he applied to her majesty's piper—a fine stalwart Highlander; and on being asked what kind of article was required, his lordship said in reply, "Just such another as yourself." The consequential Celt readily exclaimed "There's plenty o' lords like yourself, but very few sic pipers as me."

A Modern Dumb Devil (D.D.)

Mr. Dunlop happened one day to be present in a Church Court in a neighboring presbytery. A Rev. Dr. was one day asked to pray, and declined.

On the meeting adjourning, Mr. Dunlop stepped up to the doctor, and asked how he did. The doctor never having been introduced, did not reply.

Mr. Dunlop withdrew, and said to a friend, "Eh! but is' na he a queer man, that doctor; he'll neither speak to God nor man?"

A Curiously Unfortunate Coincidence in Psalm Singing

In the parish church of Fettercairn, a custom existed, and indeed still lingers in some parts of Scotland, of the precentor on communion Sabbath reading out each single line of the psalm before it was sung by the congregation. This practice gave rise to a somewhat unfortunate introduction of a line from the First Psalm. In most churches in Scotland the communion tables are placed in the centre of the church. After sermon and prayer the seats round these tables are occupied by the communicants while a psalm is being sung. On one communion Sunday, the precentor observed the noble family of Eglinton approaching the tables, and saw that they were likely to be kept out by those who pressed in before them. Being very zealous for their accommodation, he called out to an individual whom he considered to be the principal obstacle in the passage, "Come back, Jock, and let in the noble family of Eglinton"; and then, turning again to his psalm-book, gave out the line, "Nor stand in sinners' way."

Living With His Uncle

A little boy had lived some time with a penurious uncle, who took good care that the child's health should not be injured by overfeeding. The uncle was one day walking out, the child at his side, when a friend accosted him, accompanied by a greyhound. While the elders were talking, the little fellow, never having seen a dog so slim and slight in texture, clasped the creature round the neck with the impassioned cry, " Oh, doggie, doggie, and did ye live wi' your uncle, tae, that ye are so thin ? "   [7]

Pulpit Familiarity

A pastor of a small congregation of Dissenters in the west of Scotland, who, in prayer, often employed terms of familiarity towards the great Being whom he invoked, was addressing his petition in the season of an apparently doubtful harvest, that He would grant such weather as was necessary for ripening and gathering in the fruits of the ground ; when suddenly, he added, " But what need I talk ?   When I was up at Shotts the other day, everything was as green as leeks."

A Churl Congratulated

Hume went to a newspaper office, and laid on the counter an announcement of the death of some friend, together with five shillings, the usual price of such advertisements.   The clerk, who had a very rough manner, demanded seven shillings and sixpence, the extra charge being for the words: " he was universally beloved and regretted." Hume paid the money, saying, gravely, " Congratulate yourself, sir, that this is an expense which your executors will never be put to."

Touching Each Other's Limitations

There once lived in Cupar a merchant whose store contained supplies of every character and description, so that he was commonly known by the sobriquet of " Robbie A' Thing." One day a minister who was well known for making a free use of his notes in the pulpit, called at the store asking for a rope and pin to tether a young calf in the glebe.

Robbie at once informed him that he could not furnish such articles to him.

But the minister being somewhat importunate, said : "Oh ! I thought you were named ' Robbie A' Thing,' from the fact that you keep all kinds of goods."

"Weel, a weel," said Robbie, "I keep a' thing in my shop but calf's tether-pins, and paper sermons for ministers to read."

" Having the Advantage "

The Rev. Mr. Johnstone, of Monquhitter, a very grandiloquent pulpit orator in his day, accosting a traveling piper, well known in the district, with the question, "Well, John, how does the wind pay?" received from John, with a low bow, the answer, " Your reverence has the advantage of me." [7]

Giving Them the Length of His Tongue

A lawyer in an Edinburgh court occupied the whole day with a speech which was anything but interesting to his auditors.

Some one, who had left the court-room and returned again after the interval of some hours, finding the same harangue going on, said to Lord Cockburn, " Is not II—— taking up a great deal of time ? "

" Time ? " said Cockburn ; " he has long ago exhausted time, and encroached upon eternity."

Sectarian Resemblances

A friend of mine used to tell a story of an honest builder's views of church differences, which was very amusing and quaintly professional. An English gentleman who had arrived in a Scottish county town, was walking about to examine various objects which presented themselves, and observed two rather handsome places of worship in the course of erection nearly opposite each other. He addressed a person, who happened to be the contractor for the chapels, and asked, " What was the difference between these two places of worship which was springing up so close to each other?'' meaning, of course, the difference of the theological tenets of the two congregations.

The contractor, who thought only of architectural differences, innocently replied, "There may be a difference of sax feet in length, but there's no' aboon a few inches in breadth.''

Would that all religious differences could be brought within so narrow a compass.   [7]

A Process of Exhaustion

A Scotch minister was asked if he was not very much exhausted after preaching three hours.   "Oh, no,'' he replied ; " but it would have done you good to see how worried the people were.''

A Thoughtless Wish

A landed proprietor in the small county of Rutland became very intimate with the Duke of Argyle, to whom, in the plenitude of his friendship, he said : " How I wish your estate were in my county !'' Upon which the duke replied, " I'm thinking, if it were, there would be *no room for yours.*''

Sunday Thoughts on Recreation

The Rev. Adam Wadderstone, minister in Bathgate, was an excellent man and as excellent a curler, who died in 1780.   Late one Saturday night one of his elders received a challenge from the people of Shotts to the curlers of Bathgate to meet them early on Monday morning ; and after tossing about half the night at a loss how to convey the pleasing news to the minister, he determined to tell him before he entered the pulpit.

When Mr. Wadderstone entered the session-house, the elder said to him in a loud tone, " Sir, I've something to tell ye ; there's to be a parish play with the Shotts folk the morn, at——''

" Whist, man, whist !'' was the rejoinder.   " Oh, fie, shame, John ! fie, shame !   Nae speaking to-day about warldy recreations.''

But the ruling passion proved too strong for the

worthy clergyman's scruples of conscience, for just
as he was about to enter the inner door of the church,
he suddenly wheeled round and returned to the
elder, who was now standing at the plate in the lobby,
and whispered in his ear, "But whan's the hoor,
John? I'll be sure and be there. Let us sing,

> "'That music dear to a curler's ear,
> And enjoyed by him alone—
> The merry chink of the curling rink,
> And the boom of the roaring stone.'"

Relieving His Wife's Anxiety

A Scotchman became very poor by sickness. His
refined and affectionate wife was struggling with him
for the support of their children. He took to peddling
with a one-horse wagon, as a business that would
keep him in the open air and not tax his strength too
much. One day, after having been sick at home for
two or three weeks, he started out with his cart for a
ten-day's trip, leaving his wife very anxious about
him on account of his weakness. After going about
fifteen miles his horse fell down and died. He got a
farmer to hitch his horse to the cart and bring it
home. As they were driving into the yard he saw
the anxiety depicted on his wife's countenance, and
being tenderly desirous to relieve it, he cried out,
" Maria, its not me that's dead; its the mare!"

Radically Rude

Mr. Burgon, in his "Life of Tyler," tells the fol-
owing amusing story: Captain Basil Hall was once
traveling in an old-fashioned stage-coach, when he
found himself opposite to a good-humored, jolly
Dandy-Dinmount looking person, with whom he
entered into conversation, and found him most intelligent. Dandie, who was a staunch Loyalist, as well as
a stout yeoman, seemed equally pleased with his
companion.

" Troth, sir," he said, " I am well content to meet
one wi' whom I can have a rational conversation, for
I have been fairly put out. You see, sir, a Radical

fellow came into the coach. It was the only time I
ever saw a Radical ; an' he begun abusing everything,
saying that this wasna a kintra fit to live in. And
first he abused the king. Sir, I stood that. And
then he abused the constitution. Sir, I stood that.
And then he abused the farmers. Well, sir, I stood
it all. But then he took to abusing the yeomanry.
Now, sir, you ken I couldna stand *that*, for I am a
yeoman mysel' ; so I was under the necessity of
being a wee bit rude-like till him. So I seized him
by the scruff of the neck : ' Do ye see that window,
sir? Apologeeze, apologeeze this very minute, or I'll
just put your head tnrough the window.' Wi' that
he *apologeezed*. ' Now, sir,' I said, ' you'll gang out
o' the coach.' And wi' that I opened the door, and
shot him out intil the road ; and that's all I ever saw
o' the Radical.''

" Gathering Up the Fragments "

The inveterate snuff-taker, like the dram-drinker,
felt severely the being deprived of his accustomed
stimulant, as in the following instance : A severe
snowstorm in the Highlands which lasted for several
weeks, having stopped all communications betwixt
neighboring hamlets, the snuff-boxes were soon
reduced to their last pinch. Borrowing and begging
from all the neighbors within reach were first resorted
to, but when these failed they were all alike reduced
to the longing which unwillingly-abstinent snuff-takers
alone know. The minister of the parish was amongst
the unhappy number, the craving was so intense that
study was out of the question, and he became quite
restless. As a last resource, the beadle was dispatched, through the snow, to a neighboring glen, in
the hope getting a supply ; but he came back as
unsuccessful as he went.

"What's to be dune, John ? " was the minister's
pathetic inquiry.

John shook his head, as much as to say that he
could not tell ; but immediately thereafter started up,
as if a new idea had occured to him. He came back
in a few minutes, crying, " Hae ! "

The minister, to eager to be scrutinizing, took a long, deep pinch, and then said, "Whaur did you get it?"

"I soupit (swept) the poupit," was John's expressive reply.

The minister's accumulated superfluous Sabbath snuff now came into good use.

Sleepy Churchgoers

The bowls of rum punch which so remarkably characterized the Glasgow dinners of last century, and the early part of the present, it is to be feared, made some of the congregation given to somnolency on the Sundays following. The members of the town council often adopted Saturdays for such meetings; accordingly, the Rev. Mr. Thorn, an excellent clergyman, took occasion to mark this propensity with some acerbity. A dog had been very troublesome, when the minister at last gave orders to the beadle, "Take out that dog; he'd wauken a Glasgow magistrate." [7]

A Highland Chief and His Doctor

Dr. Gregory (of immortal mixture memory) used to tell a story of an old Highland chieftain, intended to show how such Celtic potentates were once held to be superior to all the usual considerations which affected ordinary mortals. The doctor, after due examination, had, in his usual decided and blunt manner, pronounced the liver of a Highlander to be at fault, and to be the cause of his ill-health. His patient, who could not but consider this as taking a great liberty with a Highland chieftain, roared out, "And what business is it of yours whether I have a liver or not?"

"Rippets" and Humility

The following is a dry Scottish case of a minister's wife quietly "kaming her husband's head." Mr. Mair, a Scotch minister, was rather short-tempered, and had a wife named Rebecca, whom, for brevity's sake, he addressed as Becky. He kept a diary and

among other entries this one was very frequent—
" Becky and I had a rippet, for which I desire to be
humble."

A gentleman who had been on a visit to the minister
went to Edinburgh, and told the story to a minister
and his wife there, when the lady replied, " Weel,
he must have been an excellent man, Mr. Mair. My
husband and I some times, too, have ' rippets ' but
catch him if he's ever humble." [7]

" Kaming " Her Ain Head

The late good, kind-hearted Dr. David Dickson
was fond of telling a story of a Scottish termagant of
the days before Kirk-session discipline had passed
away. A couple were brought before the court, and
Janet, the wife, was charged with violent, and unduti-
ful conduct, and with wounding her husband, by
throwing a three-legged stool at his head. The minister rebuked her conduct, and pointing out its
grievous character, by explaining that just as Christ
was head of his Church, so the husband was head of
the wife ; and therefore in assaulting *him*, she had in
fact injured her own body.

" Weel," she replied, " it's come to a fine pass gin
a wife canna kame her ain head."

" Aye, but Janet," rejoined the minister, " a three-
legged stool is a thief-like bane-kame to scart yer ain
head wi' ! "

Splendid Use for Bag-Pipes

A Scottish piper was passing through a deep forest.
In the evening he sat down to take his supper. He
had hardly began when a number of wolves, prowling
about for food, collected round him. In self-defence,
the poor man began to throw pieces of victuals to
them, which they greedily devoured. When he had
disposed of all, in a fit of despair he took his pipes
and began to play. The unusual sound terrified the
wolves so much that they scampered off in every
direction. Observing this, Sandly quietly remarked :
" Od, an' I'd kenned ye liket the pipes sae weel, I'd
a gi'en ye a spring *afore* supper."

Practical Piety

The following story was told by the Rev. William Arnot at a soirée in Sir W. H. Moncrief's church some years ago.

Dr. Macleod and Dr. Watson were in the West Highlands together on a tour, ere leaving for India. While crossing a loch in a boat, in company with a number of passengers, a storm came on. One of the passengers was heard to say :

" The twa ministers should begin to pray, or we'll a' be drooned."

" Na, na," said a boatman ; " the little ane can pray, if he likes, but the big ane must tak' an oar ! " [10]

" There Maun be Some Faut "

Old Mr. Downie, the parish minister of Banchory, was noted in my earliest days for his quiet pithy remarks on men and things as they came before him. His reply to his son, of whose social position he had no very exaulted opinion, was of this class. Young Downie had come to visit his father from the West Indies, and told him that on his return he was to be married to a lady whose high qualities and position he spoke of in extravagant terms. He assured his father that she was " quite young, was very rich, and very beautiful."

" Aweel, Jemmy," said the old man, very quietly and very slily, " I'm thinking there maun be some *faut.*" [7]

Deathbed Humor

The late Mr. Constable used to visit an old lady who was much attenuated by long illness, and on going upstairs one tremendously hot afternoon, the daughter was driving the flies away, saying : " These flies will eat up a' that remains o' my puir mither." The old lady opened her eyes, and the last words she spoke were : " What's left's good eneuch for them."

A Matter-of-Fact Death Scene

The Scottish people, without the least intention or purpose of being irreverent or unfeeling, often

approach the awful question connected with the
funerals of friends in a cool matter-of-fact manner.   A
tenant of Mr. George Lyon, of Wester Ogil, when on
his death-bed, and his end near at hand, was thus
addressed by his wife : " Willie, Willie, as lang as ye
can speak, tell us are ye for your burial baps round
or *square?*" Willie, having responded to this inquiry,
was next asked if the *murners* were to have *glooves*
or mittens—the latter having only a thumb-piece ;
and Willie, having answered, was allowed to depart
in peace.

Acts of Parliament " Exhausted "

A junior minister having to assist at a church in a
remote part of Aberdeenshire, the parochial minister
(one of the old school) promised his young friend a
good glass of whiskey-toddy after all was over, adding
slily and very significantly, " and gude *smuggled*
whiskey."

His southern guest thought it incumbent to say,
" Ah, minister, that's wrong, is it not ?   You know it
is contrary to Act of Parliament."

The old Aberdonian could not so easily give up his
fine whiskey, so he quietly said : " Oh, Acts of Parliament lose their breath before they get to Aberdeenshire."

Concentrated Caution

The most cautious answer certainly on record is
that of the Scotchman who, being asked if he could
play a fiddle, warily answered that he "couldna say,
for he had never tried."

A " Grave " Hint

Mr. Mearns, of Kineff Manse, gave an exquisitely
characteristic illustration of beadle *professional* habits
being made to bear upon the tender passion.   A certain beadle had fancied the manse house-maid, but at
a loss for an opportunity to declare himself, one day—
a Sunday—when his duties were ended, he looked
sheepish, and said, " Mary, wad *ye* tak' a turn,
Mary ? "

He led her to the churchyard, and pointing with his

finger, he got out: "My fowk lie there, Mary; wad
ye like to lie there?"

The *grave* hint was taken, and she became his wife.

A Spiritual Barometer

There was an old bachelor clergyman whose landlady declared that he used to express an opinion of
his dinner by the grace which he made to follow.
When he had a good dinner which pleased him, and
a good glass of beer with it, he poured forth the
grace, "For the richest of Thy bounty and its bless-
ings we offer our thanks." When he had had poor
fare and poor beer, his grace was, "We thank Thee
for the least of these Thy mercies."

A New Application of "The Argument from Design"

An honest Highlander, a genuine lover of sneeshin,
observed, standing at the door of the Blair Athole Hotel,
a magnificent man in full tartans, and noticed with
much admiration the wide dimensions of his nostrils
in a fine up-turned nose. He accosted him and, as
his most complimentary act, offered him his mull for
a pinch.

The stranger drew up and rather haughtily said:
"I never take snuff."

"Oh," said the other, "that's a peety, for there's
gran' *accommodation*."

Two Methods of Getting a Dog Out of Church

I had an anecdote from a friend of a reply from a
betheral (beadle) to the minister *in* church, which
was quaint and amusing from the shrewd self-import-
ance it indicated in his own acuteness. The clergyman had been annoyed during the course of his sermon by the restlessness and occasional whining of a
dog, which at last began to bark outright. He looked
out for the beadle, and directed him very peremp-
torily, "John, carry that dog out."

John looked up to the pulpit and, with a very knowing expression, said: "Na, na, sir; I'se just mak'
him gae out on his ain four legs." [7]

Born Too Late

A popular English nonconformist minister was residing with a family in Glasgow, while on a visit to that city, whither he had gone on a deputation from the Wesleyan Missionary Society. After dinner, in reply to an invitation to partake of some fine fruit, he mentioned to the family a curious circumstance concerning himself, viz.: that he had never in his life tasted an apple, pear, or grape, or indeed any kind of green fruit. This fact seemed to evoke considerable surprise from the company, but a cautious Scotchman, of a practical matter-of-fact turn of mind, and who had listened with much unconcern, drily remarked: "It's a peety but ye had been in Paradise, an' there might na hae been ony faa'."

A Preacher with his Back Towards Heaven

During one of the religious revivals in Scotland, a small farmer went about preaching with much fluency and zeal, the doctrine of a "full assurance" of faith, and expressed his belief of it for himself in such extravagant terms as few men would venture upon who were humble and cautious against presumption. The preacher, being personally rather remarkable as a man of greedy and selfish views in life, excited some suspicion in the breast of an old sagacious countryman, a neighbor of Dr. Macleod, who asked what *he* thought of John as a preacher, and of his doctrine?

Scratching his head, as if in some doubt, he replied, "*I never ken'l a man sae sure o' heaven and so sweert* (slow) *to be gaing lael.*" [5]

Nearer the Bottom than the Top

A little boy who attended a day school near his home, was always asked in the evening how he stood in his own class. The invariable answer was, "I'm second dux," which means, in Scottish academical language, second from the top of the class. As his habits of application at home did not quite bear out the claims to so distinguished a literary position at school, one of the family ventured to ask what was

the number in the class to which he was attached.
After some hesitation, he was obliged to admit, " Ou,
there's jist me and *anither lass*."

A Crushing Argument against MS. Sermons

A clergyman thought his people were making
rather an unconscionable objection to his using an
MS. in delivering a sermon.

They urged, " What gars ye tak' up your bit papers
to the pu'pit ? "

He replied that it was best, for really he could not
remember his sermons, and must have his paper.

" Weel, weel, minister, then dinna expect that *we*
can remember them."

Mortal Humor

Humor sometimes comes out on the very scaffold.
An old man was once hanged for complicity in a
murder.   The rope broke, and he fell heavily to the
ground. His first utterance when his breath returned
to him was, " Ah, sheriff, sheriff, gie us fair hangin'."

His friends demanded that he should be delivered
up to them, as a second hanging was not contem-
plated in the sentence.   But the old man, looking
round on the curious crowd of gazers, and lifting up
his voice, said, " Na, na, boys, I'll no gang hame to
my neighbors to hear people pointing me oot as the
half-hangit man ; I'll be hangit oot."

And he got his wish five minutes after.

A Fruitful Field

The following anecdote was communicated to me
by a gentleman who happened to be a party to the
conversation detailed below.   This gentleman was
passing along the road not one hundred miles from
Peterhead one day.   Two different farms skirt the
separate sides of the turnpike, one of which is rented
by a farmer who cultivates his land according to the
most advanced system of agriculture, and the other
of which is farmed by a gentleman of the old school.

Our informant met the latter worthy at the side of
the turnpike, opposite his neighbor's farm, and seeing

a fine crop of wheat upon what appeared to be (and really was) very poor and thin land, asked, "When was that wheat sown?"

"O, I dinna ken," replied the gentleman of the old school, with a sort of half indifference, half contempt.

"But isn't it strange that such a fine crop should be reared on such bad land?" asked our informant.

"O, na—nae at a'—devil thank it; a gravesteen wad gie guid bree gin ye geed it plenty o' butter." [7]

The "Minister's Man"

The "minister's man" was a functionary now less often to be met with. He was the minister's own servant and *factotum*. Amongst this class there was generally much Scottish humor and original character. They were (like the betheral, or beadle) great critics of sermons, and often severe upon strangers, sometimes with a sly hit at their own ministers. One of these, David, a well-known character, complimenting a young minister who had preached, told him, "Your introduction, sir, is aye grand; it's worth a' the rest o' the sermon,—could ye no' mak' it a' introduction?"

David's criticisms of his master's sermons were sometimes sharp enough and shrewd. On one occasion, the minister was driving home from a neighboring church where he had been preaching, and where he had, as he thought, acquitted himself pretty well, inquired of David what *he* thought of it. The subject of discourse had been the escape of the Israelites from Egypt. So David opened his criticism:

"Thocht o't, sir? Deed I thocht nocht o't ava. It was a vara imperfect discourse, in ma opinion; ye did well eneucht till ye took them through, but where did ye leave them? Just dauncerin' o' the sea-shore without a place to gang till. Had it no' been for Pharaoh they had been better on the other side, where they were comfortably encampit than daunerin' where ye left them. It's painful to hear a sermon stoppit afore it is richt ended, just as it is to hear ane streeket out lang after it's dune. That's my opinion o' the sermon ye geid us to-day."

12

"Very freely given, David, very freely given; drive on a little faster, for I think ye're daunerin' noo, yersell." [7]

A New and Original Scene in "Othello"

At a Scottish provincial theatre, a prompter named Walls, who, being exceedingly useful, frequently appeared on the stage, happened one evening to play the Duke, in "Othello." Previous to going on, he had given directions to a girl-of-all-work, who looked after the wardrobe, to bring a gill of best whiskey. Not wishing to go out, as the evening was wet, the girl deputed her little brother to execute the commission. The senate was assembled, and the speaker was—

Brabantio: "For my particular grief is of so floodgate and o'erbearing nature, that it engluts and swallows other sorrows, and is still itself."

Duke: "Why, what's the matter?"

Here the little boy walked on to the stage with a pewter gill stoup, and thus delivered himself:

"It's just the whusky, Mr. Walls, and I couldna get ony at fourpence, so yer awn the landlord a penny, an' he says it's time you were payin' whet's doon i' the book."

The roars of laughter which followed from both audience and actors for some time prevented the further progress of the play.

The Shape of the Earth

A country schoolmaster of the old time was coaching his pupils for the yearly examination by the clergymen of the district. He had before him the junior geography class.

"Can any little boy or girl tell me what is the shape of the earth?"

To this there was no answer.

"Oh, dear me, this is sad! What wull the minister sink o' this? Well, I'll gie you a token to mind it. What is the shape o' this snuff-box in ma han'?"

"Square, sir," replied all.

"Yes; but on the Sabbath, when a shange ma

claes, I shange ma snuff-box, and I wears a round one. Will you mind that for a token?"

Examination day came, and the junior geography class was called.

"Fine intelligent class this, Mr. Mackenzie," said one of the clergymen.

"Oh, yes, sir, they're na boor-like."

"Can any of the little boys or girls tell me what is the shape of the earth?"

Every hand was extended, every head thrown back, every eye flashed with eager excitement in the good old style of schools. One was singled out with a "You, my little fellow, tell us."

"Roond on Sundays, and square all the rest o' the week."

Rivalry in Prayer

Yarmouth, Nova Scotia, has a wide-awake Presbyterian elder of Scotch character, who, although a persistent advocate of the Westminster Confession, occasionally for convenience sake — and from an innate love of religious intercourse — attends the meetings of his Methodist brethren.

At a recent prayer-meeting that was held preparatory to a centennial service in commemoration of the progress of Methodism in Nova Scotia, the presiding minister dwelt eloquently upon the wonderful growth and prosperity of the Methodist Church, and upon the life of its great founder, John Wesley. He also expressed thankfulness that on that day there were one hundred and nine Methodist ministers in Nova Scotia. The meeting thus very decidedly assumed a denominational character, but the minister asked the good Presbyterian brother to lead in prayer at the close. The elder complied, and after thanking God for the many good things he had just heard "about this branch of Zion," he added, with much depth and feeling, "O Lord, we thank Thee for *John Knox ;* we thank Thee for the one hundred and nine Methodist ministers in our country, but we *especially* thank Thee for the *one hundred and thirteen* Presbyterian ministers who are preaching the Word of Life throughout our land. Amen."

A Compensation Balance

The answers of servants often curiously illustrate the habits and manners of the household. A bright maid-of-all-work, alluding to the activity and parsimony of her mistress, said, "She's vicious upo' the wark, but, eh, she's vary mysterious o' the victualing."

The " Sawbeth " at a Country Inn

The Rev. Moncure D. Conway, while traveling in the neighborhood of the Hebrides, heard several anecdotes illustrative of the fearful reverence with which Scotchmen in that region observe the Sabbath. Says he : " A minister of the kirk recently declared in public that at a country inn he wished the window raised, so that he might get some fresh air, but the landlady would not allow it, saying, 'Ye can hae no fresh air here on the Sawbeth.' " [11]

Scotchmen Everywhere

Was ever a place that hadn't its Scotchman? In a late English publication we find an account of a gentleman traveling in Turkey, who, arriving at a military station, took occasion to admire the martial appearance of two men. He says : " The Russian was a fine, soldier-like figure, nearly six feet high, with a heavy cuirassier moustache, and a latent figure betraying itself (as the 'physical force,' novelists say) in every line of his long muscular limbs. Our pasha was a short thick-set man, rather too round and puffy in the face to be very dignified ; but the eager, restless glance of his quick gray eye showed that he had no want of energy. My friend, the interpreter, looked admiringly at the pair as they approached each other, and was just exclaiming, ' There, thank God, are a real Russian and a real Turk, and admirable specimens of their race, too!' when suddenly General Sarasoff and Ibrahim Pasha, after staring at each other for a moment, burst forth simultaneously, ' Eh, Donald Cawmell, are *ye* there?' 'Lord keep us, Sandy Robertson, can this be *you?*' "

A Bookseller's Knowledge of Books

A Glasgow bailie was one of a deputation sent from that city to Louis Philippe, when that monarch was on the French throne. The king received the deputation very graciously, and honored them with an invitation to dinner. During the evening the party retired to the royal library, where the king, having ascertained that the bailie followed the calling of bookseller, showed him the works of several English authors, and said to him: " You see, I am well supplied with standard works in English. There is a fine edition of Burke."

The magistrate, familiar only with Burke the murderer, exclaimed : " Ah, the villain ! I was there when he was hanged ! "

" Fou'—Aince "

George Webster once met a shepherd boy in Glenshee, and asked, " My man, were you ever fou' ? "

" Ay, aince "—speaking slowly, as if remembering— " Ay, aince."

" What on ? "

" Cauld mutton ! "   [12]

Sunday Drinking

Dr. M——, accompanied by a friend, took a long walk on Sunday, and being fatigued, the two stopped at an inn to get some refreshment. The landlord stopped them at the door with the question whether they were *bona fide* travelers, as such alone could enter his house on Sunday. They said they were from London, and were admitted. They were sent bread and cheese and stout. The stout was bad, and they sent for ale ; but that being worse, they sent for whiskey. The landlord refused this, saying they had enough for their bodily necessities.

After a great deal of urging for the whiskey, which the landlord withstood, M—— said, " Very well ; if you won't sell us whiskey, we must use our own," at the same time pulling a flask out of his pocket.

This was more than the Scotchman could stand. The sin was to be committed, and there would be no compensation to its heinousness in the way of profit to his inn. "Ah, weel," he said, "if ye maun have the whiskey, ye maun, an' I'll send ye the mateyrials."

Drawing an Inference

A certain functionary of a country parish is usually called the *minister's man*, and to one of these who had gone through a long course of such parish official life, a gentleman one day remarked—"John, ye hae been sae lang about the minister's hand that I dare say ye could preach a sermon yersell now."

To which John modestly replied, "O na, sir, I couldna preach a sermon, but maybe I could draw an inference."

"Well, John," said the gentleman, humoring the quiet vanity of the beadle, "what inference could ye draw frae this text, 'A wild ass snuffeth up the wind at her pleasure!" (Jer. ii : 24).

"Weel, sir, I wad draw this inference :—she wad snuff a lang time afore she would fatten upon 't." [7]

Going to Ramoth Gilead

A sailor, who had served the king so long at sea that he almost forgot the usages of civilized society on shore, went one day into the church at his native town of Kircaldy, in Fife, where it happened that the minister chose for his text the well-known passage, "Who will go up with us to Ramoth Gilead?"

This emphatic appeal being read the second time, and in a still more impressive tone of voice, the thoughtless tar crammed a quid of tobacco into his cheek, rose up, put on his hat; then, looking around him, and seeing nobody moving, he exclaimed, "You cowardly lubbers! will none of you go with the old gentleman? I go for one."

So out he went, giving three cheers at the door, to the amazement of all present.

Why Saul Threw a Javelin at David

A High-Churchman and a Scotch Presbyterian had been at the same church. The former asked the latter if he did not like the "introits."

" I don't know what an introit is," was the reply.

" But did you not enjoy the anthem?" said the churchman.

" No, I did not enjoy it at all."

" I am very sorry," said the churchman, " because it was used in the early church ; in fact, it was originally sung by David."

" Ah !" said the Scotchman, "then that explains the Scripture. I can understand why, if David sung it at that time, Saul threw his javelin at him."

A Sexton's Criticism

The following criticism by a Scotch sexton is not bad :

A clergyman in the country had a stranger preaching for him one day, and meeting his sexton, asked, " Well, Saunders, how did you like the sermon to-day ? "

" It was rather ower plain and simple for me. I like thea sermons best that jumbles the joodgment and confoonds the sense. Od, sir, I never saw ane that could come up to yoursel' at that."

Strange Reason for not Increasing a Minister's Stipend

A relative of mine going to church with a Forfarshire farmer, one of the old school, asked him the amount of the minister's stipend.

He said, " Od, it's a gude ane—the maist part of £300 a year."

" Well," said my relative, " many of these Scotch ministers are but poorly off."

" They've eneuch, sir ; they have eneuch ; if they'd mair, it would want a' their time to the spending o't." [7]

Pulpit Eloquence

An old clerical friend upon Spreyside, a confirmed old bachelor, on going up to the pulpit one Sunday to preach, found, after giving out the psalm, that he had forgotten his sermon. I do not know what his objections were to his leaving the pulpit and going to the manse for his sermon, but he preferred sending his old confidential housekeeper for it. He accordingly stood up in the pulpit, stopped the singing, when it had commenced, and thus accosted his faithful domestic : " Annie, I say, Annie, *we've* committed a mistake the day. Ye maun jist gang your waa's hame, and ye'll get my sermon out o' my breek pouch, an' we'll sing to the praise o' the Lord till ye come back again." [7]

Maunderings, by a Scotchman

The following is said by *Chambers' Journal* to have been written by a Scotchman. If so, the humorous way in which he is taking off a certain tendency of the Scotch mind, is delicious ; if by an Englishman, the humor will be less keen, though not less fair.

I am far frae being clear that Nature hersel', though a kindly auld carline, has been a'thegither just to Scotland seeing that she has sae contrived that some o' our greatest men, that ought by richt to hae been Scotchmen, were born in England and other countries, and sae have been kenned as Englishers, or else something not quite sae guid.

There's glorious old Ben Jonson, the dramatic poet and scholar, that everybody tak's for a regular Londoner, merely because he happened to be born there. Ben's father, it's weel ken't, was a Johnston o' Annandale in Dumfriesshire, a bauld guid family there to this day. He is alloo't to hae been a gentleman, even by the English biographers o' his son ; and, dootless, sae he was, sin' he was an Annandale Johnston. He had gane up to London, about the time o' Queen Mary, and was amang them that suffered under that sour uphalder o' popery. Ben, puir chiel', had the misfortune first to see the light somewhere aboot Charing Cross, instead o' the bonnie leas o' Ecclefechan, where his poetic soul wad hae been on far better feedin' grund, I reckon. But nae doot, he cam' to sit contented under the dispensations of Providence. Howsomever, he ought to be now ranked amang Scotchmen, that's a'.

There was a still greater man in that same century.

that's generally set down as a Lincolnshire-man, but
ought to be looked on as next thing till a Scotchman,
if no' a Scotchman out and out; and that's Sir Isaac
Newton. They speak o' his forebears as come frae
Newton in Lancashire; but the honest man himsel's
the best authority aboot his ancestry, I should think;
and didna he say to his friend Gregory ae day:
" Gregory, ye warna aware that I'm o' the same
country wi' yoursel'—I'm a Scotchman." It wad
appear that Sir Isaac had an idea in his head, that he
had come somehow o' the Scotch baronet o' the name
o' Newton; and nothing can be better attested than
that there was a Scotchman o' that name wha became
a baronet by favor o' King James the Sixt (What for
aye ca' him James the *First?*) having served that
wise-headed king as preceptor to his eldest son, Prince
Henry. Sae, ye see, there having been a Scotch
Newton who was a baronet, and Sir Isaac thinking he
cam' o' sic a man, the thing looks unco' like as if it
were a fact. It's the mair likely, too, frae Sir Adam
Newton having been a grand scholar and a man o'
great natural ingenuity o' mind; for, as we a' ken
right weel, bright abilities gang in families. There's
a chiel' o' my acquentance that disna think the dates
answer sae weel as they ought to do; but he ance
lived a twalmonth in England, and I'm feared he's
grown a wee thing prejudiced. Sae we'll say nae
mair aboot *him.*

Then, there was Willie Cowper, the author o' the
Task, John Gilpin, and mony other poems. If ye
were to gie implicit credence to his English biographers, ye wad believe that he cam' o' an auld Sussex
family. But Cowper himsel' aye insisted that he had
come o' a Fife gentleman o' lang syne, that had been
fain to flit southwards, having mair guid blude in his
veins than siller in his purse belike, as has been the
case wi' mony a guid fellow before noo. It's certain
that the town o' Cupar, whilk may hae gi'en the
family its name, is the head town o' that county to
this day. There was ane Willie Cowper, Bishop o'
Galloway in the time o' King Jamie—a real good
exerceesed Christian, although a bishop—and the poet

jaloosed that this worthy man had been ane o' his
relations. I dinna pretend to ken how the matter
really stood; but it doesna look very likely that
Cowper could hae taken up the notion o' a Scotch
ancestry, if there hadna been some tradition to that
effeck. I'm particularly vext that our country was
cheated out o' haeing Cowper for ane o' her sons, for
I trow he was weel worthy o' that honor; and if Providence had willed that he should hae been born and
brought up in Scotland, I haena the least doot that he
wad hae been a minister, and ane too, that wad hae
pleased the folk just extrornar.

There was a German philosopher in the last century, that made a great noise wi' a book of his that
explored and explained a' the in-thoughts and out-
thoughts o' the human mind. His name was Immanuel Kant; and the Kantian philosophy is weel kent as
something originating wi' him. Weel, this Kant
ought to hae been a Scotchman; or rather he *was* a
Scotchman; but only, owing to some grandfather or
great-grandfather having come to live in Königsberg,
in Prussia, ye'll no' hinder Immanuel frae being born
there—whilk of coorse was a pity for a' parties except
Prussia, that gets credit by the circumstance. The
father of the philosopher was an honest saddler o' the
name o' Cant, his ancestor having been ane o' the
Cants o' Aberdeenshire, and maybe a relation of
Andrew Cant, for onything I ken. It was the philosopher that changed the C for the K, to avoid the foreign
look of the word, our letter C not belonging to the
German alphabet. I'm rale sorry that Kant did not
spring up in Scotland, where his metaphysical studies
wad hae been on friendly grund. But I'm quite sure,
an' he had visited Scotland and come to Aberdeenshire, he wad hae fund a guid number o' his relations,
that wad hae been very glad to see him, and never
thought the less o' him for being merely a philosopher.

Weel, we've got down a guid way noo, and the next
man I find that ought by richts to hae been a Scotchman is that deil's bucky o' a poet, Lord Byron. I'm
no' saying that Lord Byron was a'thegither a respectable character, ye see; but there can be nae manner

o' doot that he wrote grand poetry, and got a great name by it. Noo, Lord Byron was born in London—I'm no' denyin' what Tammy Muir says on that score —but his mother was a Scotch leddy, and she and her husband settled in Scotland after their marriage, and of coorse their son wad hae been born there in due time, had it no' been that the husband's debts obliged them to gang, first to France and after that to London, where the leddy cam' to hae her down-lying, as has already been said. This, it plainly appears to me, was a great injustice to Scotland.

My greatest grudge o' a' is regarding that bright genius for historical composition, Thomas Babbington Macaulay, M. P. for Edinburgh. About the year 1790, the minister o' the parish o' Cardross in Dumbartonshire, was a Mr. M'Aulay, a north-country man, it's said, and a man o' uncommon abilities. It was in his parish that that other bright genius, Tobias Smollett, was born, and if a' bowls had rowed richt, sae should T. B. M. But it was otherwise ordeened. A son o' this minister, having become preceptor to a Mr. Barbinton, a young man o' fortune in England, it sae cam' aboot that this youth and his preceptor's sister, wha was an extrornan' bonny lass, drew up thegither, and were married. That led to ane o' the minister's sons going to England—namely, Mr. Zachary, the father o' oor member; and thus it was that we were cheated out o' the honor o' having T. B. as an out-and-out Scotsman, whilk it's no' natural to England to bring forth sic geniuses, weary fa' it, that I should say sae. I'm sure I wiss that the bonny lass had been far eneuch, afore she brought about this strange cantrip o' fortune, or that she had contented hersel' wi' an honest Greenock gentleman that wanted her, and wha, I've been tould, de'ed no' aboon three year syne.

Naebody that kens me will ever suppose that I'm vain either aboot mysel' or my country. I wot weel, when we consider what frail miserable creatures we are, we hae little need for being proud o' onything. Yet, somehow, I aye like to hear the name o' puir auld Scotland brought aboon board, so that it is na for

things even-down disrespectable. Some years ago,
we used to hear a great deal about a light-headed
jillet they ca' Lola Montes, that had become quite an
important political character at the coort o' the king
o' Bavaria. Noo, although I believe it's a fact that
Lola's father was a Scotch officer o' the army, I set nae
store by her ava—I turn the back o' my hand on a'
sic cutties as her. Only, it *is* a fact that she comes o'
huz—o' that there can be nae doot, be it creditable
or no'.

Well, ye see, there's another distinguished leddy o'
modern times, that's no' to be spoken o' in the same
breath wi' that Lady Lighthead. This is the new
Empress o' France. A fine-looking queen she is, I'm
tauld. Weel, it's quite positive aboot her that her
mother was a Kirkpatrick, come of the house o' Closeburn, in the same county that Ben Jonson's father
cam' frae. The Kirkpatricks have had land in Dumfriesshire since the days o' Bruce, whose friend ane o'
them was, at the time when he killed Red Cummin;
but Closeburn has long passed away frae them, and
now belangs to Mr. Baird, the great iron master o' the
west o' Scotland. Howsomever, the folks thereaboots
hae a queer story aboot a servant-lass that was in the
house in the days o' the empress' great-grandfather
like. She married a man o' the name o' Paterson
and gaed to America, and her son came to be a great
merchant, and his daughter became Prince Jerome
Bonaparte's wife; and sae it happens that a lady
come frae the parlor o' Closeburn sits on the throne
o' France, while a prince come frae the kitchen o' the
same place is its heir presumptive! I'm no' sure that
the hale o' this story is quite the thing; but I tell it
as it was tauld to me.

I'm no' ane that tak's up my head muckle wi'
public singers, playgoers, composers o' music, and
folk o' that kind; but yet we a' ken that some o'
them atteen to a great deal o' distinction, and are
muckle ta'en out by the nobility and gentry. Weel,
I'm tauld (for I ken naething about him mysel') that
there was ane Donizetti, a great composer o' operas,
no' very lang syne. Now, Donizetti, as we've been

tauld i' *the public papers*, was the son o' a Scotchman.
His father was a Highlandman, called Donald Izett,
wha left his native Perthshire as a soldier—maist
likely the Duke o' Atholl pressed him into the service
as ane o' his volunteers—and Donald having quitted
the army somewhere abroad, set up in business wi'
Don Izett over his door, whilk the senseless folk
thereabouts soon transformed into Donizetti, and thus
it came about that his son, wha turned out a braw
musician, bore this name frae first to last, and dootless left it to his posterity. I ken weel that Izett is a
Perthshire name, and there was ane o' the clan some
years sin' in business in the North Brig o' Edinburgh,
and a rale guid honest man he was, I can tell ye, and
a very sensible man, too. Ye'll see his head-stane
ony day i' the Grayfriars. And this is guid evidence to me that Donizetti was, properly speaking,
a Scotchman. It's a sair pity for himsel' that he
wasna born, as he should hae been, on the braes o'
Atholl, for then he wad nae doot hae learned the
richt music, that is played there sae finely on the
fiddle—namely, reels and strath-speys; and I dinna
ken but, wi' proper instruction, he might hae rivalled
Neil Gow himsel'.

Ye've a' heard o' Jenny Lind, the Swedish nightin-
gale, as the fulishly ca' her, as if there ever were ony
nightingales in Sweden. She's a vera fine creature,
this Jenny Lind, no greedy o' siller, as sae mony are,
but aye willing to exerceese her gift for the guid o' the
sick and the puir. She's, in fack, just sick a young
woman as we micht expeck Scotland to produce, if it
ever produced public singers. Weel, Jenny, I'm tauld,
is another of the great band o' distinguished persons
that ought to hae been born in Scotland, for it's said
her greatgrandfather (I'm no' preceese as to the generation) was a Scotchman that gaed lang syne to
spouse his fortune abroad, and chanced to settle in
Sweden, where he had sons and daughters born to
him. There's a gey wheen Linds about Mid-Calder,
honest farmer-folk, to this day; sae I'm thinkin'
there's no' muckle room for doot as to the fack.

Noo, having shewn sic a lang list o' mischances as

to the nativity o' Scotch folk o' eminence, I think
ye'll alloo that we puir bodies in the north hae some
occasion for complaint. As we are a' in Providence's
hand, we canna, of coorse, prevent some o' our best
countrymen frae coming into the world in wrang
places — sic as Sir Isaac Newton in Lincolnshire,
whilk I think an uncommon pity ; but what's to hinder
sic persons frae being reputed and held as Scotchmen
notwithstanding? I'm sure I ken o' nae objection,
except it may be that our friends i' the south, feeling
what a sma' proportion o' Great Britons are Englishmen, may entertain some jealousy on the subjeck.   If
that be the case, the sooner that the Association for
Redress o' Scottish Grievances takes up the question
the better. [21]

A Leader's Description of His Followers

Old John Cameron was leader of a small quadrille
band in Edinburgh, the performances of which were
certainly not the very finest.

Being disappointed on one occasion of an engagement at a particular ball, he described his more fortunate but equally able brethren in the following
terms : " There's a Geordie Menstrie, he plays rough,
like a man sharpening knives wi' yellow sand.   Then
there's Jamie Corri, his playin's like the chappin' o'
mince-collops—sic short bows he tak's.   And then
there's Donald Munro, his bass is like wind i' the lum,
or a toom cart gaun down Blackfriars' Wynd ! "

It Takes Two To Fight

A physician at Queensferry was once threatened
with a challenge.   His method of receiving it was at
once cool and incontrovertible.

" Ye may challenge me if ye like," said he; "but
whether or no, there'll be nae fecht, *unless I gang
out.*"

" What's the Lawin', Lass ? "

The following dialogue occurred in a little country
inn, not so long ago as the internal evidence might
lead one to suppose.   The interlocutors are an
English tourist and a smart young woman, who acted

as waitress, chambermaid, boots, and everybody else,
being the man and the maid of the inn at the same
time :

Tourist : Come here, if you please.

Jenny : I was just coming ben to you, sir.

Tourist : Well, now, mistress.

Jenny : I'm no' the mistress; I'm only the lass,
an' I'm no' married.

Tourist : Very well, then, miss.

Jenny : I'm no' a miss ; I'm only a man's dochter.

Tourist : A man's daughter?

Jenny : Hoot, ay, sir ; didna ye see a farm as ye
came up yestreen, just three parks aff?

Tourist : It is very possible ; I do not remember.

Jenny : Weel, onyway, it's my faither's.

Tourist : Indeed !

Jenny : Ay, it's a fact.

Tourist : Well, that fact being settled, let us proceed to business. Will you let me see your bill ?

Jenny : Our Bill. Ou, ay, Wully we ca' him, but I
ken wha you mean—he's no in e'en now.

Tourist : Wully ! what I want is my account—a
paper stating what I have had, and how much I have
to pay.

Jenny : Did ony woman ever hear the like o' that—
ye mean the lawin', man ! But we keep nae accounts
here ; na, na, we hae ower muckle to dae.

Tourist : And how do you know what to charge ?

Jenny : On, we just put the things down on the
sclate, and tell the customers the tottle by word o'
mouth.

Tourist : Just so. Well, will you give me the
lawin', as I am going ?

Jenny : Oh, sir, ye're jokin' noo ! It's you maun
gie me the lawin'—the lawin's the siller.

Tourist : Oh, indeed, I beg your pardon ; how
much is it ?

Jenny : That's just what I was coming ben to tell
you, sir. If ye had ask'd me first, or waited till I
tell't ye, I wadna hae keepit ye a minute. We're no
blate at askin' the lawin', although some folk are
unco' slow at payin' o't. It's just four-and-six.

Tourist: That is very moderate; there is five shillings.

Jenny: Thank you, sir; I hope we hae a sixpence in the house, for I wadna' like to gie bawbees to a gentleman.

Tourist: No, no; the sixpence is for yourself.

Jenny: Oh, sir, it's ower muckle.

Tourist: What, do you object to take it?

Jenny: Na, na, sir; I wouldna' put that affront upon ye. But I'll gie ye a bit o' advice for't. When ye're gaun awa' frae an inn in a hurry, dinna be fashin' yersel' wi' mistresses, and misses, and bills; but just say, " What's the lawin', lass? "

Meanness versus Crustiness

A rather mean and parsimonious old lady called one day upon David Dreghorn, a well-known Glasgow fishmonger, saying, " Weel, Maister Dreghorn, how are ye selling your half salmon the noo? "

David being in a rather cross humor, replied, " When we catch ony half salmon, mem, we'll let ye ken ! "

Speeding the Parting Guest

It is related of a noble Scottish lady of the olden time, who lived in a remote part of the Highlands, and was noted for her profuse liberality, that she was some times overburdened with habitual " sorners." When any one of them outstayed his welcome, she would take occasion to say to him at the morning meal, with an arch look at the rest of the company, " Mak' a guid breakfast, Mr. ——, while ye're about it; ye dinna ken whaur ye'll get your dinner." The hint was usually taken, and the " sorner " departed.

" Things Which Accompany Salvation "

" What d'ye think o' this great revival that's gaun on the noo, Jamie? " asked a grocer of a brother tradesman.

" Weel," answered Jamie, " I canna say muckle about it, but I ken this—I hae gotten in a gude wheen bawbees that I had given up lang syne as bad debts."

Lights and Livers

Lord Cockburn, when at the bar, was pleading in a steamboat collision case. The case turned on the fact of one of the steamers carrying no lights, which was the cause of the accident. Cockburn insisting on this, wound up his eloquent argument with this remark: " In fact, gentlemen, had there been more *lights*, there would have been more *livers*."

Both Short

" Ye're unco' short the day, Saunders, surely," said an undersized student to a Glasgow bookseller, one morning, when the latter was in an irritable mood.

" Od, man," was the retort, "ye may haud your tongue; ye're no' sae lang yersel'."

His Own, With " Interest "

" Coming from h—l, Lauchlan? " quoth a shepherd, proceeding on Sacrament Sunday to the Free Church, and meeting a friend coming from the Church of the Establishment.

" Better nor going to it, Rory," retorted Lauchlan, as he passed on.

" The Spigot's Oot "

Lord Airlie remarked to one of his tenants that it was a very wet season.

" Indeed, my lord," replied the man, " I think the spigot's oot a'thegither."

Looking After Himself

A canny man, who had accepted the office of elder because some wag had made him believe that the remuneration was a sixpence each Sunday and a boll of meal on New Year's Day, officially carried round the ladle each Sunday after service. When the year expired he claimed the meal, but was told that he had been hoaxed.

" It may be sae wi' the meal," he replied, coolly, " but I took care o' the saxpence mysel'."

13

An Epitaph to Order

The Rev. Dr. M'Culloch, minister of Bothwell at the end of last century, was a man of sterling independence and great self-decision. To a friend—Rev. Mr. Brisbane—he one day said, "You must write my epitaph if you survive me."

"I will do that," said Mr. Brisbane; "and you shall have it at once, doctor."

Next morning he received the following : .

"Here lies, interred beneath this sod,
That sycophantish man of God,
Who taught an easy way to heaven,
Which to the rich was always given ;
If he get in, he'll look and stare
To find some out that he put there."

A Variety Entertainment

There used to be a waggish ostler at one of the chief inns at Hertford, who delighted to make merry at the expense of any guests who gave themselves airs. The manner of the ostler was extremely deferential, and only those who knew him well were aware of the humor which almost always lurked beneath his civil replies to the questions put to him. One day a commercial traveler, a complete prig, who wanted to play the fine gentleman, entered the inn, and having despatched his dinner, rang the bell of the commercial room for "boots," who presently made his appearance, when the following colloquy took place :

Commercial : " Dull town, this. Any amusements, Boots ? "

Boots : " Yes, sir, please, sir ; Musical Conversazione over the way at the Shire Hall, sir. Half-a-crown admission, sir. Very nice, sir."

Commercial : " Ah, nice music, I dare say ; I don't care for such things. Is there nothing else, Boots ?"

Boots : " Yes, sir, please, sir ; Popular Entertainment at Corn Exchange, admission one penny ; gentlemen pay sixpence to front seats, sir, if they please, sir."

Commercial: "Intensely vulgar! Are there no other amusements in this confoundedly dull town?"

Boots: "Yes, sir, please sir; railway station at each end of the town—walk down and see the trains come in."

A Descriptive Hymn

A minister in Orkney having been asked by the Rev. Mr. Spark, minister of St. Magnus, to conduct service in his church, and also to baptize his infant daughter, gave out for singing, before the baptismal service, a portion of the fifth paraphrase, beginning :

"As *sparks* in quick succession rise."

As Mr. Spark's help-mate was a fruitful vine, and presented him with a pledge of her affection every year, the titter among the congregation was unmistakable and irresistible.

A Vigorous Translation

"What is the meaning of *ex nihilo nihil fit?*" asked a Highlander of a village schoolmaster.

"Weel, Donald," answered the dominie, "I dinna mind the literal translation; but it just means that ye canna tak' the breeks aff a Highland-man."

"Before the Provost!"

The magistrates of the Scottish burghs, though respectable men, are generally not the wealthiest in their respective communities. And it sometimes happens, in the case of very poor and remote burghs, that persons of a very inferior station alone can be induced to accept the uneasy dignity of the municipal chair.

An amusing story is told regarding the town of L——, in B——shire, which is generally considered as a peculiarly miserable specimen of these privileged townships. An English gentleman approaching L—— one day in a gig, his horse started at a heap of dry wood and decayed branches of trees, which a very poor-looking old man was accumulating upon the road, apparently with the intention of conveying

them to town for sale as firewood. The stranger
immediately cried to the old man, desiring him in no
very civil terms, to clear the road that his horse
might pass. The old man, offended at the disrespect-
ful language of the complainant, took no notice of
him, but continued to hew away at the trees.

"You old dog," the gentleman then exclaimed,
"I'll have you brought before the provost, and put
into prison for your disregard of the laws of the
road."

"Gang to the de'il, man, wi' your provost!" the
woodcutter contemptuously replied; "I'm provost
mysel'."

Denominational Graves

For a short time after the disruption, an unkindly
feeling existed between the ministers of the Established Church and their protesting brethren. Several
"free" parishioners of Blackford, Perthshire, waited
on Mr. Clark, the established minister, and requested
that they might have the services of a non-Erastian
sexton.

"Will you allow us, sir," said one of the deputation,
"to dig our own graves?"

"Certainly, gentlemen," said Mr. Clark, "you are
most welcome; and the sooner the better!"

Escaping Punishment

An active-looking boy, aged about twelve years,
was brought up before Provost Baker, at the Ruther-
glen Burgh Court, charged with breaking into gardens
and stealing fruit therefrom. The charge having
been substantiated, the magistrate, addressing the
juvenile offender, said in his gravest manner: "If you
had a garden, and pilfering boys were to break into
and steal your property, in what way would you like
to have them punished?"

"Aweel, sir," replied the prisoner, "I think I
would let them awa' for first time."

It is needless to add that the worthy provost was
mollified, and that the little fellow was dismissed with
an admonition.

Passing Remarks

"There she goes," sneered an Englishman, as a Highlander marched past in his tartans at a fair.

"There she lies," retorted Duncan, as he knocked the scorner down at a blow.

Scottish Vision and Cockney Chaff

Two sharp youths from London, while enjoying themselves among the heather in Argylshire, met with a decent-looking shepherd upon the top of a hill. They accosted him by remarking: "You have a fine view here, friend; you will be able to see a great way."

"Ou, ay, ou, ay, a ferry great way."

"Ah! you will see America from here?"

"Farther than that," said Donald.

"Ah! how's that?"

"Ou, juist wait till the mists gang awa', an' you'll see the mune!"

"The," and "The Other"

When the chief of the Scottish clan, Macnab, emigrated to Canada with a hundred clansmen, he, on arriving at Toronto, called on his namesake, the late Sir Allen, and left his card as "*The* Macnab." Sir Allen returned his visit, leaving as his card, "The *other* Macnab."

"Old Clo'"

Christopher North had a great hatred of the "old clo'" men who infest the streets. Coming from his class one day, a shabby Irishman asked him in the usual confidential manner, "Any old clo', sir?"

"No;" replied the professor, imitating the whisper; "no, my dear fellow,—have you?"

Church Popularity

"How is it, John," said a minister to his man, "that you never go a message for me anywhere in the parish but you contrive to take too much spirits? People don't offer *me* spirits when I'm making visits in the parish."

"Weel, sir," said John, "I canna precisely explain

it, unless on the supposition that I'm a wee bit mair
popular wi' some o' the folks maybe than you are."

Wersh Parritch and Wersh Kisses

Kirsty and Jenny, two country lassies, were supping
their "parritch" from the same bicker in the harvest-
field one morning.

"Hech," said Kirsty to her neighbor, "Jenny, but
thae's awfu' wersh parritch!"

"'Deed are they," said Jenny, "they are that.
D'ye ken what they put me in mind o'? Just o' a
kiss frae a body that ye dinna like."

A Stranger in the Court of Session

The "Daft Highland Laird," a noted character in
Edinburgh at the latter end of last century, one day
accosted the Hon. Henry Erskine, as he was entering the Parliament House. Erskine inquired of the
"laird" how he did.

"Oh, very well!" answered the laird; "but I'll
tell ye what, Harry, tak' in *Justice* wi' ye," pointing
to one of the statues over the old porch of the House;
"for she has stood lang i' the outside, and it would
be a treat to see her inside, like other strangers!"

Wit and Humor Under Difficulties

Sandy Gordon, the town-crier of Maybole, was a
character in his way. At one period of his life he
had been an auctioneer and appraiser, although his
"louring drouth" interfered sadly with the business,
but neither poverty nor misfortune could blunt
Sandy's relish for a joke. One day, going down the
street he encountered his son riding on an ass.

"Weel, Jock," quoth he, "you're a riding on your
brither."

"Ay, father," rejoined the son, "I didna ken this
was ane o' yours tae."

At a neighboring village he had one day sold his
shoes to slake his thirst. After the transaction he was
discovered seated on the roadside, gazing on his bare
feet, and soliloquizing in this strain—"Step forrit,
barefit Gordon, if it's no' *on* you, it's *in* you."

He was once taking a walk into the country, when he met Sir David Hunter Blair.

"Where are you for to-day, Gordon?" asked the baronet.

"Sir David," rejoined the crier, with some dignity, "if I was to ask that of you, you would say I was ill-bred."

He had the misfortune once to break his leg in a drunken brawl, and a hastily constructed litter was improvised to carry him home. Still his characteristic humor did not leave him. "Canny boys," he would cry to those carrying him, "keep the funeral step; tak' care o' my pipe ; let oor Jock tae the head, he's the chief mourner."

An Affectionate Aunt

A plain-spoken old Scottish lady, Mrs. Wanchope, of Nibbey, being very ill, sent for Aunt Soph and said to her : "Soph, I believe I am dying; will you be always kind to my children when I am gone?"

"Na, na ; tak' yer spoilt deevils wi' ye," was the reply, "for I'll hae naething ado wi' them !"

A Discerning Fool

"Jock, how auld will ye be?" said a sage wife to daft Jock Amos one day, when talking of their ages.

"O, I dinna ken," said Jock ; "it would tak' a wiser head than mine to tell you that."

"It's an unco' queer thing you dinna ken hoo auld you are," returned the woman.

"I ken weel eneuch how auld I *am*," answered Jock ; "but I dinna ken how auld *I'll be*." [24]

A Law of Nature

Principal Hill once encountered a fierce onslaught from the Rev. James Burn in the General Assembly. When Mr. Burn had concluded his attack, the professor rose, and said with a smile : "Moderator, we all know that it is most natural that *Burns* should *run down Hills*."

The laugh was effectually raised against his opponent, whose arguments and assertions he then proceeded to demolish at his leisure.

Ingenious Remedy for Ignorance

When a former Prince of Wales was married, a
Highland minister at Greenock was praying for the
happiness and welfare of the royal couple. He was
somewhat embarrassed as to how he should join the
two names, but at length he got over it thus :

" Lord bless *her* royal highness the Prince of Wales,
and *his* royal highness the *she* prince ! "

Highland " Warldliness "

At a breakfast there was abundance of Highland
cheer, towering dishes of scones, oatcakes, an enor-
mous cheese, fish eggs and a monstrous grey-beard of
whiskey ready, if required; fumes of tobacco were
floating in the air, and the whole seemed an embodi-
ment of the Highlander's grace, " Oh, gie us rivers of
whiskey, chau'ders o' snuff, and tons o' tobacco,
pread an' a cheese as pig as the great hill of Ben
Nevis, and may our childer's childer be lords and
lairds to the latest sheneration." On repeating this
grace to an old hillsman of eighty, leaning on his
stick, he thoughtfully answered : " Weel, it's a goot
grace—a very goot grace—but it's a warldly thing ! "

A Paradox

On Henry Erskine being told that Knox, who had
long derived his livelihood by keeping the door of the
Parliament House, had been killed by a shot from a
small cannon on the king's birthday, he observed that
" it was remarkable that a man should live by the
civil and die by the can(*n*)on law."

A Sensible Lass

A Scottish gentleman, while walking in a meadow
with some ladies, had the impudence to snatch a kiss
from one, unperceived by the rest. She said indignantly, " Sir, I am not accustomed to such freedom."

" It will be the greater rarity, then, madam."

She flew from him, and ran towards her mother,
who, alarmed at her seeming terror, inquired what
was the cause.

" She has taken fright at a rash buss," said the gentleman.

" O, ye idiot," said the mother, " go back this instant."

She returned, smiling, and said, " Do't again, it's no' forbidden."

A Sad Loss

An old lady was telling her grandchildren about some trouble in Scotland, in the course of which the chief of her clan was beheaded.

" It was nae great thing of a head, bairns, to be sure," said the good lady, "but it was a sad loss to him."

Catechising

The minister called in upon the gudewife at Corset Hill one night, for the purpose of catechising her.

" What is the Lord's Supper, Peggy? " he inquired.

" 'Decd, sir," said the hostel wife, more intent on matters temporal than on things spiritual, "there's nae lords come this way; but I'se tell ye what a cadger's supper is—it's just a groat ; and what they leave at night they tak' awa' wi' them in their pouch in the morning."

Lord Cockburn Confounded

One day Lord Cockburn went into the Second Division of the Court of Session, but came out again very hurriedly, meeting Lord Jeffrey at the door.

" Do you see any paleness about my face, Jeffrey ? " asked Cockburn.

" No," replied Jeffrey ; " I hope you're well enough."

" I don't know," said the other ; " but I have just heard Bolus (Lord Justice-Clerk Boyle) say : ' I *for one* am of opinion that this case is founded on the fundamental basis of a quadrilateral contract, the four sides of which are agglutinated by adhesion !' "

" I think, Cockburn," said Jeffrey " that you had better go home."

" No Compliments "

An aged divine had occasionally to avail himself of the assistance of probationers. One day, a young man, very vain of his accomplishments as a preacher, officiated, and, on descending from the pulpit, was met by the old gentleman with extended hands. Expecting high praise, he said, " No compliments, I pray."

"Na, na, na, my young friend," said the minister, " nowadays I'm glad o' onybody ! "

A Sensible Servant

A very old domestic servant of the familiar Scottish character common long ago, having offended his master extremely, was commanded to leave his service instantly.

"In troth, and that will I not," answered the domestic ; "if your honor disna ken when ye hae a gude servant, I ken when I hae a gude master, and go away I will not."

On another occasion of the same nature the master said, "John, you and I shall never sleep under the same roof again ", to which John replied, with much *naivete*, "Where the deil can your honor be ganging?"

A Lesson in Manners

William Martin was at one time a book auctioneer in Edinburgh. He was no great scholar, and occasionally made some humorous blunders during the exercise of his vocation. One night he made a clumsy attempt to unravel the title of a French book. A young dandy, wishing to have the laugh at Martin's expense, asked him to read the title again, as he did not quite understand him.

"Oh!" said Martin, " it's something about manners, and that's what neither you nor me has ower muckle o'."

A Magnanimous Cobbler

At a certain country election of a member of Parliament in the Highlands, the popular candidate waited on a shoemaker to solicit his vote.

"Get out of my house, sir," said the shoemaker; and the gentleman was forced to retire accordingly. The cobbler, however, followed him and called him back, saying, "You turned me off from your estate, sir, and I was determined to turn you out of my house; but for all that, I'll give you my vote."

How Greyhounds are Produced

At a certain mansion, notorious for its scanty fare, a gentleman was inquiring of the gardener about a dog which he had given to the laird some time before. The gardener showed him a lank greyhound, on which the gentleman said : "No, no; the dog I gave your master was a mastiff, not a greyhound"; to which the gardener quietly answered :

"Indeed, sir, ony dog would soon be turned into a greyhound if it stoppit lang here."

Vanity Scathingly Reproved

Burns was dining with Maxwell of Terraughty, when one of the guests chose to talk of the dukes and earls with whom he had drank or dined, till the host and others got tired of him. Burns, however, silenced him with an epigram :

"What of earls, with whom you have supped ?
And of dukes, that you dined with yestreen ?
Lord ! a louse, sir, is still but a louse,
Though it crawls on the curls of a queen."

Gratifying Industry!

In Galloway large craigs are met with having ancient writing on them. One on the farm of Knockleby has, cut deep on the upper side :

"Lift me up and I'll tell you more."

A number of people gathered to this craig, and succeeded in lifting it up, in hopes of being well repaid ; but, instead of finding any gold, they found written on it :

"Lay me down as I was before. "

The Force of Habit

Some years ago a Scotch gentleman, who went to London for the first time, took the uppermost story of a lodging-house, and was very much surprised to get what he thought the genteelest place of the whole at the lowest price. His friends who came to see him, in vain acquainted him with the mistake he had been guilty of.

"He ken't very weel," he said, "what gentility was; and after having lived all his life in a sixth story, he had not come to London to live upon the ground."

Significant Advice

A church in the north country which required a pastor had a beadle who took an active interest in all the proceedings taken to fill up the vacancy.

One of the candidates, after the afternoon service was over, put off his cloak in the vestry and slipped into the church, in which our worthy was just putting things to rights.

"I was just taking a look at the church," said the minister.

"Ay, tak' a guid look at it," said the beadle, "for it's no' likely ye'll ever see't again."

A "Wigging"

The Rev. Dr. Macleod (father of the late Dr. Norman Macleod) was proceeding to open a new place of worship.

As he passed slowly and gravely through the crowd gathered about the doors, an elderly man, with the peculiar kind of a wig known in that district—bright, smooth and of a reddish brown—accosted him:

"Doctor, if you please, I wish to speak to you."

"Well, Duncan," said the venerable doctor, "can ye not wait till after worship?"

"No, doctor; I must speak to you now, for it is a matter upon my conscience."

"Oh, since it is a matter of conscience, tell me what it is; but be brief, Duncan, for time presses."

"The matter is this, doctor. Ye see the clock

yonder on the face of the new church? Well, there
is no clock really there—nothing but the face of the
clock. There is no truth in it, but only once in the
twelve hours. Now it is, in my mind, very wrong,
and quite against my conscience, that there should be
a lie on the face of the house of the Lord."

"Duncan, I will consider the point. I am glad to
see you looking so well. You are not young now;
I remember you for many years; and what a fine head
of hair you have still!"

"Eh, doctor, you are joking now; it is long since I
have had my hair."

"Oh, Duncan, Duncan, are you going into the house
of the Lord with a lie upon your head?"

This settled the question, and the doctor heard no
more of the lie on the face of the clock.

A Poacher's Prayer

Jamie Hamilton, a noted poacher at Crawfordjohn,
was once asked by a woman to pray for a poor old
woman who was lying at the point of death.

"I canna pray," said he.

"But ye maun do't, Jamie," said the woman.

"Weel, if I maun do't, I maun do't, but I haena
muckle to say," said Jamie.

Being placed beside the dying woman, the poacher,
with thoughts more intent upon hares than prayers,
said "O Lord, thou kens best Thyself how the case
stands between Thee and auld Eppie: but sin' ye
hae baith the haft and the blade in your ain hand,
just guide the gully as best suits Thy ain glory and
her guid. Amen!"

Could a bishop have said more in as few words?

Broader than He was Long

Mr. Dale, whose portrait figures in *Kay*, was very
short in stature, and also very stout.

Having mentioned to a friend one day that "he
had slipped on the ice, and fallen all his length"—

"Be thankful, sir," was the consolatory and apt
reply, "that it was not all your breadth!"

"Prayer, with Thanksgiving"

On one occasion, a clergyman eminent for his piety and simplicity of heart, but also noted for his great eccentricity of character, surprised his hearers by introducing the following passage into one of his prayers : " Oh Lord ! we desire to offer our grateful thanks unto Thee for the seasonable relief which Thou has sent to the poor of this place, from thine inexhaustible storehouse in the great deep, and which every day we hear called upon our streets, ' Fine fresh herrings, sax a penny ! sax a penny ! ' "

An Extra Shilling to Avoid a Calamity

A farmer having buried his wife, waited upon the grave-digger who had performed the necessary duties, to pay him fees. Being of a niggardly disposition, he endeavored to get the knight of the spade to abate his charges.

The patience of the latter becoming exhausted, he grasped his shovel impulsively, and, with an angry look, exclaimed : " Doon wi' another shillin', or—up she comes ! " The threat had the desired effect.

Putting off a Duel and Avoiding a Quarrel

At a convivial meeting of the Golfing Society at Bruntsfield Links, Edinburgh, on one occasion, a Mr. Megget took offence at something which Mr. Braidwood, father of the lamented superintendent of the London Fire Brigade, had said. Being highly incensed, he desired the latter to follow him to the Links, and he " would do for him."

Without at all disturbing himself, Mr. Braidwood pleasantly replied : Mr. Megget, if you will be so good as to go out to the Links, and *wait till I come*, I will be very much obliged to you."

This produced a general burst of laughter, in which his antagonist could not refrain from joining ; and it had the effect of restoring him to good humor for the remainder of the evening.

A Test of Literary Appreciation

Dr. Ranken, of Glasgow, wrote a very ponderous *History of France*. Wishing to learn how it was appreciated by the public, he went to Stirling's Library *incognito*, and inquired "if Dr. Ranken's *History of France* was in?"

Mr. Peat, the caustic librarian, curtly replied : " In ! it never was out !"

Ornithology

"Pray, Lord Robertson," said a lady to that eminent lawyer at a party, "can you tell me what sort of a bird the bul-bul is?"

"I suppose, ma'am," replied the humorous judge, " it is the male of the coo-coo."

A Practical View of Matrimony

"Fat's this I hear ye're gaun to dee, Jeannie," said an Aberdeen lass to another young woman.

"Weel, Maggie, lass, I'm just gaun to marry that farm ower by there, and live wi' the bit mannie on't."

Winning the Race Instead of the Battle

When Sir John Copse fled from Dunbar, the fleetness of his horse carried him foremost, upon which a sarcastic Scotsman complimented him by saying, " Deed, sir, but ye hae won the race : win the battle wha like !"

" After You, Leddies "

Will Hamilton, the " daft man o' Ayr," was once hanging about the vicinity of a loch, which was partially frozen. Three young ladies were deliberating as to whether they should venture upon the ice, when one of them suggested that Will should be asked to walk on first. The proposal was made to him.

" Though I'm daft, I'm no' ill-bred," quickly responded Will ; " after you, leddies !"

" Ursa Major "

Boswell expatiating to his father, Lord Auchinleck, on the learning and other qualities of Dr. Johnson, concluded by saying, " He is the grand luminary of our hemisphere—quite a constellation, sir."

" Ursâ Major, I suppose," dryly responded the judge.

Sheridan's Pauses

A Scottish minister had visited London in the early part of the present century, and seen, among other tricks of pulpit oratory, "Sheridan's Pauses" exhibited. During his first sermon, after his return home, he took occasion at the termination of a very impassioned and highly wrought sentence or paragraph, to stop suddenly, and pause in " mute unbreathing silence."

The precentor, who had taken advantage of his immemorial privilege to sleep out the sermon, imagining, from the cessation of sound, that the discourse was actually brought to a close, started up, with some degree of agitation, and in an audible, though somewhat tremulous voice read out his usual, " Remember in prayer——"

" Hoot man ! " exclaimed the good-natured orator over his head, placing at the same time his hand upon his shoulder : " hout, Jamie, man, what's the matter wi' ye the day ; d'ye no ken I hae nae done yet?— That's only ane o' Sheridan's pauses, man ! "

Absent in Mind, and Body, Too

The Rev. John Duncan, the Hebrew scholar, was very absent-minded, and many curious stories are told of this awkward failing.

On one occasion he had arranged to preach in a certain church a few miles from Aberdeen.

He set out on a pony in good time, but when near the end of his journey he felt a desire to take a pinch of snuff. The wind, however, blowing in his face, he turned the head of the pony round, the better to enjoy the luxury. Pocketing his snuff-box, he started the pony without again turning it in the proper direction, and did not discover his error until he found himself in Union Street, Aberdeen, at the very time he ought to have entered the pulpit seven miles off.

On another occasion he was invited to dinner at the house of a friend, and was shown into a bedroom to wash his hands.

After a long delay, as he did not appear, his friend went to the room, and, behold ! there lay the professor snugly in bed, and fast asleep !'

Prof. Aytoun's Courtship

After Prof. Aytoun had made proposals of marriage to Miss Emily Jane Wilson, daughter of "Christopher North," he was, as a matter of course, referred to her father. As Aytoun was uncommonly diffident, he said to her, "Emily, my dear, you must speak to him for me. I could not summon courage to speak to the professor on this subject."

"Papa is in the library," said the lady.

"Then you had better go to him," said the suitor, "and I'll wait here for you."

There being apparently no help for it, the lady proceeded to the library, and taking her father affectionately by the hand, mentioned that Aytoun had asked her in marriage. She added, "Shall I accept this offer, papa ; he is so shy and diffident, that he cannot speak to you himself."

"Then we must deal tenderly with him," said the hearty old man. "I'll write my reply on a slip of paper, and pin it on your back."

"Papa's answer is on the back of my dress," said Miss Wilson, as she re-entered the drawing-room.

Turning round, the delighted swain read these words : "With the author's compliments."

A Sad Drinking Bout

The following story of an occurrence at one of the drinking bouts in Scotland, at which the Laird of Garscadden took his last draught, has often been told, but it will bear repetition. The scene occurred in the wee clachan of Law, where a considerable number of Kilpatrick lairds had congregated for the ostensible purpose of talking over some parish business. And well they talked and better drank, when one of them, about the dawn of the morning, fixing his eye on Garscadden, remarked that he was "looking unco' gash."

Upon which the Laird of Kilmardinny coolly replied, "Deil mean him, since he has been wi' his Maker these twa hours ! I saw him step awa', but I dinna like to disturb guid company !"

The following epitaph on this celebrated Bacchanaalian plainly indicates that he was held in no great estimation among his neighbors :

"Beneath this stane lies auld Garscad,
Wha lived a neighbor very bad ;
Now, how he finds and how he fares,
The deil ane kens, and deil ane cares."

Not Surprised

Benjamin Greig, one of the last specimens of tie-wig and powder gentry, and a rich old curmudgeon to boot, one day entered the shop of Mr. Walker—better known, however, by the nickname of "Sugar Jock"—and accosting him, said, "Are you no' muckle astonished to hear that Mr. L—— has left £20,000 ?"

"Weel, Mr. Greig," replied "Sugar," "I wad hae been mair astonished to hear that he had ta'en it wi' him."

Greig gave a grunt and left the shop.

The Best Crap

A baby was out with its nurse, who walked it up and down a garden.

"Is't a laddie or a lassie, Jess?" asked the gardener.

"A laddie," said the maid.

"Weel," said he, "I'm glad o' that; there's ower mony lasses in the world already."

"Hech, man," said Jess, "div ye no ken there's aye maist sawn o' the best crap?"

A Marriage "Not Made in Heaven

Watty Marshall was a simple, useless, good-for-nothing body, who somehow or other got married to a terrible shrew of a wife. Finding out that she had made a bad bargain, she resolved to have the best of it, and accordingly abused and thrashed her luckless spouse to such an extent that he, in despair, went to the minister to get unmarried.

The parson told him that he could do him no such service as marriages were made in heaven.

"Made in heaven, sir," cried Watty; "it's a lee!
I was marriet i' your ain kitchen, wi' your twa servant hizzies looking on! J doubt ye hae made an
awfu' mistake wi' my marriage, sir, for the muckle
fire that was bleezing at the time made it look far
mair like the other place! What a life I'll hae to lead,
baith in this world and the next, for that blunder o'
yours, minister!"

"Another Opportunity"

An old gentleman named Scott was engaged in the
"affair of the '15" (the Rebellion of 1715) and with
some difficulty was saved from the gallows by the
intercession by the Duchess of Buccleuch and Mon-
mouth. Her grace, who maintained considerable
authority over her clan, sent for the object of her
intercession and, warning him of the risk which he
had run and the trouble she had taken on his account,
wound up her lecture by intimating that, in case of
such disloyalty again, he was not to expect her interest
in his favor.

"An' it please your grace," said the stout old Tory,
"I fear I am too old to see another opportunity."

A Night in a Coal-cellar

One night, sitting later than usual, sunk in the pro-
fundities of a great folio tome, the Rev. Dr. Wightman
of Kirkmahol imagined he heard a sound in the
kitchen inconsistent with the quietude and security of
a manse, and so taking his candle he proceeded to
investigate the cause. His foot being heard in the
lobby, the housekeeper began with all earnestness to
cover the fire, as if preparing for bed.

"Ye're late up to-night, Mary."

"I'm jist rakin' the fire, sir, and gaun to bed."

"That's right, Mary; I like timeous hours."

On his way back to the study he passed the coal-
closet, and, turning the key, took it with him. Next
morning, at an early hour, there was a rap at his
bedroom door, and a request for the key to put a
fire on.

"Ye're too soon up, Mary; go back to your bed yet."

Half an hour later there was another knock, and a similar request in order to prepare the breakfast.

"I don't want breakfast so soon, Mary; go back to your bed."

Another half an hour and another knock with an entreaty for the key, as it was washing day. This was enough. He rose and handed out the key saying, "go and let the man out."

Mary's sweetheart had been imprisoned all night in the coal-closet, as the minister shrewdly suspected, and, Pyramis-and-Thisbe-like, they had breathed their love to each other through the key-hole. [25]

Not Quite an Ass

James Boswell, the biographer of Dr. Johnson, was distinguished in his private life by his humor and power of repartee. He has been described as a man in whose face it was impossible at any time to look without being inclined to laugh. The following is one of his good things: As he was pleading one day at the Scotch bar before his father, Lord Auchinleck, who was at that time what is called Ordinary on the Bills (judge of cases in the first stage), the testy old senator, offended at something his son said, peevishly exclaimed: "Jamie, ye're an ass, man."

"Not exactly, my lord," answered the junior; "only a colt, the foal of an ass."

A Cute Gaoler

Before the adoption of the police act in Airdrie, a worthy named Geordie G—— had the surveillance of the town. A drunken, noisy Irishman was lodged in a cell, who caused an "awful row" by kicking at the cell-door with his heavy boots. Geordie went to the cell, and opening the door a little, said:

"Man, ye micht put aff yer buits, and I'll gie them a bit rub, so that ye'll be respectable like afore the bailie in the mornin'."

The prisoner complied with his request, and saw his mistake only when the door was closed upon him, Geordie crying out:

"Ye can kick as lang as ye like, noo."

Not Qualified to Baptize

The only amusement in which Ralph Erskine, the father of the Scottish Secession, indulged, was playing the violin. He was so great a proficient on this instrument, and so often beguiled his leisure hours with it, that the people of Dumfermline believed he composed his sermons to its tones, as a poet writes a song to a particular air. They also tell the following anecdote connected with the subject:

A poor man in one of the neighboring parishes, having a child to baptize, resolved not to employ his own clergyman, with whom he was at issue on certain points of doctrine, but to have the office performed by some minister of whose tenets fame gave a better report.

With the child in his arms, therefore, and attended by the full complement of old and young women who usually minister on such occasions, he proceeded to the manse of ——, some miles off (not that of Mr. Erskine), where he inquired if the clergyman was at home.

"Na; he's no' at hame yeenoo," answered the servant lass; "he's down the burn fishing; but I can soon cry him in."

"Ye needna gie yoursel' the trouble," replied the man, quite shocked at this account of the minister's habits; "nane o' your fishin' ministers shall bapteeze my bairn."

Off he then trudged, followed by his whole train, to the residence of another parochial clergyman, at the distance of some miles. Here, on inquiring if the minister was at home, the lass answered:

"'Deed he's no' at home the day, he's been out since sax " the morning at the shooting. Ye needna wait, neither; for he'll be sae made out when he comes back, that he'll no' be able to say bo to a calf, let-a-be kirsen a wean!"

"Wait, lassie!" cried the man in a tone of indignant scorn; "wad I wait, d'ye think, to haud up my bairn before a minister that gangs oot at six i' the morning to shoot God's creatures? I'll awa down to

gude Mr. Erskine at Dumfermline; and he'll be
neither out at the fishing nor shooting, I think."

The whole baptismal train then set off for Dumfermline, sure that the Father of the Secession,
although not now a placed minister, would at least be
engaged in no unclerical sports, to incapacitate him
for performing the sacred ordinance in question.

On their arriving, however, at the house of the
clergyman, which they did not do until late in the
evening, the man, on rapping at the door, anticipated
that he would not be at home any more than his
brethren, as he heard the strains of a fiddle proceeding from the upper chamber. "The minister will not
be at home," he said, with a sly smile to the girl who
came to the door, "or your lad wadna be playing that
gait t'ye on the fiddle."

"The minister *is* at hame," quoth the girl; "mair
by token, it's himsel' that's playing, honest man; he
aye takes a tune at night, before he gangs to bed.
Faith, there's nae lad o' mine can play that gait; it
wad be something to tell if ony o' them could."

"*That* the minister playing!" cried the man in a
degree of astonishment and horror far transcending
what he had expressed on either of the former occasions. "If *he* does this, what may the rest no' do?
Weel, I fairly gie them up a'thegither. I have traveled this haill day in search o' a godly minister, and
never man met wi' mair disappointment in a day's
journey. "I'll tell ye what, gudewife," he added,
turning to the disconsolate party behind, "we'll just
awa' back to our ain minister after a'. He's no'
a'thegither sound, it's true; but let him be what he
likes in doctrine, deil hae me if ever I kenk him fish,
shoot, or play on the fiddle a' his days!'

One Scotchman Outwitted by Another

Some years since, before the sale of game was legal-
ized, and a present of it was thought worth the expense
of carriage, an Englishman who had rented a moor
within twenty miles of Aberdeen, wishing to send a
ten brace box of grouse to his friends in the south,
directed his gilly to procure a person to take the box

to the capital of the north, from whence the London
steamer sailed. Not one, however, of the miserably
poor tenants in the neighborhood could be found who
would take the box for a less sum than eight shillings.
This demand was thought so unreasonable, that the
Englishman complained to a Scotch friend who was
shooting along with him.

The Scotchman replied that "the natives always
make a point of imposing as much as possible upon
strangers; but," he said "if you will leave it to me, I
will manage it for you; for with all their knavery,
they are the simplest people under the sun."

A few days afterwards, going out shooting, they saw
a man loading his cart with peats, when the Scotchman, approaching him, said, after the usual saluta-
tion—"What are you going to do with the peats?"

"I'm going to Aberdeen to sell them," was the
reply.

"What do you get for them?"

"One shilling and eightpence, sir."

"Indeed! Well, I will buy them, if you will be sure
to deliver them for me at Aberdeen."

"That I will, and thank you, too, sir."

All agreed, the Scotchman resumed his walk for
about twenty yards, when he suddenly turned round
and said: "By-the-by, I have a small box I want
taken to the same place. You can place it on the top
of the peats?"

"That I will, and welcome, sir."

"Well, if you will call at the lodge in the evening, I
will give you the direction for the peats, and you can
have the box at the same time."

He did so, and actually carried the box, and gave a
load of peats for one shilling and eightpence, although
neither the same man nor any of his neighbors would
forward the box *alone* for less than eight shillings.

Quaint Old Edinburgh Ministers

There was wee Scotty, o' the Coogate Kirk; and a
famous preacher he was at the height o' his popularity.
But he was sadly bathered wi' his flock, for they kept
him aye in het water.

Ae day he was preaching on Job. " My brethren,"
says he, " Job, in the first place, was a sairly-tried
man ; Job, in the second place, was an uncommonly
patient man ; Job, in the third place, never preached
in the Coogate ; fourthly and lastly, had Job preached
there, the Lord help his patience."

At anither time, before the service began, when
there was a great noise o' folk gaun into their seats,
he got up in the pu'pit an' cried out—" Oh, that I
could hear the pence rattle in the plate at the door
wi' half the noise ye mak' wi' yer cheepin' shoon !
Oh, that Paul had been here wi' a long wudden ladle !
for yer coppers are strangers in a far country, an' as
for yer silver an' gold—let us pray ! "

An' there was Deddy Weston, wha began ane o'
his Sunday morning services in this manner : " My
brethren, I'll divide my discourse the day into three
heads : *Firstly*, I'll tell ye something that I ken, an'
you dinna ken. *Secondly*, I'll tell ye something that
you ken, an' I dinna ken. *Thirdly*, I'll tell ye something that neither you nor me ken. *Firstly*, Coming
ower a stile this mornin', my breeks got an unco'
skreed. That's something that I ken, an' you dinna
ken. *Secondly*, What you're gaun to gie Charlie
Waddie, the tailor, for mendin' my breeks, is what
you ken, an' I dinna ken. *Thirdly*, What Charlie
Waddie's to tak' for mendin' my breeks, is what
neither you nor me ken. *Finally and lastly*, Hand
round the ladle."

An' there was Doctor **Dabster**, that could pit a
bottle or twa under his belt, an' was neither up nor
down. But an unco' bitter body was he when there
was a sma' collection. Before the service began, the
beadle generally handed him a slip of paper stating
the amount collected. Ae day a' the siller gathered
was only twa' shillin's an' ninepence ; an' he could

never get this out o' his head through the whole of his sermon.

He was aye spunkin oot noo an' then. "It's the land o' Canawn ye're thrang strivin' after," says he; "The land o' Canawn, eh?—twa an' ninepence! yes, ye're sure to gang there! I think I see ye! Nae doot ye'll think yersel's on the richt road for't. Ask yer consciences, an' see what they'll say. Ask them, an' see what they'll say. Ask them, an' what *will* they say? I'll tell ye: 'Twa miserable shillin's an' ninepence is puir passage-money for sic a lang journey!' What? Twa-an'-ninepence! As weel micht a coo gang up a tree tail foremost, an' whistle like a superannuated mavis, as get to Canawn for that!" [26]

Glossary

Aa. - I.

Aboon. Above.
Ae. One.
Aff Off.
Afit. Afoot.
Aiblins. Perhaps, possibly.
Ain. Own.
Ane. One.
A'thegither. Altogether.
Auchteenpence. Eighteenpence.
Aught. Eight.
Auld. Old.
Ava. At all.
Awn. Own.
Aye. Always.

Babble-ment. Confusion.

Bairns. Children.
Baith. Both.
Bane. Bone.
Bauld. Bold.
Bawbee. A half-penny.
Begond. Began.
Belyve Immediately, quickly.
Ben. Towards ; towards the inner ; the inner room of a house.
Blate, blait. Bashful.
Blinkit. Flashed, glanced.
Birkies. Lively young fellows.
Blude. Blood.
Bobshanks. Knees.
Bracs. The sides of hills.
Braik. Break.
Braw. Fine, gay, worthy, handsome.
Bree. Soup, sauce, juice.
Brig Bridge
Brocht. Brought.
Brose A kind of pottage made by pouring hot water on oatmeal and stirring while the water is poured.

Bucky. Hind quarters (of a hare).
Buits. Boots.
Buss. Kiss.

Canny. Cautious, Prudent.

Cantrip. Charm, spell, trick.
Carle, carl. A man, as distinguished from a boy.
Carline. An old woman.
Cauld. Cold.
Caup. Cup, wooden bowl.
Chapping. Striking.
Chau'ders. Denoting large quantities.
Cheekit. Entrapped.
Chiel. A stripling, a fellow, a servant.
Chwal. What.
Clachan. Clan.
Claes. Clothes.
Clan Tribe.
Con'le-licht. Candle-light.
Coo. Cow.
Cuddy. Donkey.
Crackit. Cracked.
Crand. Grand.
Craw. Crow.
Crouse. Boldly, lively, brisk.
Custrin Silly.
Cutties. Short spoons.

Dae. Do.

Daft. Foolish, gay, giddy, wanton.
Daunder To wander.
Deavin'. deafening.
Dee. Die.
Deid. Dead.
Deil. Devil.
Ding. To beat.

219

Dinna. Do not.
Dittha. Do they.
Dochter. Daughter.
Douce. Sedate, sober.
Dool. Numskull.
Doup. The breech, the bottom or extremity of anything.
Dour. Bold, inflexible, obstinate, stern.
Drap. A drop ; to drop.
Drookit. Soaked.
Droon't. Drowned.
Dub-shouper. Gutter-cleaner.
Durdham. Squabble.

E'e. Eye.

E'en. Eyes ; even.
Eer. Air.
Eneuch. Enough.
E'enow. Even now.
Extrornar. Extraordinary.

Faa'. Fall.

Fack. Fact
Far cist? Where is it?
Far was't? Where was it?
Fash. Trouble.
Fut? What?
Faund. Found.
Faut. Fault.
Fecht. Fight.
Feck. A term denoting space, quantity, number ; *the feck o' them* means " the most part of them."
Feckled. Made weak.
Feine. Fine.
Ferry. Very.
Fifish. Somewhat deranged.
Fleg, fley. To frighten,
Flit, flyt. To change, to remove, to transport. Commonly used of changing one's residence.
Fluir. Floor.
Flyte, Flytings. To scold, scolding.
Fog. Moss.
Forebears. Ancestors.
Forrit. Forward.
Fortnicht. Fortnight,
Foo'. A fool, through being drunk.
Fou, fu'. Drunk, full.
Fouk. Folk.

Freens. Friends, relatives.
Fremit. Strange.
Fules. Fools.
Fund. Found.

Gaed. Went.

Gail. Way.
Gang. Go.
Gars. Causes, makes.
Gash. Ghastly.
Gar'd. Made, induced.
Gey, gay. Moderately.
Gied. Gave.
Gin. If.
Glint. Sight, glimpse.
Gowd, goud. Gold.
Gowk, golk. Cuckoo, fool.
Greetin', greetin. Crying, the act of.
Grit. Great.
Grond. Grand.
Grup. Grip.
Gude, guid. Good.
Gully. A large knife.

Hae. Have.

Haggis. A pudding, made in a sheep's stomach, with oatmeal, suet, the heart, liver and lungs of the sheep, minced down and seasoned with salt, pepper, and onions, and boiled for use.
Haist. Haste.
Hale. Whole.
Haudin'. Holding, keeping.
Haveril. One who talks habitually in a foolish manner.
Heek, heeh, high. To pant, to breathe hard ; an exclamation which expresses a condition of breathlessness.
Heid. Head.
Hemmel. A cow without horns.
Het. Hot.
Hielans. Highlands.
Hirple. To move in a halting manner, as if crippled or momentarily injured, as by a blow.
Hoo. How.
Hunner. Hundred.
Hurdham. Squabble.
Hastrin. Lascivious.

Ilka, ilk. Every, each.
Intil, intill. In, into.
Intil't. Into it.

Jalouse. Expect, guess.
Jaud. Jade.

Keeking, keiking. Looking with a prying eye, peeping.
Kame, kaim. To comb, comb, honeycomb.
Ken. To know; to be acquainted; to understand.
Kintra. Country.
Kirk. Church.
Kirsen. To christen.

Laird. A man of superior rank; the owner of a property.
Lang. Long, to long or yearn.
Langsyne. Long since.
Lawin'. A tavern bill.
Leear. Liar.
Lees. Lies.
Leeve. Live.
Leeving. Living.
Lippened. Trusted, depended.
Li-thall. Lethal, deadly, mortal.
Loon. Clown, fool.
Lugs. Ears.
Lum, lumb. Chimney.
Louring drouth. Thirst.

Mair. More.
Mairret. Married.
Maist. Most.
Maun. Must.
Meikle. See "Muckle"
Micht. Might.
Miscad. Miscall.
Modiwarts, modywarts, moudicworts. Moles.
Mon. See "Maun."
Muckle. Much, great.
Mune. Moon.

Nit. Nut.
Noo. Now.

Ocht. Ought.
Oot. Out.

Parritch. Porridge.
Pawkily, pawkily. Slily, artfully.
Pawpish. Popish.
Poother. Powder.
Pow. The head; a slow rivulet—one moving on lands nearly flat.
Provost. The mayor of a burgh or township.
Puir. Poor.

Rale. Real.
Reekit. Smoked.
Reestit. Smoke-dried.
Richt. Right.
Rippet. A difference of opinion such as to estrange; a quarrel.

Sair. Sore.
Scart. To scratch; to scrape money together; to scrape a dish with a spoon.
Sclate, sclait. Slate.
Scoonril. Scoundrel.
Sheltie. A Shetland pony.
Shoost. Just.
Sic. Such.
Sicht. Sight.
Siller. Silver.
Sink. Think.
Skalin'. Dispersing, retiring, spilling.
Skelpin'. Clapping, applause.
Skirl. To cry shrilly, shriek.
Sleekit. Smooth, shining, oily.
Sma'. Small.
Smiddy. A smith's shop, smithy.
Snceshin'. Sneezing.
Sooming. Swimming.
Sorners. Spongers, loiterers.
Southrons. Those who live in the south.
Spier, speir. To ask.
Spigot. Peg, vent-peg.
Spune. Spoon.
Stane. Stone.
Strae. Straw.
Strathspeys. A dance tune for two.
Steekit. Closed, shut fastened.
Sune. Soon.
Suppone. Suppose.
Syne. Since.

Tacket. A nail of a shoe.

Tae. The toe.
Taes. Toes.
Taigle. Confound.
Tauld. Told.
Thae. Those (just referred to).
Thocht, thoucht. Thought.
Thrang. Busy, pressed, crowded thronged.
Tift. Coolness, estrangement.
Tint. Lost.
Toom. Empty.
Trow. To believe.
Twa. Two.

Unco'. Unknown, very, extra.

Wad. Would.

Wadna. Would not.
Wansc. Once.

Ware. Trouble, fuss.
Wast. West.
Wean (wee-ane). A child, little one.
Wee. Small, little, a short time.
Weed. Wild.
Wersh. Insipid to the taste.
Wha. Who.
Whaur. Where.
Wheen. A number, quantity, division.
Whets. What is, that which is
Whilk. Which.
Wiss. To wish.
Worill. World.
Wot. To know.
Wowf. Half-mad.
Wud. Would.
Wull. Will.
Wunnering. Wondering.

Yestreen. Last night.

Yirth. Earth.